The searchlight caught me full in the face.

Lousy dream. I came awake but the light didn't go away. Someone was in my bedroom—someone shining a strong flashlight in my eyes.

"No quick moves ... This gun has a hair trigger and I am in a hurry."

"Wha ... what do you want? Money? Liquor? Whatever it is, you got it, just don't get nervous."

"What I want is *you*, MacCardle. You and your boat. Now turn on the table lamp and we'll talk."

I did as I was told, sitting up in bed. The man was standing near the door, training a very ugly pistol at me.

"That's better. We're going on a fishing trip, MacCardle. To Nassau. Only neither of us is coming back. Nassau, then Jamaica, then Trinidad. From Trinidad it's a quick trip to Venezuela. By that time, I'll be Esteban Dario from Barcelona ... Got all the papers to prove it— terrific passport, picture and everything. Too bad you won't see it— setting off—halfway to Nassau."

Also by Tucker Halleran
available in paperback from
St. Martin's Press

A COOL, CLEAR DEATH

SUDDEN DEATH FINISH

Tucker Halleran

ST. MARTIN'S PRESS/NEW YORK

Triskidekaphobia is the irrational fear of all things pertaining to the number thirteen. That's why there isn't a chapter thirteen in this book. With apologies to all logic enthusiasts and with thanks to an indulgent publisher.

—Tucker Halleran

SUDDEN DEATH FINISH

Copyright © 1985 by Tucker Halleran

Library of Congress Catalog Card Number: 85-1704

ISBN: 0-312-90483-5   Can. ISBN: 0-312-90484-3

Printed in the United States of America

First St. Martin's Press mass market edition/December 1986

10 9 8 7 6 5 4 3 2 1

For Julie and John—
Both, creatures wise and wonderful

The highest of renown
Are the surest stricken down.
But the stupid and the clown,
They remain.

Eugene Fitch Ware
"Paresis"

1

The bullets lay in a precise rank on the kitchen table, their brass casings dully reflecting the light from the whaler's lamp hanging in gimbals overhead: thirty-aught-six extra-velocity bullets, hand loaded and carefully crimped, deadly accurate over a range of more than a thousand yards. Their heads, tapering to a needle-sharp point, gave final testimony to their lethal purpose. In effect they said, If this job's botched, you can bet the mortgage it won't be our fault.

The rifle being reassembled by the marksman's patient, deft fingers had been produced by the Springfield Armory as part of its July 1924 production run. Now only an expert could have guessed at its origins.

For ease of carrying and mobility, three pounds of the wood in its stock and forearm pieces had been stripped away. A knurled, Olympic-style pistol grip had been grafted on its underside. Its iron front and rear sights had been removed, replaced by an ultralight, precious-metal telescopic sight powered for night sight by a small battery pack. In short, the marksman had taken one of history's most dependable weapons and converted it into the most lethal killing machine in the world.

"Ready?"

"Just about. Gotta check the scope first. Do me a favor and turn out the lights."

"Done. What *is* that music? Sounds weird in the dark."

The marksman sat silent in the captain's chair, thoughts composed, waiting for night vision to establish itself. Finally he rose, walked to the window, and peered through the telescopic sight, focusing on objects at short, medium, and long range. Perfect, just perfect; the guys that built this really knew what they were about. "Flip on the lights, everything checks out. And that 'weird music', as you call it, is Mendelssohn's 'Violin Concerto in E Minor,' the Francescatti version. It relaxes the soul."

"For somebody in your line of work, it's strange, that's all."

The weapon, armed but with the safety on, slid easily into the specially tailored gun case with the easy-carry handle. They walked out together, closing and locking the door carefully.

"You're sure this is the only way to handle the problem?"

"Got a better one, lay it on me."

"What if it doesn't come off tonight?"

"We try again tomorrow night. Keep trying."

"We don't have all the time in the world, you know."

"Tell me about it."

*   *   *

Across town, on the fourteenth floor of the only high-rise building in Cypress Beach, someone else was working late as well, although bent on quite a different course.

He'd called home, apologized to Linda, asked her to give Betsy and Little Tom a hug, said he'd be along as soon as he could, that he hoped it would all be worth it someday. God bless Linda, he thought, no complaining, no recriminations, she'd just said, "Now look-ayere, Tom Horton, if it were slow horses or fast women you were after, I'd put up a fuss. You've gone farther, faster at that law firm than anybody since they started it. You're good at what you do and we're all mighty proud of you. Get home when you can and I'll have some supper waiting on you. Got a surprise too; Aunt Ellie sent me a nightgown from Paris—a sure-fire scandal—don't be too long."

He hung up, leaned back in the big leather swivel chair, smiling. You just been rabbit lucky your whole life, boy, he thought, and she's the biggest bit of all the luck. He was the first of three generations of Hortons not to get his law degree at Stetson, going instead to the University of Virginia. It disappointed his father, The Judge, and enraged his grandfather, but it turned out to be the smartest thing he'd ever done. In addition to discovering there was more to the world than South Florida, it gave him the chance to meet and mix with students from all over the world—and best of all, it had given him Linda.

He'd taken a ride through the hill country in the MG one day, top down to clear his head after a particularly vexing session on constitutional law. Mind elsewhere, he'd lost it in a bend, slewing sideways across the road and through a section of stringer fence, knocking himself cold as a cod in the process. He awoke to behold the angriest and loveliest woman he'd ever seen.

"If you were trying to make life hard for me, kiddo, you couldn't hardly have done any better. Damn horses see that fence you tore up, they won't stop till they get to Tennessee."

"I'm sorry, ma'am, d . . ."

"Sorry won't keep those idiots from bolting, buddy, now climb on out of there and help me restack these stringers. Then we'll ride up to the house and get Parker to tractor that darlin' little car out of here."

It was to be the first of many times he'd spend on the wide, shaded veranda that encircled the house, an ice pack on the lump where the steering wheel got him, a cold can of Budweiser to feed the inner man. He found out the Avenging Angel had a name—Linda—and best of all, that it was *Miss* Linda. She'd spent two years at Hollins, came home when her mother died to help her father through the first couple of weeks and hadn't ever gone back.

He met her father, a retired state senator, whom he liked

on sight, got invited to dinner, and began the relationship that resulted two years later in a wedding ceremony under the enormous willow tree dominating the front lawn.

Six years ago, he thought, time *really* does fly when you're having fun. Now there were Betsy and Little Tom to share it all with, too—lucky, just rabbit lucky.

Well, best get to it, be here all night otherwise. He plowed away at the stacks of papers and folders and documents on his desk, making appropriate notes to his secretary as to their disposition the next day, scribbling reminders for her to put in the follow-up file for action. He finally turned to the task that ended every working day for him: summing up thoughts on the day's activities in a spiral-ring diary. Diary keeping was new to him when he joined the firm—the Senior Partner had said it wasn't mandatory, but that *he* had found it a helpful way to recap daily progress, as well as provide some history as projects unfolded.

So he tried it, found it worked for him, and had kept diaries ever since. For him they were not simply historical records; he often used them as a method to express half-formed ideas, options, and plans—some of which changed markedly as his involvement in each case deepened. Early on, he discovered a secret drawer in the Williamsburg desk in his office. It was really a drawer within the main drawer of the massive old piece. Because of the nature of his diaries, he kept the current one locked away in the secret drawer, taking finished ones home with him for safekeeping.

He opened the desk, got out the diary, quickly ran through the past weeks' entries, and paused for a minute to collect his thoughts before beginning to record.

He was particularly troubled by two of his current projects, for very different reasons. On one, he was concerned about the physical well-being of a client. In the last meeting the client had been almost incoherent, then had swung into a tirade, including a personal attack on him. Maybe it's physical, maybe it's a case of a screw loose, can't put my finger on it. Can't let that go on much longer, though. Wonder what that strange phone message was this afternoon? Check it tomorrow.

The other project concerned him most. He was becoming increasingly appalled at the depth of moral degradation he was becoming exposed to, and the impact it had and could have on the community and all its residents. God knows I'm no bluenose, he thought, but these guys have gone too far, much too far. We've got to put a stop to this kind of thing once and for all before they get every one of us.

He wrote steadily, carefully, pausing occasionally to review the entries, then yawned, looked at his watch, and decided to call it a day. Locking up the diary, he put his jacket on and left the big briefcase behind. Enough work for one day; I think I earned my keep. He turned out the lights, closed up the office, and got on the elevator down to the underground parking lot.

He always used the twenty-minute drive home as a kind of separation process, a way to put the workday behind him and to anticipate family activity to come. He shared some business-related thoughts with Linda, appreciating her ability to get to the heart of things, but in the main he tried to keep the occupations apart. It is an occupation to run a family, particularly mine, and you have to work just as hard at being a Daddy as you do at becoming a Partner. Otherwise, what's the worth of it?

A nightgown from Paris, umm um—bet she's a knockout in it. Linda had kept her figure marvelously, despite two kids in five years. Happily, he found himself still aroused and excited by the promise of the firm body whether in a nightgown or a bathing suit—hell, even in a poncho she'd look superb. Okay, Mademoiselle Fifi, Le Great Lovaire, Tomas, is on zee way!

The headlights picked up a car parked catercorner across from his house, pointing back toward the main road. Two heads close together—he dimmed the headlights in courtesy and as a sort of a salute to romance. Kids had to find someplace to get it on. Have a good time, folks, but be careful about it. There's more than enough of that stuff going around these days.

He parked the car, turned off the lights, and walked toward the front door with the two flanking carriage lanterns. She *did* stay up, he thought, as his head exploded in an all-consuming flash of light.

*   *   *

"Okay, that's got it, let's get the hell out of here."

"You sure?"

"Positive. Blew up like a pumpkin."

Lights began coming on in the neighborhood, sleepy people attracted by the noise, stumbling out to find the cause, seeing nothing—since there was nothing to be seen.

Save at one house, where a welcoming wife leaned against her front doorway, sobbing as if she could never, ever stop.

2

On a glorious Sunday afternoon in the middle of September we were rolling home from West End, Grand Bahama, aboard *Smollert's Folly,* at a comfortable three thousand RPMs, the *Folly*'s big beam making short work of the mild swells, giving us a smooth run with no chance of broken crockery. I'd put us on a southwest course for the Hillsboro Inlet, kicked in the automatic pilot, tuned the big Emerson radio direction finder to station WQIS in Cypress Beach. WQIS is a 50-KW clear-channel station, which makes it the RDF operators' dream, even if their taste in music leaves something to be desired. In fact, it leaves a lot to be desired unless you're heavily into Zulu war chants—but from a navigational standpoint it's absolutely first cabin.

Ollie Morse—actually Admiral Oliver Hazard Morse, USN, Ret.—was lounging in one of the fighting chairs aft, feet cocked up on the starboard cockpit coaming, periodically tossing the last bits of bait squid over the rail, which was probably why every seagull in South Florida was flying convoy for us. Ollie's handsome niece, Cass, had volunteered to keep bridge watch so we didn't run into anything, but really to make sure we didn't get creamed by one of the speed freaks in the sixty-five knot cigarette boats they use to court suicide on the weekends.

Handsome is an inadequate word to describe Cass. Stunning is closer, spectacular probably the best choice. A shade over six feet tall, a hundred thirty-five pounds without an ounce of fat, the model's face that had paid her way through Wellesley, all crammed into an aqua-colored bikini that set off her deep tan perfectly. When we'd topped off the fuel tanks at West End earlier in the day, the old *Folly* got service the likes of which she'd never seen in her entire life. The pump jockey nearly made a career out of putting in fifty gallons. If I hadn't sent Cass below on a made-up errand, we'd probably still be there. Lascivious devil, no shame to him whatsoever.

I reminded myself that friends' relatives were high on my personal no-no list; besides which I was giving away sixteen or so years, which didn't put me in the Humbert Humbert class, but would look somewhat peculiar to the narrow minded.

I estimated remaining running time to the Hillsboro Inlet at a little over two hours, so I dropped down into the galley to retrieve Coke for the Intrepid Helmsman and me, and a frosty bottle of Saint Pauli Girl Beer—a German export topped only by Wernher Von Braun—for Ollie. Came topside, handed Wonder Woman her Coke and went aft to take up station in the other fighting chair across from Ollie. I told him the beer locker was in good shape, not to be bashful about refills, and that Cass seemed fully in control minding the wheel. So we sat in the sunshine, watching the squadrons of gulls wheeling overhead, sipping away, and generally feeling good about things—worldwide. Anchors aweigh my boys, anchors aweigh. . . .

* * *

Two weeks earlier, we had sat in the breakfast nook in my house at Lighthouse Point, surrounded by super-official-looking charts Ollie commandeered from an old pal at the Key West Naval Station. The coffee, and a box of Dunkin' Donuts had made the option selection process even more enjoyable.

My first choice had been to start with Bimini—which is close—then over to Nassau and on to Eleuthera, which I'd never seen but heard was truly special.

Ollie thought otherwise, "Too much for your first major cruise, Cam. You're okay—even pretty good—on the Intracoastal and for our short-haul day trips, but this is different. Too long and too much empty water. I know we've had a mild season so far but those things can blow up quicker than a Catholic bride. If one does blow up, best we have a hole we can run to in a hurry.

"I agree with you on Bimini. It's right to hand and I know a couple of ring twisters from the class of thirty-six who run a marina there—you'll like them both. Plus you'll see some pretty wild craft over there, the big Matthews and Rybovichs and such, quarter of a million dollars per.

"Then we'll swing through the Northwest Providence Channel and run up into the lee of Great Abaco. There'll be a little bonefishing there, not much, but some, and a good chance for swimming and scuba and just hacking around.

"Now for a favor. I have a niece who's spending the week of the thirteenth on Grand Bahama. If we started out Monday of that week we could pick her up at West End Saturday afternoon. Save her a plane fare and we'll probably be tired of looking at each other by then."

So that's what we did, leaving Great Abaco behind, picking our way through Little Bahama Bank above the main island, running along the coast, and puttering into West End at four thirty that Saturday, sunburned, tired, and completely at peace.

A couple of years back, I met a guy named Ted Rowe at a party. He made a living sailing a ninety-foot, three-stick schooner through the West Indies, carrying charter customers.

"You wouldn't believe what happens on some of these cruises," he said, "I think the only thing close to it must be taking people on safari in Africa. Civilized, successful folks can turn into monsters at sea . . . drunks, tyrants, whiners,

would-be lovers, the whole kit and kaboodle. I've finished
more than one cruise where nobody but the crew was speaking to each other. I've boiled it all down to the Ted Rowe
Rule: The ultimate test of friendship is the ability to coexist
more than three days at sea on a charter boat."

I'd understood the theory then, and with Ollie watched it
work in practice. Thirty-six feet of boat is not a lot of room;
there are literally times when you feel you're living in the
other person's back pocket. Surprisingly, Ollie showed some
major talent as a cook, which was fortunate since my idea of
self-prepared fare is to add a slug of chianti to a tin of Dinty
Moore's beef stew. So Ollie did the cooking and I tended to
the more disagreeable chores of dishwashing, garbage disposal, and the like.

We seemed to pass the Ted Rowe test just fine—Ollie
certainly did and I hoped I held up my end as well. Ollie is a
world class yarn spinner—which helped—but he was also
good at saying nothing when silence was clearly the best
course of action, and he even got me talking about myself,
which is something I do very rarely.

We'd anchored in the protected cove of a small island off
Great Abaco after a full day of sun, open water, and a marvelous two hours' worth of an unexpected school of dolphins,
one of which was about to be our supper. When we secured
the *Folly* fore and aft, I went below and built us two hefty jars
of Navy Grog, cheating some by using a bottle of mix, but
making up for it with a healthy dollop each of the good
Mount Gay rum.

We sat working on the grog watching the sun go down,
with just enough breeze to discourage any mosquito activity
when Ollie said, "If my instincts weren't so good, I'd swear
you were AWOL from the French Foreign Legion. In all the
time I've known you, you've hardly said two words about
yourself."

"That's because talking about me bores me silly. I'd
much rather spend time figuring out what other people are
about."

"Commendable, at least directionally. Far too many people got it the other end to. Look—I know you were in the Marine Corps and I know you played pro football—even saw you one time when you came down to play the Dolphins. I also know you're close with that Reverend Graham fella up in Boca Raton and that's where it stops. If it isn't being too nosy, what causes a young guy like you to live in South Florida like us retireds?"

"In a way I *am* retired. I played six and a half seasons for New York until they got my knee and turned me into Super Gimp. I was lying in the hospital feeling terminally sorry for myself until Billy showed up and dragged me down to Boca to rehabilitate the knee and slap some sense into my skull."

"That's not his real name is it? *Billy* Graham?"

"No, his real name is Gerry, the Right Reverend Gerald R. Graham, to be precise. He and I were in the Marine Corps together, from Parris Island to 'Nam. He's a helluva guy."

"What keeps you busy when you're not helping me clobber pompano?"

"You mean do I have a job? Not really. A little of this, a little of that. I do some scouting for New York during the season; pay's lousy but the job's fun. My dad left my brother and me some money, not a fortune, but enough to live on. I've got it in a tax-free municipal bond fund my ex-wife, the banker, told me about, so Uncle Sugar gets as little as my accountant can hold him to."

"Ex-wife? I didn't know you'd been married."

"Painful topic. She's a terrific person. Her name is Lydia . . . Lydia Longstreet Vance . . . from Charlotte, North Carolina. I christened her the Pearl of the Piedmont, all my friends call her Pearl—drives her parents nuts, they think it sounds too undignified. We were married almost four years; football and a couple of other things broke it up. This pleasure barge we're bucketing around in is named after her lawyer, Stead Smollert—truly the Willie Sutton of divorce lawyers. I call her *Smollert's Folly* because its about the only thing he *didn't* get."

"Don't you do some work for that lawyer, Dick Ellis?"

"Legwork investigation, pretty routine stuff. Dick covers my expenses and puts me on a per diem compensation. Last thing I did for him was to locate a young heiress—one of the Wentworth family—you know, the headache tablet king. Lisa Wentworth. I'd have been better off if they'd paid me in pills.

"Took me three solid months to find her. I tracked her all over Florida, then to Texas where she'd been for a while, then Mexico City, Acapulco, and Mazatlan. Finally found her in one of those unpronounceable towns—all Xs and Zs and Ls—in Yucatan. She was in one of the resort hotels there, shacked up with a lifeguard, blowing Mexican Gold like they were Marlboros. She wasn't exactly overjoyed to see me. Told me to get lost. Said tell her family to get stuffed, down to the last nephew.

"So, I got lost. Went back and gave Ellis the address and the messages, told him it was going to take dynamite to move that lady out of Yucatan. All I got out of the trip were some hairy plane rides and a case of the Aztec two-step—it took a month to get rid of it. Why are you laughing?"

"It doesn't sound like the typical private eye, you know, with the false business cards, the sort that trips up the villain, the fastest gun in town, that kind of thing."

"Don't get me wrong. I've read every Travis McGee book John D. MacDonald ever wrote and I'm the biggest sucker in the world for James Garner on "The Rockford Files" reruns. Sure there are people like that but not me—I'm just not clever enough. Besides, private investigating, at least what I've done of it, is pretty mind-crushing material, just hours and days of plodding away, asking questions, following up, reporting back. Nothing fancy and not very steady work either. I'm glad I don't count on it to keep the wolf away.

"Dick arranged for me to get a license—mostly because cops aren't too crazy about having civilians bumping around their turf—so it's Angus Cameron MacCardle, part-time PI. Exciting, huh?"

"Containable, son, although I'm sure it's more than you

make it out to be. Got a proposition for you, though. If you construct two more of those lethal concoctions and get the hell out of my galley, I'll make the best dolphin dinner you ever ate. Deal?"

"Done deal, Admiral, and high time too, if I might say so."

*   *   *

After mooring in West End, Ollie had gone ashore in search of a phone, while I washed down the *Folly*, coiled her lines up, promised the metalwork a polish job next week, and went below to try to make the cabin look respectable after a week's worth of not too tidy use by the pair of us. I even shaved and changed clothes, having already decided we'd have the final supper ashore, no matter how good Ollie was in the galley.

When I got back topside, Ollie and his niece were standing on the pier looking down at me—holding hands. It was quite a picture: the slim, lovely young woman and the craggy-faced, white-haired man right out of *The Ancient Mariner*. As they looked at each other, though, it became instantly clear that this was, indeed, a very special relationship.

I waved them on down to the wharf's loading platform, boathooked the *Folly* flush against the lip and handed them both over the side. After the introductions, I took drink orders, announced that we would eat shoreside, my treat, and suggested to Ollie that he might want to stop being a contestant in the "Ernest Hemingway Look-Alike Contest."

"You weren't making noises like that when the big wind hit us, Captain Ahab, but I guess I can dig up something, seeing as you're paying for dinner, long as I don't have to wear a tie."

Cass wanted Perrier—with lime if I had it, which I did, albeit the last of the stock we'd packed aboard a week ago. In honor of the occasion, I made a shaker of martinis which sat on the chart shelf with a thin sheen of perspiration beading its metal.

Waiting for the admiral to emerge, I asked Cass how her vacation had been, what her impressions were of Grand Bahama.

"In a word, bor-ing. My girlfriend got sun poisoning on day two. The hotel doctor popped her into bed for forty-eight hours and she went home Friday. Every male I've seen so far is either married, gay, or something out of an X-rated movie plot. Talk about tacky—I think the word must have been invented to describe Freeport. The whole thing is early Southern California Fake Spanish.

"I did find one nice place, though, and I suggest we go there tonight. It's called the Royal Poinciana Beach Club, just outside of Freeport—easy ride in a cab from here.

"They tell me the Mafia owns it. Honest to goodness. They say you can't get a reservation to stay there in January or February—it's a sort of reward for the troops for a job well done, I guess. Anyway, it's very nice and . . . ah, Uncle Ollie, don't you look handsome. With the two of you I think I'm finally going to enjoy at least one night in this distressing place."

The cab ride wasn't quite as easy as Cass had made it sound. It was more like long, expensive, and potentially bad for your health. After we missed the seventy-eighth chicken by at least two millimeters, I leaned back, closed my eyes, and listened to them chattering away happily back and forth. Didn't open the eyes until we got there, either. Much safer.

She hadn't exaggerated in describing the Royal Poinciana, though; understated it, if anything. It was a big, sprawling, two-story building with dark timber and gleaming whitewashed facades. Inside, the floors were all cool, dark marble, high ceilings, and arches throughout, creating a feeling of openness and relaxation. The place was absolutely spotless, showing zero signs of wear, anywhere. If this was owned by the Mafia, I hoped they'd be kind enough to send me a list of all their other properties.

The maitre d' bowed us through the dining room to a corner table overlooking the ocean, handing around leather-bound oversized menus with the choices written in a purple calligraphic style. A lovely mocha-colored waitress took our drink orders, repeating them in a particularly musical cadence. I wondered on her origin. Cass said probably Haitian.

"Evidently, some time back, the Head Bahama won an election with a platform based on the slogan 'Bahamas for the Bahamians.' After that all the service jobs were restricted to Bahamian residents. They tell me everything came to an absolute standstill. Apparently your average Bahamian doesn't give a fig if the sun comes up—which is terrific for his stress quotient but not so great for service. Most of the maids, waiters, porters, and whatnot in all the good hotels were Haitian. Slowly, the managers are starting to feed them back into the system; illegal as sin but nobody seems to be complaining."

"Wherever did we pick up that little footnote to history?"

"From the piano player in the lounge here. He's been on Grand Bahama over twenty-five years—I'd guess he's seen it all—what there is to see, that is."

After dinner we went to the lounge to hear Cass's piano player—quite good if you like calypso music, which I do. It also gave us, at least me, the opportunity to prepare for the cab ride home. Four double Tia Marias on the rocks made me pliable enough not to wince as the local version of Mario Andretti tried to break the land speed record for 1955 Chevrolets.

We dropped Cass at her hotel, told her we'd be by at nine next day to pick her up please to be packed and checked out you're welcome we had a wonderful time, too.

Back to the *Folly* to sleep, perchance to dream. Ollie, no doubt, of the days of derring-do. I, made of less stern stuff, of the snapping, deep brown eyes and the slim figure of the model with the peculiar name.

*   *   *

Nearing home, I took over the wheel. The Sunday afternoon traffic began to build—the big fishing boats first then a

variety of sail and power boats, finally a smattering of red and
white diver-down buoys floating above the reefs. The RDF
had been right on the button, I thought, recognizing the distinctive shape of the Boca Raton Hotel and Club Tower as we
slid south. For about ten minutes until the bridge opened we
milled around the Hillsboro Inlet, then tucked the *Folly* in
line, proceeding at low, low speed into the Intracoastal and
turning south toward Lighthouse Point.

The first canal to starboard, then three more canals, a
port turn, and we were home. End of a voyage. A curious
admixture of feelings. Glad to be home; sorry it's over. It'll
be great to take an honest-to-God shower; will you ever forget that blue marlin tail-walking in Little Horseshoe Sound.
New places, new sights, new friends. All imprinted on the
mind, to be retrieved like Kodachrome slides, for reviewing
when things got dull. Good old *Folly*—you took every mistake a rookie skipper could throw at you and handled them
all, got us home safe as a church. Have to do it again. Soon.
Yessir, real, real, soon.

Ollie and Cass offered help with the washing-down
chores, but I said they'd hold till tomorrow, better to come on
inside for a farewell drink and a call to the redoubtable Mrs.
Morse to say they had arrived and were on their way and
should be home in time for supper.

Ollie went over the starboard rail, seabag in hand, me in
tow just behind. Cass jumped down lightly from the foredeck
where she'd coiled the mooring line . . . and almost broke her
neck, pitching forward face down, with a little gasp of pain.
Ollie got to her just as she sat up, cradling an ankle, rocking
back and forth and making little mewing sounds. The fall had
roughed up her knee badly, the scraped skin an ugly feature
against the honey tan.

"You okay, Cass? What happened, sweetheart?"

"I don't know, everything looked safe, and then my foot
just gave way."

"Let me feel it . . . All right, nothing broken—just a
good hard fall. Can you stand up?"

"I think so. Ooooh, that smarts, penalty for being such a klutz, I guess."

She hadn't been a klutz at all. I'd walked over to where she'd fallen and found out why. A board in the forward section of the dock had worked loose, I could rock it back and forth easily with my foot. Probably a rotten section in the supporting beam. Wonderful, another back-breaking chore if I had to rip all that up. But at least she hadn't gotten badly hurt, give thanks for little favors.

She leaned on both of us all the way to the house, where I broke out the first-aid equipment and patched up her knee.

"Cass, if that ankle blows up on you, go get it checked by a doctor—that's what insurance is for. I'm sorry as hell."

"Not your fault. Think I'll skip the Perrier this once. Could I please have a medicinal gin and tonic?"

Easily done, along with a mug of grog for the admiral and me. They waved off the offer of a second drink and I walked them to the door, Cass limping most noticeably. Thanked Ollie for all his help, accepted the invitation to dinner Thursday, waved as the big Cadillac pulled away.

Unfortunate ending for an otherwise perfect trip.

I found it was getting on toward eight o'clock and that I was bone weary. Eggs and bacon time, quick, easy, and reasonably nourishing for a Sunday supper. I finished cleaning up the kitchen, listening to the Yankee-Red Sox game on WIOD, thinking how good a wide bed was going to feel.

Just before turning in, I checked the answering machine on my telephone. I got it after realizing I would probably be spending extended periods of time away from home and adhering to my Scottish upbringing that said three months of an answering service would more than pay for the machine. Besides, it's tax deductible.

The weekly catch was a mixture of social calls, invitations, and offers to sell me everything from Arthur Murray dance lessons to a cemetery plot for two at Shady Lawn. Really.

I noticed that Dick Ellis had called, first on Thursday then every day since, including today. Three times today.

Each message the same. "Urgent you call me as soon as you can."

That, too, could wait until tomorrow. I needed another Lisa Wentworth like Custer needed a few more Sioux. Call you tomorrow, Dick. Right now, I've got bigger and better things to do. Like twelve hours of sleep. Maybe a dream or two.

Exeunt all, *without* alarums.

3

"Rise and shine, boys and girls, it's seven ayem on a beeyootiful Gold Coast Monday. Monty Drew comin' to ya on the big QIS, the mighty six ninety. Right after the news, I'll be back to play this week's *numero uno*, 'You Made Me Go All The Way,' by Fata Morgana and the Camelots!"

Oh, come now.

I'd set the alarm for seven last Monday, needing the time for last-minute preparations for our trip, and forgotten to re-set it last night. Why it was tuned to the mighty 690 was anybody's guess. I flipped the switch mercifully provided by some geniuses at GE and made Monty go away—hopefully forever. Rolled over and promptly went back to sleep, eventually getting up at a much more civilized nine fifteen.

I shrugged into the big, blue terry robe the Pearl had given me—the one that always makes me feel I'm off to do battle with Muhammad Ali. Shuffled out to the kitchen to see about breakfast. The larder was a long way from overflowing on this beeyootiful Monday morning. Knowing I'd be gone for seven days, I'd purposely run to rock bottom all the stock that could get stale or sour, so this was not going to be a breakfast to remember. Fortunately, I'd remembered to stow a box of English muffins in the freezer; there was one last tin of tomato juice that had somehow survived my Bloody Mary friends. That plus a pot of coffee would have to do it: not great, but maybe enough to get me to the supermarket.

I carried it all out to the breakfast nook, slid into the long bench seat nearest the wall phone, picked it up, and called Dick Ellis. Miz Jane, his superefficient secretary, told me he would be in court all day, was most anxious to see me, would certainly phone in, at which time she'd give him the message, would I be home the rest of the morning? Yes, I would, thank you very much, nice to talk to you, too.

In my living room is a monstrous, six-cushion couch one of my puckish friends christened the USS Lexington, in honor of its aircraft carrier dimensions. Armed with a second mug of coffee, I turned on the television set and sank back into the Lexington to watch Merv Griffin while I sorted through an action plan for the day.

I picked up on Merv when I was in the hospital, right after they'd made hash out of my knee. I think he's the very best of the talk show hosts—principally because his guests seem genuinely comfortable with him. Consequently, he is able to get the best out of them, which may contain a lesson for all of us. Ever notice how truly few good *listeners* there are in the world? Think about it, see if you don't agree.

This morning's lineup included Joan Rivers, Judy Collins, an author who'd written a book entitled *Twenty Days to a Slimmer You,* and an aspiring young comedian who did for his craft what Jack the Ripper did for door-to-door salesmanship.

Rivers was her usual hysterically funny self, Collins's contralto as haunting and beautiful as ever, while the would-be comedian and the author provided welcome periods of inattention to help the day-planning process.

I started by returning all the phone calls that required returning—which weren't many—called Billy to check in and reaffirm dinner tonight, ended with a mission of pure pleasure.

"Cypress Beach Racquet Club, Good mo-orning."

"Henny Youngman here."

"Oh, Cam, you nut, how long you going to hold that one over my head?"

"Only another twenty, maybe thirty years, Carole."

"How was the Great Nautical Outing, Sir Francis?"

"Pretty good, mostly thanks to Ollie. At least I didn't hit anything or drown us. Look, the reason I called was to check your barbecued ribs quotient."

"Low, My Captain, dangerously low."

"Thought so. Mine too. How about Rubino's, tomorrow night, pick you up at your place around six thirty?"

"Sounds good to me, I'll be the tall blonde in the lobby wearing bib and rubber gloves."

"Don't get gussied up on my account."

"No fear of that. See you then, hon."

"Bye, Carole."

Carole Cummings is one of the great bonuses that life as a sort-of-private eye has provided me. I had met her in the course of trying to uncover who murdered one of Billy's parishoners—a woman named Laura Morgan. When I got involved, the police were holding her husband, Ralph, on a Murder One count and he had undoubtedly the worst alibi I've ever heard—past, present, and probably forever. One of the few contact points we had was a tennis pro at the Cypress Beach Racquet Club who'd been a friend of Laura's. Ralph had given me his first name—Dana—but drew a blank on the last name. So, I'd called the Club to find out. Enter Carole Cummings.

"Dana Shepherd?" she'd asked.

In typical smart-ass fashion, I asked how many Dana's they *had* over there.

Non-typical response, "Oh, my goodness, it's Henny Youngman. I can't tell you how much I've enjoyed your work."

On and on in similar vein.

At the end of the conversation, I'd hung up laughing, impressed by the deft way she'd handled me, and by her basic irreverence. The physical part turned out to be no less impressive, the blonde hair worn in a ponytail that only great cheekbones, jawline, and ears can get away with; the athlete's figure crowned with an impressive pair of what the Pearl used to refer to as "upper frontals."

Our relationship, now eighteen months old, maintained the ease and warmth it began with, a no-holds, no-pressures, no-undying-promises kind of mutual understanding. Carole liked the outdoor life too, the swimming, waterskiing, fishing, and just-lazing-in-the-sun parts most of all.

In turn, she'd taught me to play bridge—the best of all card games—not making fun of my mistakes early on, bringing me along in a confidence-building way, to a point where we could now play competitively with all save those who make a lifetime career out of amassing master's points.

The physical part of the relationship had developed comfortably as well, into one of no demands, no quid pro quos, just a thoroughly mutual enjoyment. A time had come when it just seemed natural to go to bed together and we had—with neither shame nor shyness—drawing pleasure from each other, waking grinning in the morning. The finest kind.

My marriage, at least after Stead Smollert had done with me, had soured me on the institution, but now I was beginning to have second thoughts. Might not be the world's worst idea, big fella. Sure, you can get along without Carole, but do you really want to try?

The telephone rang, giving me an excuse to delay grappling with that issue; it was Dick Ellis.

"Where the hell you been? Trying to outdo Magellan?"

"Seven days doth not a circumnavigation make, Counselor. Got back Sunday night, noticed all your messages, so here I am. What's up? And let me tell you right now, if it's another Lisa Wentworth number, thanks, but no thanks, Dick."

"Lisa Wentworth? This is a lot grimmer than Lisa Wentworth the worst day she ever saw. I'm down at the courthouse, jammed to the ears, be here for the balance of the day. I've got to see you, though, want you to get going right away. You remember the Pelican's Roost, don't you? It's that good saloon, three, four blocks from here. Meet me there at five thirty, can do?"

"Sure, but why all the urgency?"

"No time to explain. Due back in court just about now and this one warrants time to describe. See you at five thirty and thanks."

I spent the remainder of the morning playing househusband, dumping the sea-salted clothes into the washer, calling to reinstate delivery of the *Fort Lauderdale News-Sun Sentinel,* cleaning up the breakfast debris. Opened all the windows and doors, started the two big Hunter ceiling fans whirring to drive the musty stale smell of reconditioned air out of the house. If I had my druthers, I'd turn off the air conditioning permanently, but one of the go-withs of living on the water is high humidity. Exposed to it too long, the rugs start to grow, clothes take on a wet-bathing-suit clamminess, and you might even start the wallpaper peeling, to mention a few. I could risk a couple of hours, though—anything to get rid of the shut-in-air quality.

Just after noon, I stopped my heavyweight contender impersonation, put on clean shorts and polo shirt, kicked on the beat-up old Topsiders that live by the front door, and went off to Pantry Pride, shopping list in hand, to replenish the grocery supplies.

I got back, stowed all the goodies appropriately, and discovered I'd forgotten to write down stew meat for tonight's supper. Typical. Back to the market, pick up the stew meat, stand for half an hour in what they laughingly call the express line, watching elderly women try a variety of scams involving too many packages, coupons, out-of-date sale ads, and permutations of all three. You have to be there to believe it. Incredible.

The *Folly* got most of the afternoon, which was only fair after her performance at sea. What the brochures, the magazines, and the salesmen don't tell you—particularly the salesmen—is that maintaining a boat of any size takes a regimen of constant attention; particularly if you use the boat a lot and want to grow old together gracefully.

The oil had at least fifty hours on it so I changed that, in both engines, oil filters as well. Diesel fuel is more efficient than gasoline, but much dirtier—another little tidbit the manufacturers aren't quick to point out—so that meant a new fuel filter for each. Belt replacement and tightening chewed up another hour. I had batteries to top off, electrical wiring and connections to be checked. Finally, I could replace the deck plates, wipe my hands off on a piece of waste, and turn my attention to the cosmetics. First a general hosing down to get rid of most of the salt. It gets blown everywhere and it eats away at virtually everything. Then application of a light marine detergent—scrub down fore and aft—a washoff of the soap scum, and squeegeeing to minimize water spotting.

Four thirty by the time I got to the metalwork, which is a project all by itself, requiring special cleaners, polishes, and endless patient drudgery. Don't do today what you can put off until tomorrow—a maxim to be lived by, and the only answer in this case, if my appointment was to be kept on time.

I gave the *Folly* a final fond pat on her quarter rail, went inside to shower off the body and try to restore a sense to my own cosmetics, at least what sense could be made.

Wrapped in one of the terry bathsheets I phoned Billy, told him about my meeting with Ellis, reminded him he had a key to the house, just come by when he felt like it, I'd probably be back around eight. I realize it seems a little peculiar to let someone else have a key to your house, particularly another man, but Billy is my closest friend and, the last time I looked, Episcopal priests weren't leading the league in crimes of any nature.

In deference to my appointment, I decided my usual dress code of khakis and polo shirt wouldn't make it, though—like Ollie—I drew the line at a necktie. Fortunately, most of South Florida agrees with me, even most of the best places, making me glad not to be a salesman for Nat's Nifty Neckwear or whoever had the tie franchise down here.

A tattersall button-down shirt, light gray summer-weight worsted slacks, the navy-blue linen blazer with the Lighthouse Point Yacht Club insignia on the breast pocket. Black, over-the-calf socks, the Bally loafers with the gold miniature stirrups over the instep. Laid-Back Establishment. Enough to get me into the Boca Raton Club, more than enough for the Pelican's Roost, but not so much that it looked as if I were trying to sell something. Clothing plays an interesting role in the Eastern power structure, including the Florida Old Money crowd—understated, always understated. The Pearl had taught me that. Right after we were married, she'd torn my clothes closet apart, giving most of the contents to the superintendent with instructions to have them cleaned and burned, marched me down to Brooks, and had the clerks start all over on me from the ground up. I'd never paid much attention to clothes before, having spent most of my life in uniforms of one sort or another, but if the Big Kids put great stock in what you wore, it seemed like a pretty small price to pay for easy acceptance.

I'd had the sense to park the car in the shade of the big olive tree in front of my house so the drive downtown was relatively comfortable, the air conditioning having been given a head start. It was still uncomfortably hot as I dropped the car off at the municipal parking lot and walked to the Pelican. Inside was pleasantly dark and cool, the Muzak playing middle-of-the-road popular at a level that didn't stifle conversation. I looked through a cast of unfamiliar faces, not spotting Ellis; evidently he'd gotten hung up longer than anticipated. I went to the back and staked out a table against the wall, away from the bar where we could talk in normal tones. Then I *did* see a familiar face.

"Good to see you, Mr. MacCardle, been a long time."

"You're right, Donna, it *has* been a long time. Good to see you again. How you doin'?"

"About the same. No complaints. Pete's back working charter again, swears he's off the sauce for good. Jeff went in the Navy in August, and my other one, Debby, started high school, can't hardly believe it."

"I can't hardly believe you have kids that age, Donna. Sure doesn't show."

"Oh, go on with you, flatterer. Last time you were here, with Mr. Ellis, you talked me into singing. That was a night to recall."

"Matter of fact, Mr. Ellis is who I'm waiting for, but I don't think there's going to be much singing."

"What can I get you meanwhile? How about that Amstel beer and a bowl of mixed nuts?"

"Just the ticket. You have the memory of an elephant."

"And a behind to match, which you was kind enough not to mention. Just settle in and I'll be right back."

So I settled in, sipping the cold tangy beer, picking out the cashews and pecans to nibble on, wondering for the umpteenth time today what was important enough to have Dick drag me away from vegetating in comfort at home.

* * *

He finally showed up shortly after six, acknowledging my wave, working his way through the crowd toward our table, forced to stop periodically en route by people who wanted to ask him something, tell him something, or simply say hello.

I think sometimes that Dick knows everybody in South Florida, or at least all the people that are worth knowing. He comes by it naturally, granted his family's background. Clayton Ellis came to Florida to serve on Andy Jackson's staff when Andy was governor, before Florida was even a state. The family tree includes plantation owners, cattle ranchers, orange growers, politicians, and power brokers; integral strands in the colorful fabric of Florida's history.

Dick did a fine job at Stetson, making the *Law Review*, eventually graduating third in his class. He'd become a first-rate trial lawyer, developing a reputation and a clientele far

beyond the state borders. Already there was talk about send-
ing him to Tallahassee. Perhaps, from there to Washington.
He wore all the success easily, being one of the most unpre-
tentious people I've ever met. Knowing and working with him
made it clear to me that if he decided to go into politics, he'd
come up big.

"Hi, Cam, sorry I'm late—don't get up, I used to be an
enlisted man myself."

"That's an old joke, Counselor. Besides, I didn't even
twitch. Tough day at the office?"

"The worst. I've got two hearings going on at once—the
younger guys are really pitching in to help but today I could
have used a pair of rollerskates."

"You *do* look a little peaked."

"You don't. You look like a page out of the Land's End
catalog."

"Salt air, sunshine, and clean living, Richard. Try it
sometime and see."

"Too busy just now. Clean living, huh? You wouldn't
know clean living if it bit you on the backside."

Donna came by, patted him on the shoulder, took his
drink order, brought it back with a refill for me and another
bowl of mixed nuts. An absolute saint, even if a little broad in
the beam.

One thing I'd learned early on—there was no sense trying to rush Dick Ellis. I'd find out what was on his mind when
he was ready to tell me, not before, never by pushing. A big
mistake opposition lawyers make with him is trying to go
ahead too fast—invariably he finds a way to let them hang
themselves. So we chatted along amiably about a thousand
things—his family, my trip, the Dade/Broward proposed sta-
dium squabble, everything but the reason for his calling this
meeting. I knew it was his way of getting away from the pressures of the day, perhaps also a way of postponing telling me
something disagreeable. He really wasn't his usual chipper,
confident self today, either—he looked tired and drawn out—

those simultaneous hearings must have been taking their toll. I decided to try an oblique-angle approach.

"Much as it pains me to ask, did you ever resolve the Lisa Wentworth issue?"

"Eventually. I gave the family your report, which didn't seem to surprise them at all—and some hard-line advice they were smart enough to accept. In essence, I proposed they make her a trade: her stock, voting rights, and privileges irrevocably, in return for a guaranteed annual income of fifty thousand tax-free dollars for the rest of her life. A good deal for both sides. They get her out of their hair, and she can live well forever unless inflation really goes bananas or her taste in boyfriends gets a lot more expensive.

"Our man located her right where you said she'd be. She signed the papers with a bartender and the manager as witnesses, no questions asked, wham, bam, thank you ma'am. End of the Lisa Wentworth story. I hope it's a happy ending. God knows we've had enough of the other kind lately."

I sensed he was ready to get to the main reason for calling me and signaled Donna to bring us another round, which he grabbed at gratefully.

"Thanks, Cam, I can sure use it. Let me give you the facts as we know them, then we can go on from there, although, I must say, there are pathetically few facts involved.

"Last Wednesday night the brightest of our Associate Partners, Tom Horton, was shot and killed right in front of his house in Cypress Beach."

"Jeezuz. Prowler?"

"Could have been, but we just don't know. His wife, Linda, told us she saw his car headlights in the driveway, was going downstairs to open the door when she heard the shot."

"Shot?"

"Shot. One. Period."

"Witnesses?"

"None. Or at least we haven't been able to find one yet."

"Somebody must have seen . . ."

"If somebody did, they aren't volunteering. It was almost

eleven o'clock. I don't know about you, but most folks are in bed by then, or getting ready for it. There were four other people, neighbors, who heard the shot. One thought it was an automobile backfiring; one thought it was a loud television set; the other two actually went outside—nothing, no one."

"Why is that name familiar? I don't think I ever met him."

"Thank the Lord one of us is still functioning normally. *I* told you about him, at least a little. He was assigned the project of rewriting Ralph Morgan's will just after he and Laura married. Ralph called Tom from jail the morning after Laura was murdered and Tom came to me for help."

"You said more than that."

"I know. It's what makes this whole thing particularly horrible for me. Tom is, was, one of Harlan Horton's boys. Judge Harlan Horton. His father and mine go back forever together. When Tom graduated from law school, Dad asked me to interview him. At the time, I was a little concerned about possible conflict of interest, I mean the Judge is still active, but I was so impressed with Tom, I said the hell with conflict of interest—we could quash that pretty easily if it ever came up. Net, we hired Tom and he became one of my protégés, very much like a big brother relationship."

"Worse and worse, old friend."

"And worse still. He left a wife and two small children. The girl, Betsy, is four and a half. Feel like guessing who her godfather is?"

"Somehow I think I know."

"Right the first time. I stood with the family at the funeral Saturday, Linda with Little Tom in her arms, Betsy hanging on to my hand with both of hers. Afterwards, at the house, she asked me, 'What do we do now, Unca Dick?' I had a lump in my throat as big as a basketball. Couldn't break down there, though, had to wait until I got home. I haven't cried like that since my grandfather died, a long, long time ago.

"I went over there the next day, to explain the financial

aspects to Linda, but mostly to be with them. They'll be all right that way. Tom had his own insurance, the firm had a "key man" policy on him, and Linda has a modest trust fund from her father. We have a couple of experts in estate law so we can minimize the tax bite. They should be in good shape, even if she doesn't remarry."

"How's she taking it?"

"Much better than anybody would have a right to expect. I'm sure she has her private moments, but the public face, the one she shows the kids, is strong and brave. She's only slipped with me once, so far. At the doorway, Sunday, tears in her eyes, she whispered, 'Get them, Dick. Please, please, please. If it takes forever, please find out who did this to Tom.' I told her we would."

"Tough on you, Counselor."

"Yes, but far tougher on them. What do you do for two people whose world has just collapsed and another who's too young to understand?"

"Seems to me you're doing everything you can. I assume you want me to help."

"Please, Cam. I'm much too close to them and Tom to be even marginally objective. I have an atavistic reaction to rush out, find who did it, and kill them with my bare hands. Most unprofessional."

"But very understandable. Where do you want me to start?"

"For now, go home and think about it. We can meet in my office at nine tomorrow. I've got hearings in the afternoon, but at least we should have time to get you started."

"Want to begin earlier?"

"Thanks, I can't. Still have a law practice to run. I'll be there earlier, but I have to use the time to get ready for the afternoon. And while we're on the subject of time, it's seven thirty—I expect we'd best both be going. I'll pick up the tab."

"I'm sorry, Dick, inadequate words for such an occasion, I realize."

"Good as any. Thanks. See you tomorrow."

So we left, Dick engulfed in whatever thoughts and sorrows that beset him, I unable to shake the picture of the young mother at graveside and the little girl holding grimly to her godfather's hand.

*   *   *

"Well, it's about time. Here I am working my fingers to the bone on a super special goulash, while you're out gadding around the fleshpots with . . . hey, you don't look too hot, Cam."

"I've had worse meetings, Billy. I just can't seem to remember when."

"Well shake it off, pal. This is supposed to be a festive, welcome-home dinner. I had great visions of you and Ollie stranded on some barren little island trying to get messages out in bottles."

"Skip the levity, Padre. I'm not in the mood."

"Do we talk about it or do we spend the rest of the evening watching you play Macbeth?"

"You know, that's a hell of an insensitive thing to say . . . particularly for a minister."

"Nobody ever mistook me for Norman Vincent Peale. Now spit it out. That way maybe we can try moving the ball ahead."

So I told him the story and I probably embellished it because I have a habit of doing that when I'm feeling lousy about the world, which I for sure was. I gave him all the details of the murder itself, including the impact it was having on Dick, and ended describing the graveside picture I couldn't seem to erase from my mind. As I talked, he paced around the room, occasionally looking at me, taking it all in, the words, the gestures, and the tone of voice. When I finished, he came over, sat on the other end of the Lexington and said, "You're just too bloody suggestible. You want to take the weight of the world on your shoulders, bear everyone else's share of woe. Look, it's a terrible story, cruel, pathetic, all those dreadful things. I feel sorry, very sorry for them, including Dick. I agree, we, mostly you, Angus, have to help. But, we're not going to get anywhere if you wrap yourself in one of those black Scottish moods of yours, keening over the moors in search of shades."

It was like getting a bucket of cold water full in the face, I actually found myself shaking my head. He always knew what button to push to get the MacCardle doll operating again, and he'd just done it one more time. I *am* too suggestible—he was dead on about that, probably about the weight of the world thing too. Whatever, I had no right to visit it all on him, particularly if I wanted his help, which I did, badly.

"Macbeth? Keening over the moors? Well, then, 'Out, out, damned spot,' say I."

"That's *Lady* Macbeth's speech. No wonder you were a history major."

"Picky, picky."

"Welcome back to the real world."

"Thanks for the retrieval job, chum."

"Don't mention it. The goulash is ready, salad's in the refrigerator, garlic bread on the counter. If you can scrounge up a bottle of wine we'll be all set."

"At your service, Dominie."

The goulash was sensational. I went back to the pot twice, finally having to tip it on end to spoon out the last of the rich meat sauce. I wiped the plate clean with a slab of garlic bread, getting an almost sensual pleasure from the texture of the crust. A final glass of the slightly chilled Inglenook Navalle Zinfandel—my all-time favorite jug wine—to wash it down with. *Perfecto*. I wondered where all the appetite had come from, then realized I hadn't eaten all day—unless you count the English muffins—and I had put in a fair day's work on the *Folly*. But talk about good, Billy's goulash had just retired the word.

"You outdid yourself with that little number, chef."

"You're just happy to get a break from your Spam diet."

"I'm serious, that was just marvelous."

"It isn't very hard—like the women's magazines say, if

you can read, you can cook. The trick is in the recipe. I got it from Mrs. Morris, who claims she got it from her grandmother in Hungary. If they don't know how to make goulash, nobody does."

"Morris is Hungarian?"

"I said *Mrs.* Morris, dolt, her maiden name is probably some tongue twister that needs, as you would say, a vowel movement."

"You mean like good old Ziggy Mikalajczyk?"

"That idiot. Don't remind me. Walking mortar fire through his own people because he didn't believe his forward observer. I thought we'd all had it that day."

"Me too. I hope they chained that clown to a large mahogany desk in Youngstown, Ohio. Make me a copy of that recipe?"

"What for? Nobody around here but me . . . a-ha, don't tell me the formidable Miss Cummings can also *cook.* You'll break my lascivious heart."

"I thought lecherous friars went out with *Robin Hood*—and yes, she cooks, like a dream. Now, c'mon, we got to get to work."

We stacked the dishes in the sink for my attention later on, got mugs of coffee, and went out to the living room. Before we started, I asked Billy if he wanted an after-dinner drink. He said he would if I would, particularly if there was any Benedictine left. There is always Benedictine in my house, considered by the Pearl one of life's necessities, a rare topic on which we agreed. I poured us each a hefty beaker, knowing the sorting-out process would take a while.

"Cam, run the facts by me one more time, please."

"Okay. Name—Tom Horton. Profession—attorney. Problem—murder. Method—one gunshot. When—Wednesday, September fifteen, approximately eleven o'clock. Where—outside his house. Who—unknown. Witnesses—none. Motive—God only knows. Your move."

"Let me think. Tell you what, get a pad of paper and we

can just wander along out loud. You can take notes if anything makes sense."

"Whatever gets to you, Shylock."

"That's Sherlock and I very much doubt anything that fancy will happen, not with the mental equipment in this room."

"I'll ignore that."

"I wouldn't be at all surprised."

I'd done this before with Billy, starting when we were trying to figure out Laura Morgan's murder and proving the old bromide about two heads. The extra is that his head is far different from mine. I tend to intuition, sometimes flights of fancy, trying to connect seemingly unconnectable ideas. Billy is much more a logician, maybe from his seminary training. In any event, the dialogue process had proven helpful in the past and I hoped it would now.

We rambled back and forth over the next two hours. The gist of it, as I recall, was roughly as follows, starting with my attempt to try to provide a framework for us:

"I think we should recognize, going in, that there are any number of possible explanations for Tom Horton's murder, particularly given the extremely limited information we have. From a procedural standpoint, it seems to me we should begin by trying to eliminate options or we'll drive ourselves nuts. Make sense to you?"

"Yes, indeed. Please proceed, sir."

"Let's start by knocking out the zanies. You know, the thrill killers, like that group out in San Francisco a couple of years back. The reason is, we can't *do* anything about them unless an epidemic of it starts up. Even then it will be a police job to wire together. With me?"

"Yes. Let me try on the prowler question you asked Dick. Logic would say it wasn't a prowler. First of all we know there wasn't any stranger inside the house, or the wife—Linda, you said her name was?—Linda would surely have noticed. So, that means the prowler would have to have been outside. He hears the car, sees the headlights. Even if the headlights had picked him up, he'd still have plenty of time to make his getaway. Besides which, apparently he hadn't done anything, or at least nothing that attracted Linda's attention, then or now. So, if he hadn't done anything, it would seem to me he'd just take off. There isn't a reason to shoot someone. Make sense?"

"Eminent sense. Scratch prowlers for my money, too. I think—just a guess, I know—that our best shot is going to be someone who is or was involved with Tom Horton professionally.

"The man was a lawyer, Billy. Lawyers deal with people in a whole variety of ways. Lawyers get people convicted. Lawyers don't get people convicted. Lawyers help people, sue other people. Sometimes successfully, sometimes not as successfully as the clients hoped. Lawyers deal with divorce cases—I know all about that. Lawyers get involved with shady business deals, sometimes they even help cook them up. Lawyers may know things other people wished they didn't, wished hard enough to make them dead. And so on.

"Anyway, I'm gonna start by looking at what Horton did for Dick's law firm—all the way back to the day he joined them, if their records are that good. Bet that turns out to be the Mother Lode, ten bucks against a bent farthing."

"Maybe, Cam. At least it seems the place to start. There's one area we haven't touched on yet. It's the hard part or, put another way, the sensitive part. His personal life."

"You mean Linda? Come on."

"No. Not Linda. Not from what you tell me. But what if Horton was fooling around and got caught? Laura Morgan's sex life certainly surprised me. You remember? Maybe Horton was being unfaithful. Goodness, I don't know, maybe he was gay. Sounds far fetched, but you've got to look into it. Was he a crook? Could he have been doing something on the side besides his regular law practice? Unreported income could be a very tempting thing. Again, the point is, you'll simply have to look at his personal life, too. Even though I realize how painful that might be. I hope tact has gotten to be a larger part of your makeup."

"I'll try to keep it in mind. You done?"

"Yes. What do you have in the way of notes?" I scaled the yellow pad to him. On it I had written:

> Scrub zanies
> Prowlers—nix
> Job related—search records
> Personal life—ouch!

And in big block letters farther down the pad: VOTE FOR GRAHAM FOR D.A. THE PEOPLE'S CHOICE

"God help us all."

"I was counting on you for the big part of that. Seriously, this was more than helpful. The important notes are in my head. Nightcap?"

"No thanks. Melissa Stanfield has a hysterectomy scheduled for tomorrow morning—at age thirty two, if you please—she's scared to death. I promised I'd look in on her before they started prepping."

At the door I thanked him again—for goulash and mood altering and his thoughts on the Tom Horton problem—and told him I'd stay in touch.

He just grinned, "I'd say, 'See you in church,' but I've about given up hope on that score," and was gone.

I rinsed off the dishes and pots, put them in the dishwasher, locked up the place, and went off to bed. Dreams kept popping in and out of focus, strange dreams, combinations of grieving women, worried men, little girls, and Carole in a Giants' blue apron with red trimming and a big white "88" on her chest.

Sigmund Freud would have had a field day.

4

I got to Dick's office building at quarter of nine, parked in one of the slots marked "Visitor" in the underground lot, and checked in with the security guard, a little surprised to see it was Dan Mooney, who usually mans the lobby desk.

"How come they got you playing mole, Dan?"

"Mole? Oh, I get it, that's a good one, Mr. MacCardle. Have to remember that. We was losin' a lot of fellas down here, couldn't stand being cooped up in this little office all day, even with the radio. So the boss has us rotate the job now—one day out of five. Mole, huh, have to tell the guys that one, it sure fits all right. You hear about Mr. Horton?"

"Yesterday. I've been away for a while."

"A shame, no two ways about it. Nice young guy. Doin' real good too, he was. Never too busy to talk to you though, not like some of them young pups. Treat you like you was a goon or somethin'. Sure hope they nail the guy that did it."

"Me too, Dan."

"You have a good day, Mr. MacCardle."

I rode up to the eleventh floor, then walked through the big double doors with the brass plaque "Millington, Fox & Ellis,' into the reception area.

"Good morning, Mr. MacCardle, nice to see you again. My, my, don't we look spiffy this morning?"

Now "spiffy" is not a word you hear very often, at least, not nowadays. I tend to connect it with Van Johnson/June Allyson movies on "The Late Late Show" when I can't get to sleep. But, somehow, it seemed perfectly natural coming from Miss Evelyn, the receptionist. Miss Evelyn is a whole other number. I once calculated she must own a hundred and fifty-seven polka-dotted dresses, no two alike. Today's was green and white, and I'd never seen it before, often as I'd been here. Silver gray hair—in a bun, naturally, wire-rimmed glasses, ramrod straight posture. Right out of Norman Rockwell. Dick said she'd been here when he joined the firm, that nobody could remember when she hadn't been there, suspected she'd still be there when they carried him out feet first. A permanent institution, constant as death and taxes. A whole other number entirely.

"Good morning to you, Miss Evelyn. What a lovely dress. New?"

"Oh, my no. I've had it for ages, but how nice of you to notice. Mr. Ellis is down in the library with one of the Associates, but he left word you were coming in. Shall I ring Jane for you, Mr. MacCardle?"

"No thanks. I know the way—ought to by now."

"Very well. Have a pleasant day, won't you."

"I'll do my best."

Jane was talking on the phone as I came into the anteroom to Dick's office, her back to me, scribbling away furiously on a steno pad. She swung around, acknowledged me with a wink, held up two fingers to indicate when she'd be done. I noticed the third finger left hand was still unringed. Jane is an attractive woman—not beautiful by any means, but not a dog's dinner either—maybe just a shade too intense for my taste. I'd taken her out a few times early on, until it became quite clear she was fundamentally interested in a white gown, a condo in Boca, and lots of babies. As gently as I could, I told her I'd seen that movie and wasn't particularly keen on a rerun, not then anyway. She understood; we stayed friends: "Mr. MacCardle" in the office and on the telephone,

"Cam" when no one was around. Dick said she was far and away the best secretary he'd ever had. I could buy that in a minute.

"Hi, Janie, how's your love life?"

"Lousy. I'd even settle for a juicy obscene phone call. You?"

"You know me, lady, last of the straight arrows."

"Um hum, and Yasir Arafat is really a pacifist."

"Any coffee in this sweatshop?"

"Go on in the office. I'll bring some right after I call Mr. Ellis. What's green and red and goes a hundred miles an hour?"

"A frog in a Waring blender?"

"You sophisticated types know *all* the punch lines."

The office looked the same as always. The richly paneled walls were broken only by the floor-to-ceiling bookcases, with their rows on rows of law books. The prints on the wall were Currier and Ives—scenes of America from much more innocent times. A dark, wine red carpet ran wall to wall, complementing the leather sofa and armchairs, setting off the mahogany desk and end tables. A butler's tray stood in front of the sofa, flaps down, with an antique brass inkstand in the middle. The office was a reflection of its occupant—solid, conservative, secure.

Jane returned, bearing coffee and a message.

"The boss said he'd be along in about ten minutes, for me to keep you occupied 'til then. I almost told him that was a perilous mission, but I didn't."

"C'mon, Janie, I'm just a working stiff."

"I know. The boss had me tearing the place apart yesterday, getting ready for you. You've got a pile of reading ahead of you, dear heart."

"The more the better. We sure don't have a whole lot to go on, as is."

"What a horrible thing, I mean, with his wife and those kids. And what a waste. He was head and shoulders above the other Associates—would have made Partner next year at the latest. Who could do something as senseless and awful as that, Cam?"

"That's what the man's paying me for, luv; to try to help him find out."

"Well, I wish both of you all the luck in the world. The whole staff does. If you need me for anything—you know, like records and files, general information—count on it, hear?"

"Yes, ma'am, and thanks. We'll need all the help we can get."

"You got it. Ah, here's the boss—you *are* the early bird this morning, Mr. Ellis."

"No rest for the wicked, Jane. Morning, Cam. See you're all rigged out with coffee. Jane, would you bring in a pot for us, please? Then close the door and hold all my calls—anything important, I'll call back at noon. Okay?"

"Yes, sir."

He looked a lot better than he had yesterday. He wasn't all the way back, the strain still showed, but there was more strength in his voice, more color in his face, more snap in his gestures. As though reading my mind, he said, "I never thought yesterday was going to end. Those two damn hearings and then having to relive the whole thing telling you about it. I went home, had too many drinks, moped around the house, scared the hell out of the children, generally made myself useless."

"So what happened? You're a hundred percent improved from yesterday's model."

"Susan. Best damn thing I ever did was marry that woman. Never said a word. Let me go storming around making an ass of myself. Then right when we were going to bed, she reminded me that I always advise clients not to waste energy over the things they can't control, save it for the things they can. Told me it was high time I took my own advice."

"Smart lady, that one."

"I guess. Stayed up half the night thinking about it, decided she was right on the money, as usual. Figure I can be a lot more help to them if I stop tearing myself apart. And it won't bring Tom back, anyway."

"Looks like the right track to me, Counselor. Billy said to tell you how sorry he was. I had dinner with him last night and we . . ."

I took twenty minutes recapping the main points of dialogue, leaving out the part about Macbeth and the moors, because I didn't want him to worry that I'd gone around the bend. I told him about our theories, the informational needs as I saw them, and a rough plan of action I'd developed this morning.

". . . so I'll handle the police end of it. If we're lucky, it will be part of Lieutenant Hampton's caseload. If not, he can aim me at the man in charge. No objections, I'll have Jane call this afternoon to set up a meeting.

"I'll need your help with Mrs. Horton. She doesn't know me from Adam's off-ox and I'd like to talk to her this week, if possible—that is, if you think she's up to it.

"So much for outside, for now. What I need from you is a rundown on what Tom was working on when he was killed and, if you've got it, everything he did for the firm since he was hired. I realize that's a tall order."

"Not as tall as you think, but a helluva lot to plow through. I like your game plan, but as long as you're going to talk to Hampton, you might ask him about what you call the zanies. Knowing him, they've probably already checked that out. I'll call Linda tonight. If this week's good, I'll let you know when. You be at home tonight?"

"Later on. If you miss me you can put it on the box."

"Fine. In this stack of files are duplicates of the ones Tom had on his current projects—reminds me I've got to parcel those out at Partners' Lunch tomorrow. We'll get to them in more detail shortly.

"As I think you know, the heart of the legal fee compensation is the hourly rate. This firm is no exception. That includes everybody from the Senior Partners on down. We each make out a time sheet every day, listing what client was worked on, for how long. Some time ago, we put them into a microfiche system—for security and to save space. Jane can access all of Tom's for you this afternoon.

"We also have a practice of diary keeping in this firm. We don't insist, but just about everybody does it. Nothing fancy to them, just informal records of activity, thoughts, conversations, theories, and the like. I use them. I know Tom did too, because he'd often have a couple with him when he was meeting with me. I'll have Jane get them from his office for you.

"Diaries, time sheets, current projects—that's the lot. A long ton of spade work, my boy. What do you say we get into the current projects?"

"What do you say we take a ten-minute break? My back teeth are floating from all that coffee—if I don't get to the potty pretty quick, I won't be responsible for your rug."

"Fair enough. Always keep the workers happy, they say."

"Before we begin, Dick, I have a question. I've worked for you almost two years and I've never heard you say a word about Millington or Fox. They silent partners or what?"

"Very silent. They're both dead. Have been for a long time."

"Did you know either one of them?"

"Hardly. Millington died in 1890, Fox right after the turn of the century. I keep forgetting your penchant for the past. I'll give you a quick sketch so we can move on. The firm was founded in 1845 by my great-great-grandfather, Norton Ellis, with a former state senator, Eustace Millington. Five years later they brought in Howard Fox, changed the firm's name to what it is today. Fox died childless, Millington had a raft of children, all girls, so of the original partners only the Ellis strain remains."

"Has there always been an Ellis in the firm?"

"Yes. Some better, some worse than others. My great-grandfather, Wilton, almost ruined it during Reconstruction, came very close to being the only member of the family to go to jail. He wasn't all bad, though. He helped write the state constitution that's still in effect now."

"Final part of the history lesson. . . . If there aren't any Millingtons or Foxes around, why retain the name?"

"Fairly common practice in law firms. For example, we do a lot of work with a firm in New York called Cravath, Swaine and Moore. Those birds are all long gone—I can barely remember meeting Tex Moore down here one winter when I was a little kid. Lawyers are very conservative as a rule; there are times when we make bankers look positively giddy. Clients like stability in their dealings with lawyers, so the name endures even if none of the founders survive. Ready to move on?"

"Ready when you are, C.B."

"We'll just take the projects in order, then. I'm familiar with all of them, on a top-line basis. We have a biweekly meeting where all the Associates present the status of active cases. Never thought I'd be looking at them as a possible cause for murder, though. Well, let's see what we have."

The first file was the State of Florida versus Prairie Mutual Insurance. Prairie specializes in automobile insurance for the elderly—more than eighty percent of its policyholders being age sixty-five or over. Florida obviously represents a prime target for them and they'd done well here, the file indicating a coverage level in excess of two hundred thousand vehicles last year. At issue was a proposed eleven point five percent rate increase statewide, the levels varying by locality. The insurance commissioner had issued a restraining order, charging Prairie Mutual with excessive and unfairly discriminatory price increases. The company argued the increases were based on historical data and actuarial techniques that indicated the hikes were needed to cover rising costs and stay even with year-ago profits.

"Doesn't look too promising, Dick."

"Maybe not, but you'd better review it anyway. There's a fair amount of money involved—seven and a half million dollars, to be precise. That's the value of the proposed rate increase."

"I thought Prairie was a Chicago outfit."

"It is, but they sell all over the United States and the insurance industry is regulated state to state. They have their own lawyers, but it's *our* commission, so they always have a local firm assist them, in this case, us. We've represented Prairie since 1925."

"What happens next?"

"Tom and the Prairie people appealed the commissioner's order and asked that he lift it pending the appeal. It's on Peter Mann's desk—he's the commissioner—right now."

"What if he refuses?"

"Technically, we'd go to the First District Court of Appeals and ask them to block it. In practice, we'll probably negotiate something with Peter. He's a level-headed man—no pun intended. This is Prairie Mutual's first rate increase in over two years, we all know the price of cars and repairs isn't exactly static."

"Still doesn't look too promising."

"Nobody ever said it was easy. This next one I know a lot about. I think I told you we do a good deal of estate law. We have two Partners that specialize in it. Tom decided estate work was his principal area of interest as well. This one is the first we've let him handle more or less solo, though Jason Braxton is always on hand as a backstop.

"Julia Donaldson has been a client of ours for almost ten years, ever since her husband died and she moved to Cypress Beach. Old, old Florida money—a lot of it.

"You've probably read about Cy Donaldson, her husband. Reportedly, the meanest son of a bitch that ever crawled out of the Okefenokee. Real cracker stock, dirt poor, semiliterate, a temper like an alligator in heat. He was drafted in the First World War, got gassed in France, came out with a pension and a couple hundred dollars. Bought some land in the boondocks, started growing oranges—people thought he was berserk at the time. Built it to the third largest operation in Florida—only Braithwaite and Russell were bigger—most insiders say through a combination of price cutting and buying out less fortunate competitors. At one point he owned most of Sebring.

"When he died, Julia Donaldson decided she'd had it with central Florida, and bought a big house in the Playa Lago section of Cypress Beach. Before she left, she asked her lawyer to recommend someone over here. He gave her three names and she chose us, just about the time I joined the firm. I understand she's arthritic now—bedridden most of the time. Big money, Cam. I haven't reviewed the estate in a while, but it must be twenty-five, maybe thirty million by now."

"What did Tom do for her, basically?"

"Hand hold. Seriously. Go over there once a month to review her financial situation with her, like a steward's report. Sometimes bring along the trust officer Gold Coast Bank had assigned to her. Handle anything she asked for from a legal standpoint, which wasn't much according to their records . . . hello, what's this?

"Tom's notes here indicate she was talking about changing her will—details may be in his diary, they're not here. That's worth follow-up. The changes may turn out to be purely mechanical, but we're talking about an awesome amount of money."

"I will. May make sense to talk to the trust officer as well."

"The name will be in the file. Probably be easier to make that judgment once you see how much involvement there's been—no sense investing time chasing marginal leads."

"I might remind you, Counselor, everything we *have* is marginal and that may be an overstatement."

"True, but we've just started—I suspect you'll have a lot more to go on in a week or so. Now, what's next? Ah, the Follert deal. I don't imagine that will yield much, but I'll take you through it anyway."

"Follert? As in Follert's Market?"

"Yes. A success story and a sort of tragedy all in one."

"There's a Follert's right around the corner from me, in the Beacon Light shopping center. I go there all the time. High-priced but good stuff."

"That's Bob Follert's formula, quality merchandise, in attractive surroundings, with extra service. Bob thought it would let him command higher prices. Evidently he was right, this says he's up to twelve stores now—split about equally between Dade and Broward—all in high-rent districts. A very impressive old duck, indeed."

"You know him?"

"Slightly. Elks, Rotary, various civic causes—that kind of thing. Bob's in his seventies now, started his first store in the middle of the Great Depression, grown steadily ever since. Not as big as the Jenkins boys, of course, but a solid operation."

"The Jenkins boys?"

"Publix. They're all over the state, tend to be number one wherever they are. People say Charlie Jenkins has the first nickel he ever made—still goes to work everyday as a buyer at their headquarters in Lakeland. Probably jealousy talking—I played golf with Charlie one afternoon at Sawgrass, and nobody picked up a tab while he was around. Good golfer, too—played to a ten, as I recall."

"If Follert did so well, what's his problem?"

"Succession. Bob has two daughters and a son. His son is the youngest, the mother actually died in childbirth. Both the girls married well—one to a British foreign service official, the other to one of Bunkie Knudsen's former whiz kids at Pontiac. Obviously, no interest there in getting involved in the grocery business."

"And the boy?"

"That's the sad part. Russ Follert grew up wild and just kept going. He was always in trouble as a kid. Speeding tickets, fender benders, disturbing the peace, you name it. Got thrown out of Gainesville in his sophomore year, combination of bad grades and worse behavior. The University of Florida people, so the story goes, told Bob they wouldn't take the boy back if Bob gave them *four* libraries. Last I heard, Russ was over in Nassau, doing his best to drink the place dry."

"So Follert's selling out?"

"Exactly, to a big Northern combine called Grocers United. Pretty straightforward deal, it looks like, a combination of cash and GU stock—which has been doing well for quite a while. Apparently, the biggest problem is in minimizing the tax bite."

"Anything for us?"

"I doubt it, although it would be helpful to get a look at Bob's will. For example, if Russ was cut out of it that would be grounds for irrational action, not that Russ needs much help in the irrational area. Probably another wild goose chase—my hunch is that Bob will have it drawn up per stirpes."

"Per what?"

"Per stirpes. Equal thirds in this case—after taxes, expenses, liens, and any other bequests. It's Latin. Lawyers use it to keep you mere mortals off stride."

"You made it. What's the last one? That's a pretty thick file."

"The Mayor's Commission on Pornography."

"What mayor?"

"Cypress Beach. You may not realize it, but Cypress Beach has literally exploded in the last fifteen years. When I was growing up, it was a handful of retirement cottages east of Federal Highway. Today, it's wall-to-wall people, from the beach high-rises all the way west to the beginning of the Everglades. Well over four hundred thousand people, last census count."

"So."

"So. They grew so quickly they lost track of such niceties as zoning restrictions—not only a balanced ratio of commercial versus residential, but also what kinds of commercial. Go take a look for yourself. That stretch of U.S. One has to be the ugliest in Florida. It goes inland, too, particularly to the big subdivisions like Heron's Walk and Thunder Cay. It's not just the bars, the tacky fast-food places, and the used cars lots, either. There's one section called Action Junction, right out in plain view on Federal. Combination of topless clubs, massage parlors, adult book stores, and X-rated movie houses—if you can't get in trouble there, you can't get in trouble, period."

"How would Millington, Fox and Ellis get into something like that?"

"About two years ago, a group of citizens got together— businessmen and homeowners—to pressure the administration into getting rid of Action Junction and anything like it. Osgood Peters—he's the mayor—went to high school with me, was and is a close friend. Oz asked if we would lend some legal talent, and Tom Horton drew the straw. We do a lot of public service work, Cam, for free—feel as if we owe it to the communities that provide us a living. It's not all altruism either. Some projects are high visibility, with deep coverage by the media, and it doesn't hurt the firm at all to have one of our people involved."

"So, I get to look at *feelthy peectures?*"

"You probably won't be able to avoid it. Don't miss the point, though. When you get past the moral aspects of pornography, it's a big business and a highly profitable business, not exactly populated with graduates of the Harvard Business School. I'd be very surprised if the organized boys aren't into Action Junction—call them Mafia, Family, Cosa Nostra, whatever label you like. So, watch your step."

"I can't help thinking that's a pretty diversified project list. You always do it that way?"

"Yes. We try to give the Associates the broadest exposure possible, always backed up by a specializing Partner. That way, they can decide what interests them the most, while we're evaluating *them.* In Tom's case, as I said earlier, it would have been estate law, though now the point is obviously academic."

"A full morning, Counselor. Thanks for all the fillin."

"You'll get a lot more when you go through the detailed

file contents and Tom's diaries . . . It's almost noon, and my hearings start at one o'clock. If you don't mind, I'll turn you over to Jane—I need some time to see what the troops came up with this morning. You might start by taking her to lunch. Does wonders in the morale department and you'll be counting on her pretty heavily over the next couple of weeks, at least."

"Fine with me. Talk to you tonight. Luck this afternoon."

* * *

Jane and I had lunch at the Windjammer, on the Intracoastal in Pompano Beach. The Windjammer is only a year old but already building a solid local clientele, a sure sign of success in a town where most merchants make a living only during the Season.

The Windjammer was a Billy find, occasioned when its owner showed up after services one Sunday, introduced himself and gave Billy a chit for a free dinner. We'd cashed the chit together, finding the food good and the owner, Bill Breakey, an interesting, entertaining host.

Breakey had been a marketing biggy in New York who took early retirement to come to Florida and pursue a lifelong ambition to be a saloon keeper. Breakey says thirty years of selling products that turn your toilet's water blue, make every room smell like sandalwood, and kill all the bugs in the house, dead, dead, dead was more than ample penance for any crime imaginable. With his kids grown and gone, he figured it was high time to get out from under the big house in New Jersey and just follow his instincts to the sun. One of the happiest people I know.

"What's good, Cam?"

"I'd guess anything, Janie. Never had a bad meal here. Tell you what I'm having, if it's any help. Onion soup, bacon omelet, salad, a glass of Chablis. Maybe some peach melba for a topper. Nourishing, but not too heavy—won't go back to work feeling like I ate an anvil."

"That sounds perfect, except skip the omelet, please. Got to make some sacrifices. Everything else, most definitely—including the peach melba. What's on the docket for the afternoon? Or were you planning to give me the rest of the day off?"

"Fat chance—we've got a ton of things to do."

"Like what, slave driver?"

"Like pulling all of Tom Horton's time sheets, for starters. Dick said they were all on some kind of microfiche system, sound familiar to you?"

"Yes, indeedy, I was the guinea pig in charge when they first set it up. Guess they figured if I could learn it, anybody could. Course, we were a lot smaller in those days. Then what?"

"Then call Lieutenant Hampton. I want to meet with him as soon as possible. Tell him it has to do with the Horton killing."

"Wade Hampton? Cypress Beach Police Hampton? That man frightens me to death."

"He is pretty imposing—pleasant enough when you get to know him, if he's on your side, that is. Turn on the charm, kid—he'll never lay a glove on you."

"Well, okay, but don't be surprised if I come running for help. That voice alone gives me the shivers. Anything after that, assuming I survive?"

"Dick mentioned some diaries—evidently that's standard practice with all the lawyers there. He said he was sure Tom maintained them. Would you dig them up, please?"

"You think of all the neat assignments. That office hasn't been cleaned out yet. We're waiting until Mrs. Horton is up to it. I'll feel like a grave robber.

"Gotta be done, luv, I wouldn't know what I was looking for or even where to begin looking. Into each life . . ."

"Yeah, I know, this is beginning to look like a rainy day and a half. Anything more, I hope not?"

"Mechanical chores and easy. I'll need some cartons to

take the stuff home in, one for the project files, one for the diaries, I guess. However many it takes for the time sheets."

"That I can do. What do you want to lug all that stuff home for? We can set you up just as easily in the law library. Handier too."

"Too handy. Rather be home where it's quiet; if I have any questions, I'll either phone or come in to the office. Besides, I won't have to be wearing this monkey suit."

"I think you look very handsome."

"Miss Evelyn said 'spiffy.'"

"Miss Evelyn would."

The afternoon's activities sorted out, we turned to lunch, which more than lived up to the quality standards I'd told Jane about on the way. Under its thick cheese cover, the onion soup was scalding hot, pleasantly pungent. The omelet hit the ideal balance between fluff and substance, its bacon filling crisp and tasty. Finally, peach melba and cups of an espresso rich enough to eat with a fork.

"Could a working girl be permitted a polite belch? Of satisfaction, naturally."

"Certainly, and the operative word is working—so, let's get at it. Almost two o'clock."

"Right, Mr. Legree."

I spent the balance of the afternoon in Dick's empty office, sorting through the project files he'd summarized this morning. It was mostly an orientation session; I knew each item would have to be looked at individually and carefully. It was quiet and close in the office, telephone switched off, the only sound in the room the steady tick of the grandfather clock in the far corner. By four thirty, I'd almost succeeded in putting myself to sleep, when Jane came in.

"Would you like some warm milk and a pillow?"

"Funny, funny lady. How did you do?"

"So-so, maybe a little better, but not a hundred percent. In no particular order: Lieutenant Hampton will see you at eleven, Thursday morning. He said, quote 'I can hardly wait,' close quote. Wonder what he meant by that."

"Never mind, it's my problem. What else?"

"Here's the box for the folders you're snoozing on. The time sheets are in two cartons down in the security guard's booth—thought I'd save you the trouble. There are two cartons because we have one of the Generation I microfiche systems. It doesn't know how to retrieve selectively, that is, just give you Tom Horton's hours This one gives you his, plus everyone else's that was on that particular entry. That's why two. Sorry about that."

"No big deal. A little more time consuming, but much better than no records at all. How about the diaries?"

"They're gone, Cam. I ransacked the office, didn't turn up even one. It's very strange."

"Could anyone else in the office have them?"

"I doubt it. There'd be no need, Tom's projects won't be reassigned until this week's Partners' Lunch. I don't know *where* they could be."

"Don't fret over it. Dick plans to call me tonight, I'll see if he has any bright ideas. Meanwhile, why don't you take the rest of the day off?"

"All fifteen minutes—there's no limit to your gratitude, is there? Anyway, I always stay late when Mr. Ellis is in court. He'll come in or call in before he goes home. I'll tell him about the diaries then."

"Thanks, luv. Also for all the hard work."

"Nothing, Cam. Don't be a stranger."

*   *   *

I picked up the box of folders, went down to the parking level, and got Dan Mooney to help me take the time-sheet cartons over to the car and stow them.

Drove home carefully through the rush hour traffic, keeping special watch for the little old people who make right-hand turns from the outside lane. I was listening mindlessly to the sports talk-show man on WIOD, anticipating having dinner with Carole.

Still, the thought tugged at me—why were the diaries missing? Were they deliberately removed, maybe destroyed? If so, by whom?

As if we didn't have enough problems already. Gilbert and Sullivan wrote "a policeman's lot is not a happy one"— they should only try private investigating.

5

I gave the doorman my name and told him who I'd come to see. By now, that information was extraneous, but Nick the Surly had the duty and no amount of prior appearances was going to deter him from doing his security routine. He called upstairs, evidently got the necessary assurances, and told me I could go up—I was expected. He looked almost disappointed, seeing yet another "Wily Doorman Foils Would-Be Rapist" headline go a-glimmering; I felt like the prisoner out on parole for Mother's Day—"make sure you're back by sundown, boy." A demeaning practice, but one becoming more prevalent daily in South Florida, mute testimony to a rising crime rate and an increasingly wary citizenry.

Carole was in the doorway of 6C when I got off the elevator, waving at me with the clenched fist, up and down gesture the Marines use in combat to tell the troops to get a move on. She ushered me in, closed the door, and moved easily into my arms for a kiss—which started out as a Good to See You Again, but progressed to the point where I began to wonder about postponing dinner.

She broke off, pausing to look up at me, the wide green eyes slightly out of focus. "Whoa, Captain, I've heard about you horny sailors."

"What would you think about a midnight supper?"

"The last time we tried that there wasn't *any* supper and I'm starved, haven't eaten all day."

"Man does not live by bread alone."

"May I write that down? Okay, one fast kiss—then I feed Toby and we'll go."

"A hard bargain, lady."

Toby rubbed against the back of her legs, making himself thoroughly unctuous while she opened the can of cat food and put it into his dish on the counter. She carried the dish over to the corner of the kitchen, Toby, step for step with her, making sure it wasn't all a hideous dream, bunting at her hand with his head as she set the dish down.

"Talk about starved, don't you ever feed him?"

"Twice a day, every day. He's just a gluttonous beggar. There, I guess he likes it all right. The store was out of what I usually give him, so tonight he's dining on Tuna Medley Delight—who *thinks* of those names?"

"Some demented advertising copywriter who never owned a cat. Are we ready?"

"Ready for what?"

"Ready for dinner. As I recall, that was what you said you wanted."

"For now."

I looked at her across the table of our booth in Rubino's, watching the candlelight trace her features, bringing out soft highlights in the golden hair. Class, if we are going to try to define "lovely," we can start and end right here; we'll have done our job. I noted fondly she'd worn the gold sand-dollar pin I gave her last Christmas, set off nicely against the emerald green of her blouse. She must have known I would notice it; impulsively, I reached over the table and held her hands, meeting her eyes as her head swung up from reading the placemat menu.

"You *have* been away a long time. I hope you realize this will make eating terribly difficult, sir."

"The hell with eating. Let's go off to Tahiti and raise coconuts—just the two of us."

"An intriguing idea, if somewhat malnutritious. Oh, it's so good to see you again."

"I love you, Carole."

"Please. Don't, Cam. Don't push. Please. I'm just not sure I'm ready for it. It might not be fair . . . for either one of us. Not yet."

When I first met Carole, she was going through the final stages of divorce proceedings, watching the marriage she thought would last forever melt as quickly and finally as a child's snowman in April. She had been very leery of all contact at first. Constantly on the alert for double meanings and anything that hinted at aggression. A former Delta stewardess, she had met, flown with, and eventually married a Delta Tri-Star captain who, unbeknownst to her, had absolutely no intention of severing a coast-to-coast dalliance network over such a minor matter as a wedding ring. When the stories got back to her, mostly through the Old Girl Grapevine, she confronted him—outraged. He'd apologized, promised it would never happen again, then picked up his out-of-town life as if nothing had happened, even bagging two of the storytellers for good measure. Still, she put up with it, wanting desperately to make the marriage work, becoming less and less sure of herself as the infidelity score mounted. One night he hit her during an argument, knocked her down, and stalked out of their apartment.

When he returned, she was gone. No note. No forwarding address. He didn't bother chasing after her, either, simply complied with her lawyer's requests, signed all the papers, told the lawyer to wish her well, thanks for not asking for alimony, lots of luck—perhaps the last, the worst rejection.

So, she has a right to be cautious, I thought; she has a right to withold commitment. Most important, she's a friend. So, ease up, dummy.

"Baby back ribs, baked potato, blue-cheese dressing, onion rings, carafe of rosé. Sound close?"

"Italian dressing for me. Otherwise, sign me up."

The service is fast at Rubino's, as fast as the food is good.

Spare ribs are best eaten piping hot, so we devoted primary attention to that task, making a quick task of dinner, sitting back contentedly, watching the waitress make the mountain of dishes go away, lingering over the last of the cold, dry rosé. Rubino's doesn't serve dessert—their only drawback—but I devised a way to prolong the moment.

"Let me buy you dessert at home. I've got Häagen-Dazs butter pecan, and I'm sure we can find something in the after-dinner-drink locker, too."

"Lead on, Captain. I make a fool of myself over butter pecan."

We made camp in the living room, with dishes and coffee cups on the glass-topped table that flanks the Lexington, the stereo barely audible in the background, playing a tape I'd made—combining Baez, early Glen Campbell, Judy Collins, and Kristofferson favorites—and talked idly about a thousand things.

She stopped me right in the middle of my tale of the great wind off Grand Bahama, scooting backwards across the couch, coming to rest with an arm around my neck, her head tucked into the angle of my shoulder.

"Thank you, Cam, for a lovely dinner, for this, and . . . just for caring."

I shushed her with a gentle kiss which grew into a series, each logically suggesting another. I traced the outline of the lovely jaw with my finger, sighed, went back for more. My hand was busy with the bone buttons of her blouse when she pulled away, leaning back, looking at me almost shyly.

"Wow, Cam. Umm, um, um. No, don't, please. Humor me. How about a swim? Please?"

Wonderful. Just wonderful. "Well, if you want a swim, a swim you'll get. Probably good for us at that. It wasn't exactly what I had in mind, honey, but . . ."

"Don't be cross. My things in the same place?"

"I haven't moved them. Still in the guest-room closet."

Sometime after the first couple of times Carole had spent the night, I suggested she keep some changes of clothing here.

I wanted her to move in, but she wouldn't accept; the smaller solution was something she could live with. I grumbled my way into the master bedroom, tugged on trunks, and huffed out to turn on the underwater pool lights and get the big, fluffy bathsheets out. I wondered what in the world was taking her so long, walked inside to find out. She was standing in the guest room, wearing a particularly nasty-colored coral robe someone had left—a robe I keep meaning to throw out, admiring neither color nor owner. She'd unclipped the ponytail, her hair fully free, almost waist length, highlighted by the light of the little lamp on the bureau. She heard my steps and turned to face me, undoing the robe and shrugging it off, standing nude in the pool the robe made round her feet.

"It's a Zero-kini. . . . I hope you like it."

There weren't any words, none asked for, none given. I led her through the darkened hallway to my bedroom. Held her, standing in my arms, savoring the exquisite sensitivity of flesh on flesh everywhere we met. I brought her with me, gently down, into a warm sea of tactile exchanges, of kissing and caress. A smooth joining, the slow rhythms of mutual giving, a sweet, gentle culmination. Winding down, lying beside her, holding her still, watching over her as she drifted off.

We woke sometime during the night, as if by simultaneous alarms, holding to each other, clinging, repeating the process by which we all began—coming lovingly, finally to the same end.

The best of all endings. Arms tightly bound around me, her head snugged securely in the hollow of my neck. I heard her whisper then, a soft, fierce sound, "I love you, Cam MacCardle. With all my heart and all my mind and all my soul."

How was *my* day? Do you really have to ask?

* * *

The black bear came at me on the dead run, with that deceptive, shambling stride that masks its speed. Too late to run, too late even to grab an arrow from the quiver on my back. I threw the bow away, drew the sharp hunting knife from its scabbard, leaned forward in the semi-crouch my father had taught me so long ago, braced myself for the inevitable assault. Never make the first move, I remembered his saying, not with bears. Counterattacking is your only chance. The bear sprang, locking me in a rib-crushing clasp, its hot fetid breath stinking in my face. Only one move left. Work the knife hand free, take the killing shot at the base of the neck. With the last of my energy, I wrenched my arm clear, raised it to strike and . . . woke up, pawing away at the tangle of bedclothes wrapped around me.

The hunter is mighty and will prevail. Where the hell did all *that* come from? We'd talked about many things last night but Indians hadn't been one of them. Symbolism, probably, but symbolizing what? And where was Carole? Oh, of course, it's a weekday, she's gone to work.

I heard an insistent drumming sound, apparently from the bathroom, got out of bed to investigate. The clouded glass of the sliding shower door did little to mask the outlines of its inhabitant. Mighty fine outlines, chief, mighty fine, indeed. With the cunning and stealth acquired in a hundred moons of campaigning, the hunter stalked his quarry, eventually cornering the maiden next to the waterfall, not acknowledging that her screams of terror were, in reality, giggles. Dragged the maiden back to his lodge and violated her thoroughly, as was the custom in his tribe.

"You are an absolute mental case, Cam. This bed will take a week to dry out. But it *was* fun—we ought to do that more often. Ready for some breakfast?"

"Don't you have to go to the club?"

"It's Wednesday. Wednesday and Sundays are my days off. Remember? Now, let's see, eggs over easy, very crisp bacon, marmalade with the toast, and black coffee?"

"Mind like an IBM computer, darling. Sounds fantastic."

Shaving, I realized I hadn't called Ellis last night, and resolved to do that first thing lest he think I was totally irresponsible, instead of just semi. I wrestled into the big blue robe, padded out to the kitchen, kissed the cook, picked up the phone, and called in. Jane answered.

"The boss is out of the office, but I know what he wanted to talk to you about. What's that singing in the background?"

"Must be the radio."

"Sure it is. The a cappella festival, no doubt. Anyway, the boss reached Mrs. Horton, told her who you were and why you were involved. She can see you any time after three tomorrow. You got the address?"

"No. Give it to me, please, Janie."

"It's Seven Twelve Northeast Arbor Drive in Cypress Point. It's easy to find. Go to the stoplight on Federal opposite the Bartlett Shopping Mall. Take your next right and go three blocks to Arbor Drive. Turn left, and Seven Twelve is midway up on the left—there's a sign on the lawn with their name on it."

"Sounds easy enough. Any word on the diaries?"

"Linda has them. I'm *so* relieved. She found them in a box in Tom's study. She'll give them to you tomorrow."

"That *is* a break. Anything else?"

"No. Yes. Mr. Ellis wants to know if you can have dinner with them Friday night. At seven. Their house."

"Please tell him yes. I'll look forward to it. You have a good day, now."

"You too, and good luck. See you now."

I hung up and helped the cook transfer all the breakfast makings out to the booth, sliding in opposite her, making an approving circle of an index finger and thumb by way of appreciation for her labors. Carole asked what the phone call was all about. I gave her the bare-bones details, including what I was doing or, at least, trying to do.

"That's just awful. That poor woman. And those little kids. Nobody's safe anymore these days. That sure outweighs my plan. I was hoping we could turn today into a holiday. Forget *that*; you've got more important things to do."

"I don't know, honey. I only got started yesterday, nothing much to go on yet. Two meetings coming and the diaries I was asking about should give us a lot more direction, but they're not until tomorrow. Let's declare it a half-holiday."

"How so?"

"I have a mechanical task that has to be done—sort through all the records that show how he spent his time at the firm. At this point, it's a real no-brainer. I won't know what the entries mean without the diaries and input from Ellis."

"Want me to help?"

"No. Really better for me to do it by myself. I figure it'll need three, four hours at the most. Why don't you take the car, do whatever you want, wind up getting us the jumbo bucket of the Colonel's extra crispy, slaw and stuff. We'll take the *Folly* out poking around, maybe do some snorkeling, have a picnic supper out there."

"Sounds great to me, but look, *I* really don't have anything that needs doing. Let me do *something*.

"Could you stand a little menial chore? The metal fittings on the *Folly* could stand cleaning and polishing—they got pretty drenched last week."

"Housemaid's work, less mentally demanding?"

"Get out of here, lady."

"Teasing, darling. I'd be glad to. Where do you keep all the cleaning and polishing goop?"

"In the dock box, just beyond the bar. You *are* an angel."

"Can't be any harder than juggling hot trays at thirty-five thousand feet. I'll get to it right after breakfast."

So that was how we spent the morning, digging through the seemingly endless stack of time sheets, occasionally pacing the room to clear my head, pretending not to notice the crew person in halter and short shorts bounding around the *Folly*'s decks.

The job really *was* a no-brainer, but it had to be done. I took a yellow pad and wrote each person or company mentioned in a column on the far left indicating, by marks and cross-hatches, the hours against each as they came up on the chronological sheets. Hours of sheer mechanical drudgery. I barely noticed the tuna sandwich and iced tea Carole put on the coffee table, waving thanks to her and plunging back into the stack of records.

As a sort of a start, I went back and picked out the entries with the most marks. Meaningless names. At least, meaningless now. Mayor's Commission, Donaldson, Prairie Mutual, and Follerts were familiar territory. Rol-A-Gard Corporation, Linton Development, Mrs. Edward Alden, Morton Giles, and Top Flight Productions were not, but they were the ones most heavily worked. No particular pattern either, the work generally having been spread through five years, although with major concentrations for each project confined within a one- to two-year period.

The gloomy thought occurred that there might be no correlation between raw numbers of hours spent and possible murder motives. Theoretically he might have spent two hours on some project and gotten killed because of it. Theoretically. I reminded myself that theoretically, hummingbirds can't fly. The odds were that hours spent times nature of activity would produce what we were looking for. Time to close up shop and turn to happier activities. I stored my work sheets and summary in one of the time-sheet cartons, dragged both of them over near the desk against the far wall, went to see what Carole was doing.

I found her packing picnic supplies in the big Igloo ice chest, humming away while she stowed various food, beverage, and condiment items deemed necessary for transportable civilized living.

"All done? Good. Just about finished with this part, too."

"You *have* been a busy little beaver, madame."

"That's not all, either. C'mon, let me show you the fruits of me toil."

She took me by the hand and led me out through the pool area, down the sloping ramp to the dock, eeling aboard the *Folly* as naturally as if she lived there. She'd done quite a job. The metalwork looked as good as new, shining in the sun, in right-out-of-the-package condition. Wordlessly, she pointed at the cabin door. I swung over the edge of the hatch cover and dropped below. The galley had been cleaned to within an inch of its life, looking like something out of *Good Housekeeping*. Bunks were made, bulkhead lamps aligned; she'd even cleaned up the head. I clambered on deck.

"You don't exactly do things half way. It looks terrific, honey. If I didn't know she was an inanimate object, I'd swear the old *Folly* was smiling. I think you made a friend for life."

"Oh, pooh, it was fun. I've never really noticed the downstairs before. That's the cutest little kitchen, everything in miniature and all, like a dollhouse, almost. And a real stand-up shower in the bathroom, it's like a small apartment."

Downstairs, kitchen, bathroom—words that would send Ollie into a coma. The terminology would come with time— below, galley, and head aren't too demanding. And she had done a spectacular job.

"Okay, crew, let's get this half-holiday in gear."

"Aye, aye, My Captain."

For variety's sake and to show her some very impressive homes, we ran up the Intracoastal to Boca Raton, then out through the inlet there—which can be very tricky, particularly in a quartering wind, but was smooth as glass today. I ran offshore for about a mile, swinging to starboard and proceeding south, paralleling the coast. I stood at the wheel, pointing out landmarks to her, comfortably aware of her hand on my shoulder, the closeness of her standing beside me.

"What's that up ahead? See? That big gray shape—you can just barely make it out."

"Not sure, but I'll bet it's the *Nimitz*. I read she was here, lying off Port Everglades."

"Nimitz?"

"Flattop. Aircraft carrier. One of the biggest in the world. Named after a World War Two admiral, commander of the Pacific Fleet—later chief of naval operations. Did a lot to make things go our way. Want to run down and see her close up?"

"Is it dangerous?"

"Only if we open fire first."

"Cam!"

Impressive as we kept closing the distance, the *Nimitz* was awesome when she loomed up over us, as if someone had learned to float the Empire State Building. I had no idea what her complement was, probably enough to populate a small town. There was no flight-deck activity going on, but dungareed seamen were rushing everywhere, evidently carrying out some kind of drill. Carole had gone forward to the peak for a better look. Our third circuit took us past the enormous fantail, crowded with men waving and cheering at the pretty girl. She loved it, smiling and waving back, I was glad she couldn't read lips, having some idea of what goes on in young sailors' minds.

I took the *Folly* offshore, well out of traffic, put her on a reverse heading, indicating to Carole that she take over. Apprehensive at first, she overcorrected to each move we made. Then she got the rhythm of it and the wake began to straighten out as we barreled along northward.

"Oh, this is so much fun, Cam. Bet I could learn to drive this boat in nothing flat."

"You will, honey. Only takes a little time—then you'll be up there with the best of them."

I took over just south of Cypress Beach, easing inward, anchoring a mile off shore, near Little No Name Reef. We spent the next hour snorkeling, watching the streams of brightly colored fish, keeping an eye out for barracuda, that quick, silent predator who hits anything moving. Then back aboard for happy hour, sitting in the fighting chairs, bobbing in the gentle swells. Miller Lite for Carole, iced tea for Captain Caution.

"Thought you were a beer man?"

"I am, honey. Ashore. Probably a phobia with me, but I don't drink on the water unless we're secured for the night. I don't care if nonworking personnel aboard get drunk as billy-goats—I figure there are enough ways to get in trouble out here—without adding another element."

"A good phobia. Makes me feel even more secure."

I looked over to see if she was teasing but the look in her eyes and her tone of voice told me she really meant it, really did feel secure, that—no matter where we were—we could always be comfortable with each other. Comfortable—a funny, clunky word to describe a romantic relationship—but I knew it outranked all the rest of the words for me and, evidently, for Carole as well.

Suddenly, I realized how much I wanted to share with her, how much I wanted to know about her—feeling, somehow, that the knowledge would help bring us even closer together.

So, with the bull elephant lack of tact that ensures no one's ever going to mistake me for a delegate to the UN, I plunged in: "Honey, give me the Carole Cummings Story. I mean the part before you were making life wonderful for America's travelers. I'm talking all the way back and don't skip the details—the long course is more than fine by me."

"A pretty average story, I guess. I am, as you know, a native Floridian, an increasingly rare breed these days. I was born in Bee Ridge."

"*Bee Ridge*?"

"Whose story is this anyway? I was born and raised in Bee Ridge, proud of it. It's a little town on the West Coast, just below Sarasota. My father was in the wholesale fish business, a small operator but we lived well enough. Went to grammar school there, then to the big regional high school, two towns over outside Danielton."

"Cheerleader?"

"If you keep interrupting . . . that was a *big* school and I wasn't nearly pretty enough to be a cheerleader. Some day, when I get up my nerve, I'll show you the yearbook. I was a shoo-in for Miss Plucked Chicken."

"I'll take odds against that one."

"You'll lose, believe me. Anyway, what I really wanted to be was a baton twirler but I kept dropping the darn thing. Even then, I was blind as a bat—my glasses kept falling off and they finally made me stop before somebody got skulled. I wound up being a flag team member, you know—the high boots, the tall hat and all. They must have figured I *couldn't* drop a flag."

"Brothers or sisters?"

"Nope. Only child. Evidently my mother had some female troubles that would have made having more children dangerous. Too bad for my dad; he wanted a boy in the worst way. I often wondered why they didn't adopt. My grades in high school were good enough to get me a limited scholarship to FSU, in Tallahassee. Four good years. I liked my courses, met some really nice people, joined a sorority, had my first love affair. You remember, you can cram a lot of living into four years when you're young."

"Love affair? I'm jealous already."

"You needn't be. Warren Oates. Halfback for the Ole Seminoles. I thought he was the world wrapped up in one human being. Threw me over for a girl in my own sorority—a redheaded tramp with big boobs, Rita Something-or-Other. I wanted to die. Last I heard, Warren was a playground director in an elementary school in Fort Pierce. Never did graduate. When the football season was over so was Warren's college career. Not the brightest man I ever met."

"Then what?"

"I'd majored in American Studies—combination of art, literature, music, history, politics, and so on. All American-centered. It doesn't really prepare you for anything specific, and I didn't feel like going to graduate school. Delta had a pipeline into my sorority. Four or five girls from there had become Delta flight attendants. So, I interviewed with them when they came to the campus in the spring. They offered me the job and I took it."

"The American Studies major sees America, eh?"

"Something like that. The rest I think you know."

"How about your folks?"

"My mother died the first summer I was home from Tallahassee. An aneurysm that came out of nowhere. One minute sewing a patch on my sorority blazer, the next minute gone. At least she didn't feel any pain. I never did wear that blazer again, but I still have it—packed away somewhere."

"And your father?"

"Dad sold the fish business a couple of years ago, got enough so he's fixed for life. He moved up to Stimson River, near Anclote Springs, has a little cottage near the beach. I tried to get him to come over here, but he wouldn't have any part of it. He's living over there near a bunch of retired Greek fishermen and spongers, independent as a hog on ice. You'll like him. You're the same in a lot of ways."

"I'll look forward to it, luv."

Appetites sharpened by the salt air, we pigged out on the Extra Crispy and fixings, down to the last bare bones. Gathered up the debris, got coffee from the oversized Thermos, watched the sun go down while digesting, the radio playing calypso softly in the background.

This time I suggested a swim, Carole agreeing instantly. As long as it was dark and she did have her Zero-kini with her, no sense in not getting it wet. I lit the running lights to make sure we didn't get creamed by some idiot and dived over the side after her.

"How do we get back on, Cam . . . here, quit that, you lecherous devil."

"We swim back to the stern. See that wooden transom there? That's a diving platform. It'll hold you. Then there's a grab ring right above it. Throw a leg over and you're home free."

I watched her sail gracefully up and over the rail, following along behind. Guided her below and tucked us both into the shower to rinse off the salt. At least that's what I told her at the time.

I walked her to the front door of her apartment, kissed her goodnight, and turned over her health and welfare to Nick the Surly. I'd wanted her to spend the night, but she'd argued tomorrow was a working day for both of us and besides, Toby would be likely to explode, particularly if old Mrs. James in 6A hadn't fed him and taken care of the litterbox.

But, before she went in, she turned and took both my hands, her big eyes wide and shining, "It was a perfect holiday, Cam. Perfect, perfect, perfect."

I couldn't have said it better myself.

6

I bounded out of bed, full of energy and purpose, dedicated to getting the most out of the full day that lay ahead. Drew the curtain back from the sliding glass door to the patio and felt like going back to bed. It was raining. Not the torrential rains the locals call "frawg stranglers," but a gray, sullen rain, from sodden skies that looked quite capable of keeping it up all day. Rain is one of the few things God didn't get quite right. The wise gardener never waters a lawn during the day, knowing it brings the grasses' tender roots into the brutal exposure of the sun. God is the wisest gardener of all; why didn't He set it up so it only rains at night? Think about it.

Deciding I was incapable of solving such a cosmic problem at nine o'clock in the morning on an undistinguished Thursday, I sought some temporal relief. My television set is hooked to a cable system that is a true cornucopia for killing time. It has a channel from Atlanta, from New York, and from Chicago. A sports channel, two movie channels, a Spanish channel. Even a French channel, which always astounds me because I can't believe there are eleven real Frenchmen in all South Florida. It also has a weather channel—twenty-four hours of broadcasting a radarscope picture, with a subhuman voice-over. I switched it on, watching the long sweep arm of the radar going around the circle, putting up an endless series of blips as it encountered rain clouds. The robot voice said, "Broward County can expect a ten-percent chance of rain, current temperature eighty-four degrees, winds from the southwest of six to eight knots, barometer thirty point oh six and rising, drying conditions excellent."

Where was he broadcasting from, Peru? All the silly bastard need do was stick his hand out the window to see how reliable *that* forecast was. Further proof that meteorologists, as a species, are marginally brighter than palm trees—though not nearly as productive.

It was quite clear I was not going to be able to start off this day properly without spiritual guidance, so I picked up the bedside phone and dialed the familiar number. "Cypress Beach Racquet Club, Good Mo-orning."

"I love you."

"Um, me, too, definitely yes."

"People there, honey, can't talk?"

"Scads, I'm afraid."

"Well, anyway, I just called to say I love you."

"Me, too, sir, please be assured of that."

Now I could get going.

Aware of the radar man's forecast, I picked out a rainy day outfit. The trousers a wee bit ratty, blazer slightly threadbare, shoes the pair that hoped I was going to resole some day. Not so bad that little old ladies would try to give me quarters, but not the front of the closet, either. Sufficient unto the day.

When I got downtown, the covered parking section of the municipal lot was full, naturally, so I pulled up to the attendant's booth in the outside lot. Took the time stamp stub, reached into the back seat and extracted the big red, white, and blue umbrella with the Giants' logo on it—a going-away present they didn't know they gave me—surrendered the car, and squelshed off to police headquarters, feeling water beginning to seep up into my socks.

Sergeant Serkin was waiting for me in the lobby—the same Serkin who'd taken Ralph Morgan's statement the night

Laura was murdered. A huge man, running slightly to fat, but an experienced and reliable pro.

"Hey, MacCardle, long time no see. You ain't changed much. What's it been, two years?"

"Just about. You've changed some. Losing weight?"

"A little. It's the weight liftin', you know, pumpin' iron like that guy Arnold Swarza . . . never can say that name right."

"What do you go now, two eighty?"

"Eighty-five. Boss got on me pretty good when I went over the big three, said he didn't want no fat cops lookin' like they was takin' it easy."

"He should know better in your case."

"He don't push us no harder than he does himself. A workin' fool, that man. What you seein' him about today?"

"Tom Horton killing."

"Lord God, MacCardle, you don't pick the fat pitches to hit, that's for sure. If you thought that Morgan mess was hard, you ain't seen nothin' yet. We got zero on this one, I mean zee-row."

"Doesn't sound too encouraging."

"It ain't, no part of it. Let's get goin', boss'll have my butt for bacon if he catches us jawin'. He went over to the Commissioner's for a nine o'clock, told me to take you up to his office. You can wait on him there."

"Coffee machine still working?"

"We thrown that miserable sumbitch out. Boys bought one of them Mr. Coffee things. Cost you a quarter, though—this ain't the Salvation Army."

Hampton's office hadn't changed at all, as I suspected, its principal occupant regarding anything out of the norm with a distaste bordering on hatred. The huge map of Greater Cypress Beach, the flags, the gunmetal-gray steel desk, and the two uncomfortable straightback wooden chairs hadn't moved a millimeter. The "B-Quick-Or-B-Gone" sign still sat on the desk, precisely aligned between his metal nameplate and the in-out trays. A cold, plain pipe-rack, no-nonsense office—perfect environment for a hard-nosed, get-things-done man.

Before I decided to get involved with the Morgan thing, Ellis had described Lieutenant Hampton to me. "Wade Hampton has fifteen solid years on the force. Started as a patrolman and worked his way up not as quickly as some, but he made it. Never a hint of any wrongdoing, no influence peddling, no brutality, no corruption. He may not be very imaginative, but he's a thorough, by-the-book, superconscientious cop—and a good one."

Experience proved he was all of that and then some.

"Good morning, Mr. MacCardle. Sorry to be late, meeting ran a little longer than I thought it would."

"Good morning, Lieutenant—say, I didn't know you *owned* a white shirt."

"I do trust you didn't come all the way down here to talk about my clothes. If you must know, a white shirt is standard operating procedure for senior officers at commissioner's meetings. What else is on your mind?"

"Dick Ellis asked me to help look into Tom Horton's murder, with the Department's permission, of course. I was hoping it was part of your caseload."

"This *is* my lucky day. Yes, I have that miserable case, and now I've got to worry about you bumbling around in it. Some people get all the breaks."

"Now, come, Lieutenant. I didn't bumble around on the Laura Morgan deal and not on the Mullins case either. Give me some credit."

"I'll give you credit. Credit as the luckiest man I've ever met. Credit for a mild case of evidence withholding plus one outright breaking-and-entering—which, fortunately, occured outside my jurisdiction."

"You're a hard man. I was only trying to help."

"In the long run, you did—whether by good luck or good mangement doesn't make much difference. Truth be told, I can use your help. Hell, I could use a half-trained chimpanzee right now. You see that map? That's four hundred thousand souls looking to the department for protection, for law enforcement. We have the lowest cop-per-capita rate of any major metro area in Florida. The budget's drier than a well in the Sahara. Even if we had the money, it's getting tougher every day to attract quality people. Who wants to risk getting their ass shot off for fourteen thousand dollars a year?"

"Tough stick to shoot."

"You don't know the half of it. Didn't I see in the records you got your ticket?"

"Ellis wanted me to. Said it might make things easier—particularly in strange territory. Came in handy in Mexico, those *Federales* are very big on official credentials."

"So I hear. Well let's get after it, not that there's a whole hell of a lot to tell. Sorry damn thing, understand he was a bright guy, close to Ellis. Let me dig out the file."

"How's your son doing, Lieutenant?"

"Beau? He's doing all right. Got a scholarship to Miami. Played second string his freshman year. This fall they got him playing linebacker, said it's messed up his head some. Learning to play defense and all."

"He'll last longer. Take it from me."

"Well, you'd know about that, all right . . . Here we are, and it isn't very much. In one week's work we've turned up exactly no clues, no leads, no witnesses. We have zero prints—finger, foot, or tire. We don't even have a bullet. We have a piece of one, but not enough to tell what it was. The medical examiner believes, from the size of the frontal wound, that it was at least a thirty caliber. Trouble is, we could impound every weapon in Florida without getting a ballistics match—there just isn't enough bullet to go on.

"The one thing we know is he didn't kill himself—the paraffin test on his hands was quite conclusive. Clean as a whistle. Which leaves us with the larger problem."

"Is that kind of killing unusual? I mean, I would hope so."

"What you're asking is, did we compare the MO on this with records. *First* thing we did. Computer came up almost blank. Only thing comparable happened four years ago up in Martin County, perpetrator's in Raiford right now, will be for the rest of his life. So, it is rare, unless you throw in gang style killings. Those characters are constantly knocking each other off, although not with as much finesse as this."

"Could this have been a hit job? Mob ordered?"

"Sure. Could have been a crazed nun, too. I'm telling you we flat don't know. Had my way I'd white-ticket the file—anything comes in, fine, but we've got other things we got a better shot at solving."

"Who is the investigating officer? Serkin?"

"Not him. He was here sitting on his butt, eating Oreo cookies and drinking milk when it happened. The investigating officer is Sergeant Ordonez, first name's Cipriano."

"Does he speak English?"

"Only bigoted thing I ever heard you say MacCardle. Yeah, he speaks English. Better than you do. Four years at the University of Pennsylvania, graduate degree in criminology."

"Beg your pardon."

"You should. His shift was up at noon, according to this duty roster. Ought to be back by now. Millie, call downstairs for Ordonez. Tell him I want him up here on the double.

"Give me five minutes with him, MacCardle, so he doesn't think you're just another troublemaking Anglo—although there are days when *I* have my doubts about that. From then on, he'll be your principal contact until you give up or get lucky. Obviously, I hope for the second. If you need me, go through Ordonez; he knows how to get me, anytime."

When Ordonez appeared, I was put off somewhat by his physical appearance. Five-seven, at the most. Around a hundred fifty, wiry but not at all the Departmental mode. I always thought they hired by bulk, if Serkin and Hampton were representative. After the introductions, as bidden, I waited outside, impressed, perhaps a little depressed at the hum of activity going on in the room.

"Mr. MacCardle, Sergeant Ordonez has graciously consented to let you buy him lunch. You can tell him what you're up to then. Just remember one thing, Mr. MacCardle, Mr. Private Investigator MacCardle, you are still a civilian. Anything out of line, the Department will be all over you like a cheap suit. Oh, by the way, nice to see you again. Please extend my sympathy to Mr. Ellis."

"The pleasure was all mine, Lieutenant."

*   *   *

We went clattering down the marble staircase together, the little cop and I luncheon bound. I had to admire Hampton's motive; this was a much easier way to break the ice than peering at each other over a crowded desk in the squad room. I stopped at the bottom of the staircase.

"Where to, Sergeant Ordonez? I've got a car if we need it."

"Better call me Chip, Mr. MacCardle. Everyone in the Department does and if you phone in asking for *Sergeant* Ordonez, it'll take you three times as long to get me. It's a sort of code."

"Good deal. My name's Cam, the Mr. MacCardle thing is a little too formal for my taste. Again, where to?"

"Forget that trash Hampton put on you about buying my lunch. You don't have to do that."

"I want to. That is, if you have the time."

"I've got the time. I just don't feel like going very far in the monsoon out there. Tell you what, if you like hamburgers, there's a place two blocks from here called Mickey's. Best hamburgers in Cypress Beach. Retired cop owns it, won't let any of us pay for anything. Only place in town Hampton will let us go freebee."

"Lead on, Chip—squeeze under the umbrella."

Mickey's looked as if it had been transplanted from Third Avenue in New York. I'd eaten in dozens like it when we lived there. Smell of stale beer, sawdust on the floor, battered furniture, no menu save the entrees for the day chalked up on the blackboard over the bar. The man at the stick recognized

Ordonez as we walked in, smiled, waved us to a booth in the very back.

"It looks like hell, but the roaches won't get you and the chow's good. Not fancy, but a lot of it. Hey, Rembrandt, a little action please?"

A thin spidery man appeared at our table, wearing a serving apron with a towel draped over his left arm.

"Rembrandt, this is Mr. MacCardle. Cam, Rembrandt. I want a large mug of Michelob. You?"

"Sign said they have Beck's on draft. Make it Beck's for me—the light, please."

"Rembrandt was a forger. Made some of the best-looking bond and stock certificates you ever saw. Captain Stewart had one framed in his office before he retired. I don't know his real name; he doesn't seem to mind the Rembrandt tag, though."

"That's a switch, an ex-cop hiring an ex-con."

"Probably. Everyone who works here has done time. Been that way since Mickey opened up. He says they're so grateful they make good, loyal employees. I think he's just a sentimental slob trying to do his own rehab job."

Another beer and two gigantic cheeseburgers later, I knew a lot more about Sergeant Ordonez, first name Cipriano. A pretty impressive story. He was born in Cuba. Moderately well-to-do middle-class family. Father, a physics professor at the University of Havana. Evidently, the Professor was well tuned in politically, sensed the "Island Paradise" might go down the tube, and started taking steps against that possibility. He began shipping as much money to a Miami bank as he thought wouldn't attract attention, used the rest to buy rare stamps and gold coins. Came home one night and announced they were going to spend the Easter holiday in Florida. They packed their bags with sportswear. Chip, two sisters, Mamacita, and the Professor got on the plane and went on holiday. Not until they were safe in their Miami motel did the Professor tell them they weren't going back and why. The money was enough to buy them a small frame house near the Orange Bowl, in what would shortly become Little Havana. Then the tough part started.

"The man could not get a job, Cam. Here he was, advanced degrees in higher mathematics and physics, a tenured position at a large university, not Enrico Fermi, but not the village idiot either. Mama went to work as a waitress at Howard Johnson's. He finally caught on with a lawn maintenance company, mowing grass. Tough times, I remember— long while before I could look a bean in the eye without shuddering."

Presently the Professor discovered a hidden talent for landscaping. People began asking for him when they contracted with the company. Shrewdly, Mamacita realized they were using him, convinced him to go out on his own. By the time Chip reached his teens, there were gangs of workers on jobs in Dade and Broward Counties, the father planning, supervising, inspecting, keeping the quality-control high. Mamacita and the CPA took care of the rest. There was ample money to move the family out of Little Havana, to put the children through college, and to pay for Chip's graduate work.

"So the money part worked out okay," Chip said, "but the whole process broke his heart. He couldn't believe he'd taken his family to America, 'Land of Opportunity,' and seen the bigots do their best to put him down, keep him down. He's still bitter about it."

"Can't say I blame him."

"Some of joo Jankees are so understanding, how joo say, 'bloody heart leeberals'?"

"Can it, Cipriano. I had a bunch of *Cubanos* with me in 'Nam. Tough-ass troops, didn't back down from anything."

"Nobody ever said we were bright, just stubborn. Anyway, after I got the degree, the FBI wanted me to interview, plus some guy with a four-phone-number call routine in Virginia—didn't take too long to figure out who they were. Meanwhile, all hell was breaking loose in South Florida, a situation which isn't going to get better in a hurry, so I figured my place was here."

"Little idealistic?"

"A lot idealistic, and I'm paying for it, at least financially. But they keep moving me along in the department. I want to be in a position to help the most people, mine and other Latins, when the time comes, which it will."

"I wish you well."

"Thanks, wish *us* well on *this* one. You know what we have so far, where are you?"

"Slightly north of nowhere. Let me tell you . . ."

I outlined what Dick and I had discussed. Told him about the current projects files, the time sheets, and the diaries, how I planned to try piecing them together. I mentioned my meeting this afternoon with Linda Horton.

"I think you should handle that on your own. We took her statement the night he was killed, but beyond that we haven't talked to her in any depth. Besides, two strangers at once is probably too much. Plus, you've got an edge, being connected with Mr. Ellis. Please let me know if you turn up anything.

"The process you describe sounds fine, fair amount of work involved, but maybe productive. Better than what we have now, for sure. Let me know when you want to get us involved or if you need help. Meanwhile, Mrs. Ordonez's youngest child is going home to get some sleep."

"Will do. Good to have you aboard."

"Let's hope we can do some good."

I paid for my part of the meal, reclaimed my car, and started north for my meeting with Linda Horton. Thinking about the intense little man, with the self-mocking smile; feeling not quite so alone in the world anymore, with him to share the load.

*   *   *

"Do you remember Willis Kane, Cam?"

"That is not a man you forget, Linda. We called him Kamikaze Kane, wildest football player I ever saw. He was a rookie the last year I was with the Giants. A reserve linebacker. We used him mostly on the special teams, that's where he got the nickname. On kickoffs he was always first down the field to break up the blocking wedge. Threw his body at them, head first. He's still with the Giants, God alone knows why. Kamikaze Kane—a true madman."

"Same old Willis. You know there was a time when I was thinking about marrying him. Daddy didn't want the first part of that, said Willis would never live to see thirty."

"When was that?"

"In college. I went to Hollins, in Virginia. Willis was at Washington and Lee, which is right close. Met him at a freshman mixer, went with him for two years after that, until my mother died and I went back to the farm. He came out a couple of times at first, but somehow things weren't the same anymore, then Tom happened and that was the end of it for good. He got me into some crazy things, old Willis did."

"That I could believe with no trouble."

"I 'member one time, the spring of my sophomore year, we went to a costume party at one of the W&L fraternity houses. Willis didn't have an invitation, neither one of us had costumes, and Willis was drunker than seven owls, but he was by God goin' to that party. We got turned away at the door by a monstrous policeman 'cause we didn't have costumes. In the front yard the boys had planted a little tree, a sapling, really—you know, held up by wires and all?"

"Got the idea."

"Willis stormed over and just pulled it right out of the ground, tree, roots, wires, the whole thing. Tucked me under one arm, held the tree behind us with his other hand, marched up to the guard and told him they had to let us in—we were goddamn reindeer."

"That's gorgeous, Linda. Sounds like our man to a tee."

"More iced tea? No, just sit, I'll get it. Be right back."

I hadn't known what to expect. Truth be told, I had dreaded the meeting. I'd conjured up a dreary picture—the

bereaved widow, gaunt with strain, fighting back tears, ultimately dissolving when I posed the first question. I wasn't
even close.

What I got was a vivacious bundle of energy who controlled the situation from the time she opened the door. She'd
led me into the living room, plunked me down on the sofa,
poured iced tea for both of us, saying she'd heard so much
about me from Dick she felt she already knew me. Now we
were chattering away as if we'd been friends for years.

It wasn't *all* a big ho-ho, though. Early after the introductions were out of the way, I'd told her how sorry I was about
her husband. Linda had accepted graciously, the clear gray
eyes not wavering for an instant.

"Tom was a wonderful guy, Cam. I'll love him for the
rest of my life. I saw the Senator simply wither away after
Mama died. I remember how awful it was for all of us around
him. Well, I'm not goin' that way. In the first place, Tom
would hate it. He always did everythin' one hundred percent
and he expected no less from us. So that's what we'll give
him.

"Yes, we hurt, especially me, 'cause I knew him longer.
Yes, it will be hard goin' on without him, particularly for the
kids. And yes, there'll be times when you just have to sit
down and cry. But, we're not going to give up. No professional widow, no snivelin' children, living half lives. He gave
us six marvelous years and nobody can take them back. We're
Tom Horton's family, always will be. We'll bloody well carry
on the way he would hope and expect us to. He was, and
remains, our strength. We *will not* let him down."

Talk about your basic tone-setter.

*   *   *

When Linda came back with the iced tea, I asked her
about the diaries. She was gone just a minute or so, returning
with a shopping bag in her hand. "It's all I could find to put
them in, Cam. Tom had them stacked together on a shelf in
the bookcase in his study. He was a meticulous kind of guy,

always givin' me grief for not putting things back where they belonged. So, as far as I can tell, these are all of them, anyway, all there are in the house."

I turned the conversation to the main point of my visit, asking Linda if she could think of anything in Tom's personal life that could have any bearing.

"Cam, I've been thinkin' about that for a week. It must have been somethin' to do with his business, something he never told me about. He wasn't perfect, nobody is. Tom was a very competitive person, at his job, at sports, even card games. I expect he ruffled some feathers. But nothin' I'm aware of would cause someone to *kill* him.

"I even went so far as to consider another woman—you know, your brain does funny things sometimes, particularly now. I rejected that one right away, not because of pride or ego or anythin'—it just wasn't Tom's way. He was so honest it was almost a fault with him. Sometimes people thought he was blunt, but it was just that he wouldn't have a thing to do with somethin' that wasn't honest, wasn't true. I believe before he got involved with another woman, he would have come to me and said, 'Hey, Babe, I got a problem.' No. It had to be somethin' else."

"Anything he said, Linda, any conversations you can remember, anything particularly troubling him?"

"Nothin' out of the ordinary, that's why it's so frustratin'. Nobody wants to know the truth more than I. Won't get a good night's sleep until we finally know. If tearin' off an arm would help, I'd do it. But, I can't think of a single solitary reason why anyone would want him dead. Not one."

There didn't seem much point in carrying on the conversation. Not that Linda wasn't game, but I'd run out of questions and she obviously had nothing to volunteer. So I thanked her for seeing me. Gave her my telephone number. Took the shopping bag of diaries and went home in the ten-percent probability of rain.

A gallant, gallant lady. I hoped on hope we wouldn't disappoint her.

7

Ever have a day when nothing seems to go right? I mean, where things *start* off poorly and just keep going downhill? I had one Friday and it wasn't even the thirteenth—just a plain, average Friday that got worse as it got longer.

I might have guessed it when there wasn't any hot water for shaving. It generally takes a little while for the hot water to come up. As I stood at the sink, hand under the water's flow, looking at myself in the mirror, I realized it wasn't ever coming up until I did something about it. Shaving with cold water is bad enough. What was worse was knowing the plumber and electrician's bills to fix the hot water heater would cover a semester at Princeton. Not an auspicious beginning.

So I thought I'd treat myself to a make-up breakfast, starring that hideously expensive delicacy, Canadian bacon. Mistake number two. Reaching into the oven to flip the little pieces over on the broiling pan, I seared the back of my wrist, not enough to worry about major medical, but sufficient to produce a slight smell of charred MacCardle and an instant throbbing pain. I read somewhere that the best remedy for this kind of thing is to apply ice—numbs the affected area and stops potential blistering. Went to the refrigerator, dug out some ice cubes, wrapped them in a dishtowel, held it against the tender wrist.

Standing in the kitchen playing Mayo Clinic, I heard a familiar sound—that of the garbage truck receding—and realized I'd forgotten to put out the trash. It would be Monday before he returned, which meant that this week's accumulation plus the normal party weekend lot would turn the garage into some form of billygoat heaven. Enough to reduce strong men to tears.

Instead, I called the robber plumber, who said he thought he could get around to me in a week or so, what with being so jammed up, you know how it is, Mr. MacCardle. I didn't care how it was. All I knew was I had to have hot water for the weekend, knowing at least one guest who does not function well unless able to begin the day with a hot shower. We finally negotiated a price which would move me up the list, get the problem resolved today, and ensure a Jamaican vacation for the robber and his entire clan. Not in anybody's Holiday Inn, either.

I called Carole, recounted the horrors of the day to date, told her I was seriously thinking about taking up thumbsucking. As expected, no sympathy. Just a line of cheap chatter about clumsiness in general, plus some commentary on my culinary shortfalls in particular. Hard-hearted woman, made me wonder what I saw in her.

I dragged out the time sheets, my preliminary work sheets, and the shopping bag of diaries, stacking them on the coffee table for ready reference, and plunged in, or at least, tried to: apparently the phone was determined to ring all day. No thank you, Merrill Lynch, my investments were being taken care of. No free dance lessons, Arthur Murray, yes, I understood what I was passing up. No, I didn't want an estimate on repairing the roof, I had it redone last year. Of course, I was delighted I'd won the GE toaster oven, but going to Delray Beach to look at time-sharing condominiums was out of the question, even if it meant forfeiting such a prize. And so on.

I was reading a particularly interesting section of one of the diaries when the doorbell rang. Muttering assorted oaths,

I stalked to the front door, threw it open, growling. About four feet worth of ten-year-old girl stared up at me, sufficiently startled by my appearance to stifle speech, thrusting a grubby book of raffle tickets at me, ready for instant flight. At fifty cents a crack I could help St. Michael's Overseas Mission and maybe win a Pontiac Grand Prix. My choice of colors. I'm as lucky at games of chance as the world travelers who opted for the *Titanic*'s maiden voyage. But for two dollars, I could make this latest attention drain go away. Hopefully, get back to work. I bought the book.

I read the diaries through, nonstop. Then went back and started cross-matching them against numbers of hours spent on individual projects, tempered by the nature of the work involved. Slowly, some pattern began to emerge, still crude, but at least a series of beginnings.

From the list of current projects, I made a judgment decision to eliminate Prairie Mutual Insurance and Follert's Markets. Dick's guess on the outcome of the insurance price increase had been correct, per usual. The diary notations indicated a compromise was in the final stages. The company was pledging a lesser increase in return for the allowance of a retroactive date of effect to the day of the initial notification to policyholders. It was in the commissioner's lap currently, with all indicators pointing to his signature. Down One.

The Follert's deal was a straightforward take over, cut and dried, with asking price and method of payment amenable to both parties. Further work was already in progress to assure the lowest possible tax burden, but it was a done deal for all intents and purposes. Dick could decide whether to pursue the angle on Mr. Follert's will; otherwise there wasn't anything there of promise to us. Down Two. Which left the Mayor's Commission and the Donaldson estate alive on the current projects list.

I followed a similar elimination process with the projects dredged up from the time sheets. Struck out Linton Development and Top Flight Productions along the way.

Linton Development was a series of unbroken successes,

the story of a journeyman carpenter who was in the right place at the beginning of the land and housing boom that began in the fifties. Horton's involvement had been extensive, but was essentially limited to a variety of closing documents on shopping centers, apartment complexes, and land tract acquisitions. Nice for Mr. Linton, not so hot for us.

Top Flight Productions was a negative image of Linton Development: people who began with a lot of money and managed to lose most of it in a vain attempt to convert the Fort Lauderdale area into America's center for television commercial production. Tom's work with them centered on the creation of a holding company, then several subcompanies, and a disheartening number of Chapter Eleven bankruptcy actions, as advertising agencies stubbornly clung to the practice of funneling work through the big production houses in New York and Los Angeles. Whether the ball game is won, lost, or rained out, the lawyers always get paid, I thought. Must be a moral there somewhere for the youth of America in career planning.

Of the balance, three still looked promising: Rol-A-Gard Corporation and two cases labeled by individuals' names, Mrs. E. A. Alden and Morton Giles. I went back into the appropriate diaries for more detailed substantiation.

The Alden case was a particularly messy divorce action. There was no question as to cause or guilt. Mrs. Alden's operative evidently had enough photographs to fill four issues of *Penthouse,* assuming a lenient posture by their editorial board. As the proverbial woman scorned, Mrs. Alden was determined to make her former husband's financial life as difficult as possible. The settlement stripped him to a barely survivable base, with cost of living and escalator provisions that indicated a not very healthy future for him as a capitalist. He had threatened both Mrs. Alden and Horton with bodily damage in court, a part of the written record. All uttered in the heat of the moment, for sure. But—people have been killed for less, I thought, remembering my own homicidal urges against the Pearl's attorney.

Rol-A-Gard Corporation was the child of two men from Buffalo, New York: Seth Cutler and his partner, Paul Goodman. Together, they'd started a small company dealing in protective window and door covers. The company grew quite nicely, fueled by the housing expansion, with an unexpected but welcome bonus provided by homeowners increasingly concerned with the zooming levels of vandalism and break-ins. Goodman took care of the purchasing and manufacture; Cutler was the Company's financial man. Sales were produced through a combination of local, small-space advertising, satisfied-customer referral, and telephone solicitation—like those that had driven me up the wall all morning.

Things were going along beautifully until Mr. Cutler and his auditor began noting a decline in their rate of profit. Absolute profits continued to grow, but not in line with sales increases. Cutler eventually narrowed his investigation down to Purchasing, discovering a simple but effective system of order padding to one principal supplier who, under oath, also admitted to having agreed to a kickback arrangement benefiting Mr. Goodman even more.

After the infliction of various tax penalties, the government had agreed to provide shelter for Mr. Goodman for a period not to exceed five years, at the Tallahassee Federal Correctional Institution, the catchall for various white collar criminals. As with the unfortunate Mr. Alden, Goodman had threatened retaliation to everyone involved, from his partner to Judge Seward, who was presiding, Horton being somewhere in the middle. The diary indicated that Goodman was now free on parole, having served three of the five years' sentence.

Morton Giles had been run over by a bus. That he was jaywalking at the time, well above the legal definition regarding alcoholic intake—both unvolunteered facts which surfaced at the hearing—did not deter him from asking twenty million in damages from a combination of Broward County, Deerfield Beach, the Mass Transit Division, and Alexander Brophy, bus driver.

The jury, no doubt swayed by the distressing picture of a man permanently confined to a wheelchair, went beyond the evidence and awarded Giles one hundred thousand dollars. The appellate court subsequently reduced the amount to fifty thousand, the judge urging Mr. Giles's acceptance since he really had no legal rights whatsoever.

Already bitter, Giles had left the courtroom in a rage, vowing he would "get every damn one of them, if it takes the rest of my life." He'd begun by harassing the judge with telephone calls at home, finally forcing the man to change his telephone number and issue a cease and desist order against Mr. Giles this spring. It seemed logical that Tom Horton would be another target eventually and the timing fit.

I went back and sorted through what I had, deciding to give each candidate a probability ranking, compiling this list:

PROJECT NAME	POTENTIAL
Rol-A-Gard Corp.	1
Mayor's Commission	2
Morton Giles	3
Donaldson Estate	4
Edward Alden	5

Arbitrary judgments, perhaps way out of line, but we had to make a start. These seemed the most promising.

The diaries had been extremely helpful in compiling the list, not simply by providing information, but by the tone of the writer's remarks. For example, increasing mention of the name Angel Diaz occurred in those sections relating to the Mayor's Commission. The associative words "bloodsucker," "society cancer," "child perverter," and the query, "potential drug dealing network?" made me quite anxious to meet Mr. Diaz and helped push the project high up on my priorities list.

I was stowing the last of the diaries away when something peculiar caught my eye. The dates on the front indicated coverage from July 14 to September 8. Horton had been killed on the 15th. That meant five working days unaccounted for, no-

tably September 9, 10, 13, 14, and 15. I had his daily history
from the day he joined the firm. It seemed inconceivable he
would suddenly abandon the practice. So, there must be a
newly started diary missing. But where? Jane had gone
through his office and Linda had been sure she'd given me all
of them. Then if not at home, not in the office, where could it
be? How about a briefcase, birdbrain; maybe he took it home
to work on that night. Easy enough to find out.

"Now that you mention it," Linda told me, "he must not
have brought that bag home. Right queer, 'cause he almost
always had it with him. After the police got done with the car,
they gave me everything they took out of it. No briefcase. Is it
important?"

"Maybe. Anyway, don't worry about it. It's probably in
his office. It's after five thirty now, I'll call Jane on Monday.
I'm sure she'll find it."

That had to be the answer. Tom was too methodical for it
to be anything else. Five missing days—wonder if they are
important? At least I could find out how he spent the time;
the time sheets could take care of that.

A big block of time on the tenth on Donaldson, almost a
full day. Otherwise the hours divided almost equally among
the balance of the active projects. Why so much time against
Donaldson. What did that mean?

Again, the time sheets had the answer, although it took a
while to make the connection. The tenth was a Friday, specifically, the second Friday in September. Looking backward,
month by month, the pattern cleared—a major block of Donaldson hours on the second Friday, fourteen consecutive
months. What had Dick said? Hand holding. So that fit; the
diary would undoubtedly confirm it. Just have to wait until
Monday, no other choice.

I went off to take a murderously expensive shower, looking forward to dinner chez Ellis.

*   *   *

"Just my imagination, Susan, or is the house unnaturally
quiet tonight?"

"We're operating with a skeleton crew. The twins are off on a Brownie field trip to Disney World, Ricky's upstairs getting ready to spend the night at a friend's. You're getting a sort of a pick-me-up supper tonight."

"Productive day at home, Cam? Jane told me you turned down our offer of a spot in the library."

"You don't know the half of it."

I launched into an account of ma journee, complete with disasters—man-made and natural—of tribulations major and minor, stopping only when I realized Dick was bent double howling, with even the reserved Susan unable to suppress a face-splitting grin.

Monumental insensitivity, rare in people of such good breeding.

"Hi, Mr. MacCardle, that's an ugly-looking burn on your arm. Betcha can't guess what I'm doing tonight."

"Hi, Rick, I give up, what *are* you doing?"

"My friend's father's a real football nut. He's got videotape cassettes of all the Pro Bowl games. Me and my friend . . ."

"My friend and I, Ricky."

"Aw, Mom. Anyway, Mr. MacCardle, *we're* gonna watch the game when you scored the touchdown. Some thrill, huh?"

In deference to my blinding speed, the other team had assigned me single coverage that night; the free safety helping cover an assortment of far more lethal targets. When I ran my fifth pattern, the cornerback had fallen down, some say from laughter, so I was all alone in the end zone when the ball arrived. If I'd dropped it they would have run me out of New Orleans.

But the dreams of youth are to be nurtured.

"It certainly was, Rick. Never forget that one, for sure."

"Whaddya think of the Dolphins this year?"

"They look good to me—great draft, winning pre-season record. They're off to a fine start—that St. Louis win was a big one."

"Yeah, but I wish they'd settle on one quarterback like Marino, he's terrific."

"I don't know. Shula knows what he's doing. You can't knock the results, not so far, anyway. Are we still on for the Giants game next month?"

"Yessir, I'd go on a broken leg. Well, goodnight, Mr. MacCardle, hope your burn gets better, nice to see you again."

He was off in that whirl of sound, energy, and motion only twelve-year-olds can sustain, scooping up the aqua-and-orange Dolphin kit bag, the slam of the front door punctuating his flight.

"Harness that boy to the TVA he could light up half of Tennessee."

"He's a handful. Now that it's just us old folks, you about ready for food?"

"Right behind you, ma'am."

Susan's "pick-me-up" supper started with a puree mongole, followed by a hefty London broil with scalloped potatoes and an endive salad, finished with pecan pie with a crust so fragile it had to be homemade. I told her I was all for these informal little picnics and, long as it was so easy, we probably ought to do this every Friday.

Susan shooed us off to the den to talk while she finished clearing up the dishes. I summarized the work part of the day for Dick, ended up with my list of possibilities and priorities, asked him what he thought. He lit the always-on-hand pipe in a series of acrid billows, looked past it at me, thoughtfully.

"Appears reasonably sound to me, Cam. I agree with the logic of trying to eliminate apparent 'no potentials.' The list looks like the best we have to go on. I might quarrel a little with the priorities, but you're the one doing the legwork, so I guess you ought to be the one calling the shots. I'm glad we started filming the time sheets, they seem to have been somewhat helpful."

"A godsend. One question. If the firm doesn't bill on

something like the Mayor's Commission, why indicate the hours?"

"A variety of reasons. There's the question of control; if the hours started getting really out of hand, we'd want to know why—after all, we are trying to run a law firm. Our people's time and talent are the only product we sell. Keyed to the first reason is profit-center accounting. We need to know which clients and which lawyers are money makers— plus the converse—so that there will be a profit pot to split at the end of the year. Finally, it's a sort of internal ethics code for us. We've never been challenged, but if we were, I'd like to be able to prove we weren't sluffing nonrevenue hours over onto a paying client. Now, what about next steps?"

"Check in with Ordonez, for openers. I'll need to reference him if any of these people get stubborn about not talking to me. Then, I sit down with the telephone and start calling— try to fit together an appointment schedule."

"Good on both counts. Why not do it from my office? I'll be in court all day Monday, as usual. Jane can give you a hand coming up with telephone numbers and whatnot. Also, it would give you a chance to go through Tom's briefcase. I think you're right. I think there is another diary. Chances are you'll find it there. I'll tell Jane to expect you around ten, unless that's a hardship. No? Good, then that's done. Let's go see what the cook is up to."

The cook was sitting on the couch in front of the family room television set, watching the end of "Casablanca," blubbering like a schoolgirl. Dick got us all an after-dinner drink and we sat in solemn silence until the credits started rolling up the screen.

"How many times have you seen that movie, darling?"

"I've given up counting. The ending gets me every time. It's a three-boxer for me—Kleenex sales must skyrocket around here every time they show it. A classic, gentlemen, take it from a connoisseur."

"Big bash this weekend, Cam?"

"Modest bash. Carole and I are helping Billy out with his Single-Parents Group. Cocktail party Saturday at my house. Billy says it makes them less inhibited with each other to be in a social situation. Last one I went to, I had a tough time spotting any inhibitions, but I guess he knows best. Sunday, as ever, a day for rest and good thoughts. How 'bout you?"

"Enjoy the unaccustomed peace. Do some chores. Maybe get Miss Teardrops here to play eighteen holes. I'll take her to dinner at the club if she doesn't beat me too badly. Incidentally, Cam, that Single-Parent thing sounds like it might be a help for Linda Horton at some point down the road. We're having them over for a cookout Sunday. Maybe I'll mention it to her then. Are there any restrictions? I mean the Hortons are old-line Southern Baptist stock?"

"You know Billy—it's welcome one, welcome all. Last of the big shepherds. Just let him know when the timing seems right. No problems at all."

The big grandfather clock in the front hall began to bong the hour. Subconsciously, my mind picked up the count. Five, six, seven, it was eleven o'clock. Tell the nice people thank you for a splendid dinner, good luck with the golf, talk to you Monday.

I did all that and drove home, feeling uncharacteristically pleased with the day's efforts. Remembered the old Chinese proverb, "The journey of a thousand miles begins with a single step."

We'd taken that first step today, a solid one in my view. Ancient Chinese One, grant the balance of the journey will be smooth.

Fat chance of that, methinks.

8

"Oh no, not glazed donuts, Cam. I can put on a whole dress size just looking at those things. Get thee behind me, Satan, and you too, you wicked, wicked man."

"Sustenance for the working classes, Lady Jane. How about I get me into the inner sanctum and you hustle up some coffee, get a head start on the day."

I took the big leather chair behind the vast expanse of Dick's desk, feeling like the bloated J. Pierpont Morgan himself. Sell those two million shares short, I don't *care* if that company goes under. U.S. Steel. A group of parvenus, serve them right. Upstarts.

"Where are *you*, Cam?"

"What do you mean, where am I? All right, you got me, this office does strange things for my imagination."

"Not too strange, I hope. Everything's laid out on the coffee table. I brought my pad in case you want me to take notes."

Over our mini-breakfast I asked Jane to get me the files, or summaries better yet, for Rol-A-Gard Corporation, Morton Giles, and Mrs. Alden. I also asked her to make an appointment with both the mayor and Mrs. Donaldson, no particular time, sooner the better.

"Is Tom Horton's office locked?"

"Yes. We're still waiting for Mrs. Horton to come down and clean out his personal effects. I have the key in my desk—I'll get it for you first thing. Why do you need to go in there? I thought we'd gotten everything of any use."

I told her about the five unaccounted-for working days, my theory about a missing diary, and our guess as to where it might be. She did away with the meal remains, brought me Tom's key, suggested I start there while she was digging into the files and making the first telephone calls. Fine, but I had something to do first.

*   *   *

"Good morning, Chip Ordonez, please."

"Doesn't come off watch until noon, May I have him call you then?"

"If you would, please. My name is MacCardle, the number is five—six—four six thousand, extension four twelve."

"That local, Mr. Cardle?"

"Local enough, and the name's MacCardle, M–A–C–C–A–R–D–L–E."

"Sorry, sir, I'll have him call you."

*   *   *

The briefcase was on a credenza off to the left of his desk. A big, belting leather job with two combination locks for the snaps, looking as if it had rendered years of faithful service from all the acquired stains, scrapes, and wear marks. The dull gold monogram was still legible, T.H.H. Now, if only the bloody thing opens . . . otherwise we'll have to get a locksmith.

Both snaps popped back easily. I opened the case, took everything out of it, and spread the contents across his desk. No diary, nothing that even vaguely resembled one. Calendar, date book, pads of yellow paper, a pocket calculator. A box of sharpened pencils, pictures of the family, list of all his credit card numbers, a little case with business cards in it. Equipment for a thorough, well-prepared man. But, damn it, no diary.

"There has to be one, Jane, I just know there is."

"Is it that important?"

"Probably not, but you know me. Loose ends bother small minds."

"Then let's try to tie up a few. Here are the files you asked for. When we close out a project, the lawyer assigned to it does what we call an Executive Summary. Those are on top in each file, details behind if you need anything more.

"Hizzoner will see you in his office Wednesday at two. I got Mrs. Donaldson. Really, I got a very icy woman named Smithers. Veddy British, veddy clipped accent, evidently she's Mrs. Donaldson's companion, made it sound like a title. You have a ten o'clock date tomorrow to see her—Mrs. Donaldson, that is. La Smithers says to keep it short, apparently the old girl is 'a bit off her feed,'—I'm quoting. Directions on getting there are in this folder. I think you know where Cypress Beach City Hall is?"

"I do and thanks a bunch, Janie-O. You're a true wizard."

"We aim to please. Happy reading."

* * *

The summaries contributed a little more to my knowledge bank, not a great deal, but at least some more nuts and bolts stuff that would save digging time.

Edward (Ned) Alden had worked as a television time salesman for station WPBF–TV, in West Palm Beach. Done reasonably well at it, if the Xerox copies of his W–2 forms were any indicator. After the divorce, he'd moved to Charlotte, North Carolina, where he was employed by station WTHS-TV, address and telephone number included. I hoped he was still there—anyway, if not, they could tell me where he'd gone. He'd been a very good boy, paying his alimony and child-support payments on time, from the divorce until they closed the file six months later. You're a better man than I, Mr. Alden, I thought, recalling several particularly unpleasant exchanges with the avaricious Mr. Smollert.

The Rol-A-Gard summary did not provide the whereabouts of Paul Goodman, terminating while Mr. Goodman was still in residence at Tallahassee. The address and telephone number for the corporation were included; evidently it had still been in business when the recap was prepared. So, two ways to get at that one. Call his former partner and if that failed, the correctional institution probably had a system for keeping track of its alumni.

There was no summary on Morton Giles; apparently that case was still being treated as open. At least the file itself was sequential and it wasn't all that voluminous. Mr. Giles's current listed address was 11 Cove Lane, Balmy Breezes, Florida—wherever the hell that was—the telephone number didn't indicate it was out of the 305 area code. Jane will know.

His financial picture was not very bright. The firm had charged him the minimum fee acceptable by bar standards. Nevertheless, if he'd invested the entire settlement with a highly canny manager, he could expect an annual income from it of about four thousand dollars, not exactly the domain of the idle rich. The file indicated he was currently self-employed, probably a euphemism masking the fact that all too many people *don't* hire the handicapped.

"My day to go to lunch early, Cam. Can I get you anything?"

"Please. Ham and swiss on rye, no mustard. Coke. Maybe some potato chips if they have the little bags."

"Turn up anything from the files?"

"Some. Do me a favor, see if you can get hold of Morton Giles when you get back from lunch. Here's the number. Where in the world is Balmy Breezes?"

"See, greenhorn, you don't know everything. It's a trailer park. On U.S. One, just north of Boca Raton."

"I've been by there. *That's* Balmy Breezes?"

"You got it. Sounds a bit better than it looks. How about the Alden and Rol-A-Gard projects?"

"I'll do those. Even we Biggies aren't afraid to get our hands dirty."

"My heart leaps up. See you around twelve thirty, Santa."

Ingratitude. Shaking my head, I reached for the telephone.

*   *   *

"Rol-A-Gard . . . the Name You Trust."

"Mr. Seth Cutler, please."

"May I tell him who's calling?"

"My name is MacCardle."

"Just a minute, please."

I was on hold, listening to canned music through the receiver, a detestable practice becoming all too common. You don't even get your choice of music. This was "The Blue Danube," which always reminds me of a rollerskating rink in Paoli, Pennsylvania, and a night when I almost sprained both ankles at once trying to impress Debby Bowen, far and away the prettiest girl in my high school class.

"Mr. MacCardle? Mr. Cutler says he doesn't know you. Can you tell me what this is in reference to?"

"Please tell him it's about Mr. Goodman. Mr. Paul Goodman."

*   *   *

Back to "The Blue Danube." I picked myself up, did my best to ignore the snickering and pointed fingers, watched mournfully as Debby left arm in arm with the captain of the football team. *Sic transit gloria mundi.*

*   *   *

The voice on the other end verged on apoplectic. "Goodman? That shmuck is in no way associated with this company, his teeth should only drop out at Seder."

"I know that, Mr. Cutler. I only want to talk to him."

"Talk? To Goodman? You want a *gonif* lesson maybe?"

"*Gonif*?"

"Thief, crook, robber. Three years of profit that putz cost

me. Three years of no vacations, three years of Sylvia whining about her ratty mink, three years of *tsuris* his Chanuka present was. Him you need to talk to like Adolf Eichmann."

"Please, slow down, Mr. Cutler. Do you remember Tom Horton . . ."

"The lawyer. Of course I remember him. Such a fine young man, a real tragedy . . . you think Goodman is involved? I wouldn't be surprised."

"I don't know. That's what I'm trying to find out."

"You said *Mister* MacCardle. You're not a police officer?"

"*Working* with them—the Cypress Beach Police. Check on me with Sergeant Ordonez if you want to."

"No need. You sound like an honest man—which is more than I can say for Goodman, he should only be deported."

"Can you tell me where he is? How I can get hold of him?"

"No. If I knew where that *shtarker* was I would go to a surgeon for a lobotomy, so I wouldn't remember. Sorry I can't help you find him, may he be sent away for life."

"Well, thanks anyway, Mr. Cutler."

No information, but I'd acquired a whole new vocabulary. Shmuck, gonif, putz, tsuris, shtarker. Maybe Mr. Breslo at the Book Nook could help me translate, but I had a strong hunch they weren't character-reference words.

I caught Ned Alden on his way to lunch. He was cooperative, but extremely wary. What was it all about, why couldn't we handle it on the phone, why did I need to come all the way to Charlotte, was this somehow tied in with his former wife? He thought that was all settled. Sure he'd see me, but the schedule was lousy, hope you understand. Out of town for the rest of the week at an American Broadcasters' Association Convention in Las Vegas. Selling swing through the major Los Angeles and San Francisco advertising agencies after that, coming back Thursday night. Out-of-town sponsors coming in for a weekend junket—National 500 NASCAR race on Sunday, tours, parties, and dinners—everything at the dead run. Only open time he had was lunch on Friday, the first. So, we settled on that. At his suggestion, we agreed to meet in the main dining room at the Radisson at one o'clock, table would be in his name.

An unexpected bonus. I'd gotten involved with NASCAR through Bobby Evans, the late Laura Morgan's brother and a top-flight race driver. Through him, I'd met the big names in that most demanding sport—Richard and Kyle Petty, Cale Yarborough, Darrell Waltrip, Harry Gant, the whole lot. Bobby's racing team had taken great care of me at Daytona, particularly his assistant, an affable giant named Boomer Mays, who'd been my tour guide, mentor, and mother hen. I'd also met Ben and Sally Reed, two of the world's nicest people. Ben used to run the track at Dover, Delaware, moving into the upper echelons of the NASCAR headquarters staff. Call him and see if we couldn't get together, might as well mix some pleasure with the business. Then there was the question of the Pearl to consider. Hell, long as you're in the neighborhood. Take her to dinner, see if she wanted to go to the race. No matter what, you are still friends, right? Make a note to call her, too.

The buzzer broke my train of thought.

"Yes?"

"Mr. MacCardle, there's a Sergeant Ordonez on 412 for you."

"Thanks, I'll take it."

It was a long call. I took Chip through the details of my Friday meeting with Ellis, outlined the projects, the rationale for choosing them, and my subjective priorities.

In the middle of the conversation, Jane came in with my bag lunch. I waved her over to the couch, indicating to her to pick up the extension phone on the end table.

I told Chip about the meetings already set up—Alden, Mrs. Donaldson, and the mayor. Invited him to come with me on the last.

"Thanks, Cam. It's still too early for me to get involved. Sounds like you're doing all right, for a blunderer, that is."

"I smell Hampton behind that crack."

"Seriously, you're looking good. Anything I can do to help?"

"Two things. I can't seem to locate a Mr. Paul Goodman. He went to prison in the Rol-A-Gard scandal. I talked to his partner, his ex-partner that is—most definitely ex. I got the impression he'd love to have Goodman's head for a bowling ball, but no help. Doesn't know where he is."

"We can probably get a line on him through his parole officer. Didn't think of that one, huh? That's why they pay me all this money. We'll put somebody on it this afternoon. That was easy. What's the other one, Cam?"

"A name keeps popping up on the Mayor's Commission project. Man named Angel Diaz, mean anything to you?"

"Not by itself. Angel Diaz is like Joe Smith, must be hundreds of them in South Florida."

"His full name is Angel Obregon Diaz, that help?"

"It might if you pronounced it right, Anglo. That's O–Bray–Gon, joo Jankee."

"Eighty-six the Rich Little routine, would you, Chip? This guy gets a lot of ink in the files."

"Spoilsport. What else do you know about him?"

"Mid-forties. No home address given. Seems to own some X-rated movie houses, couple of adult book stores and a bar, all in that section called Action Junction."

"I know it—all too well. That's helpful. The Vice or License Bureau people maybe can give us a line on him. Meanwhile, we'll shove Mr. Diaz onto the computer, see if the Knowns or Suspected files have anything. It'll take a while, though. I'll get someone started. Go grab some beauty rest and pick up whatever they have this evening when I come back on. You home tonight?"

"Far as I know."

"Talk to you then, *chico*."

A smartass, natural born, dyed in the wool smartass. Why hadn't I thought about the parole officer, Vice, and the

License Bureau? Because you're not trained to think that way, Charlie Chan. He is. Thank goodness.

"Take a break, Cam. Eat the lunch the nice lady brought you. Can't think on an empty stomach."

"Thanks, Janie, I will. What do I owe you?"

"Three fifteen. You're only going to bill us for it anyway, so I'll take it out of petty cash and save the bookkeeping."

"Fine. Don't forget to call Mr. Giles for me. Fit him in wherever the schedule's blank."

"I won't forget. Enjoy."

Her instincts were good. I *was* hungry. The deli sandwich was a young mountain of shaved ham, the Swiss cheese nice and smoky. Crisp chips, cold Coke, who could ask for anything more? Then, as the Pearl so often said, I *am* easily pleased.

Speaking of the Pearl. I got Charlotte Directory Assistance, asked for the number of the Wachovia National Bank. Yes, I knew they had lots of branches, the main office number, please.

"Ms. Vance's office, may I help you?"

"I'd like to speak to her, please. My name's MacCardle."

"The nature of your call, please, Mr. MacCardle?"

"Tell her I'm cutting off the alimony payments."

"Hi there, Angus, what a nice surprise."

"I'll Angus you, *Mizz* Vance. Still going out with that no-neck cretin that smells like a still—Carter something?"

"Your vocabulary is improving, darlin'. Cretin. A big word for you. Must be doing the *Reader's Digest* tests again. Carter does like his little nip—he also owns the biggest insurance company in town."

"Each to his own taste, the old lady said . . ."

"I know, as she kissed the pig, Cam, you *surely* didn't call to check on my social life. What's on your mind?"

"I'm coming to Charlotte the night of the thirtieth, be there through Sunday. Part business, part fun. I was hoping you might be free for dinner and/or, if you wanted, to see the National Five Hundred with me Sunday."

"National Five Hundred, what's that?"

"You live in Charlotte and you don't know? It's a major stock car race. C'mon it'll be fun."

"*That's* why I couldn't get hotel rooms. I'd love to but no can do. It's Big Lydia's seventy-fifth birthday, people comin' in from all over. The whole Longstreet clan, plus assorted friends. Why don't you come on out?"

"Because, as you know all too well, sweets, your father thinks I'm a shiftless ingrate since I wouldn't go to work for him. Your mother despises me and the rest of the clan makes me feel as welcome as a plague of cotton borers. I have a high pain threshold, but not *that* high."

"How you exaggerate. There may be a teeny bit of hostility, but not nearly . . ."

"Teeny, my foot. They'll come after me like Captain Ahab. Thanks, Pearl, maybe next time, okay?"

"Your choice. Anyway, 'preciate you thinkin' about me. Let me know if you change your mind. Bye now."

So, bachelor weekend in Charlotte. Carole couldn't get that much time off, so we'll just have to tough it out. Done it before. Dangerous, but not fatal.

Jane came boiling into the office, a Jane I'd never seen before. Hair mussed, jaw set, fists on hips, glaring at me.

"It's about *your* friend, Morton Giles."

"My friend? Never laid eyes on him in my whole entire life. What's the problem?"

"That's the nastiest man I have ever had the misfortune to talk to."

"Bad language?"

"No, bad attitude. Rotten attitude. He'd paid our exorbitant fee, weren't getting another penny out of him. Shyster lawyers who couldn't win one when it was handed to them. Overpriced stuffed shirts too busy making money to do their jobs properly."

"Sounds like a real sweetheart."

"Those were just starters. Yes, he'd heard about Tom. What was that to him? One less lawyer. Tough luck, but not as tough as being in a wheelchair forever, thanks to us."

"Wow!"

"I know. I wanted to strangle him. He said you could come by any time tomorrow afternoon, or any afternoon. The mornings he saves for cha-cha lessons and volleyball."

"Looks like you drew the short straw, kid. Sorry. I had no idea."

"I know. I'm just letting off steam. An utterly vile man. You still want to see him?"

"Might as well share the fun. I'll see him tomorrow, get it over with as soon as I can. Buy you a drink to make up?"

"Two. I'll need them to wash out the taste. Five thirty? I'll come in and get you."

*   *   *

Our introduction to Morton Giles. I'm no psychiatrist, but that sounded like a double scoop of hatred with maybe a sprinkling of old fashioned paranoia. A volatile mixture, perhaps capable of producing enough hatred to kill someone. Anyone. But particularly Tom, if he held him responsible for his trouble. Find out tomorrow, I guess. Could be a long afternoon.

I spent the rest of the day re-reviewing the files, with special emphasis on Mrs. Donaldson and my friend Giles, getting ready for tomorrow.

I suddenly realized I had forgotten to call Ben Reed. Better to do that on Dick's WATS line than from home. Punched out the number, caught him just as the NASCAR switchboard was closing for the night. The enthusiastic voice hadn't changed a whit. Yes, he remembered me, hard to forget people who called every other year. Certainly he was going to Charlotte, he and Sally would be there from Wednesday on. Forget about trying to get a hotel room—I could have one of the block NASCAR had reserved at the Radisson. Thursday night wasn't a problem. Sorry, they were booked up socially but Saturday night the STP and Champion Spark Plug people were having a big dinner, more than welcome to go with them to it. Tickets, pit, and garage passes would be in an envelope in my box at the hotel, got to keep you steady customers happy. I hung up, grinning.

*   *   *

"Daiquiri for the lady, I'll take a Busch beer and some mixed nuts if you have them. Potato chips? Fine."

"Since when do you drink Busch? I thought you were strictly an imported beer man."

"Call it a sort of a debt of fealty. I just finished talking to Ben Reed at NASCAR—he's got me all set up for Charlotte. The NASCAR people go out of their way to use the sponsor's products. You know—Winstons, Gatorade, Pepsi, Mountain Dew, Skoal, and so on. Their beer is Busch. Figured it was the least I could do."

"Well here's to a good day's work—with the exception of that detestable man."

"Here's to *you*. You did all the tough stuff. Janie, I hate to prolong the agony, but talk to me a little more about Giles. Not what he said it, more how he sounded, any other impressions you got about him."

"He made me highly nervous. I mean, he doesn't even know me but he was almost attacking me, like I'd caused all of his problems *personally*. High-pitched, whiny tone of voice, talks like a machine gun. I don't think he listened to a word I said, just let me finish and then came at me again."

"A little off the wall, maybe?"

"A lot off the wall, if that call was typical of his basic outlook on life. I think you better be very careful when you see him tomorrow."

"Yes, Mother."

*   *   *

I drove Jane home, over her protests that it was out of my way, the bus was fine; dropped her off, promised I'd check in late in the afternoon, post-Giles. Drove back to Lighthouse Point mulling over how best to spend Monday night alone.

A Hungry Man Salisbury Steak TV Dinner and a half a bottle of Chianti that had miraculously survived Billy's group of inhibited single parents over the weekend. Frank, Dandy, and Howard, live from Pittsburgh, would bring me the Steelers and Raiders. *Good* ball game. There *are* worse ways to go, believe me.

Ordonez called just as I was trying to dig the last of the crumb cake out of its little compartment in the dinner tray.

"That you, Cam? Sounds like you're talking through a blanket."

"Sorry, last of my supper. How did you do?"

"That sounds better. Got a line on your man Goodman. Grab a pencil and paper. Okay?

"He lives in Coral Gables. Has an apartment in a residential hotel called Flamingo Walk. Thirty-two hundred North East Fourteenth Avenue. No, I don't know where that is. You'll just have to find it for yourself. Telephone number is eight–five–six seventy thirty–six."

"Nicely done, Chipper, that'll save a bunch of digging. Anything come up on Angel *Oh-Bray-Gon* Diaz?"

"Spoken like a native; there may be hope for you yet. Just a preliminary, all of it bad news. Born in Puerto Rico, started showing up on the Bayamon rap sheets from age thirteen on. Moved on to San Juan in his twenties, always on the fringes of the big action. Picked up a nickname there. "*Gorrion*"—it means sparrow in Spanish. Literally, that is. It also means garbage eater, picker at dung, scavenger—that kind of thing. Not too heroic."

"Any more?"

"Not much, at least not now, but we'll keep at it. Evidently, they rousted him off the island about ten years ago, told him to get going and keep going. Guess the San Juan boys didn't care *where* he went as long as he *went*."

"What's the noble citizen done in the States?"

"Being compiled. I ought to have it tomorrow. I had one retriever do international, another one do domestic. The Sparrow's our Diaz all right. *Muy penoso*, a bad actor. When you see that one, I go along for the ride, not *just* because I'm such a superb linguist."

"Modest, too."

"Cam, this is the kind of guy that gives all of us a bad name. A steak dinner bet that his file shows he's into all kinds of nasty things, undoubtedly with a crew of troops who won't be candidates for the Social Register. No offense, but he's a little out of your league."

"I'll take your word for it. Can you call me tomorrow night with whatever they turn up? I'm seeing the mayor Wednesday—like to know everything I can beforehand."

"*Con gusto, senor*, my pleasure."

I fell asleep on the couch at halftime, despite Howard's attempts to make highlights film sound like the coming of World War III. Missed a helluva game, too, Oakland pulling it out on a field goal with seventeen seconds left—had to read about it in the paper.

Phooey.

9

Let's see now, go north to the traffic light at the first main intersection. Take a right. The house is the last on the right before a roundabout, which either deposits you at the Playa Lago Club or shunts you over a little bridge, out onto A1A. Bingo! Good job, Lady Jane.

The house was completely screened from the road by an enormous stand of boxwood hedge which must have shared its youth with Ponce de Leon. I swung through an arch sculpted from the hedge onto the semicircular, crushed-shell driveway in front of the house. Crushed shell. Probably cost more than you made the last year with the Giants, fella, playoff bonus and all.

It was a two-story house, rare for this part of Florida, cream-colored stucco, terra cotta Spanish tile roof. The windows shaded by collapsible, canvas awnings—predating tinted glass and air conditioning—marked with an Old English "D" in a wreath, the only visible indication of the owner's name. When you've got it, you don't need to flaunt it. I expected an Arthur Treacher type to answer the doorbell, but that didn't happen, far from it. Instead, I was met by a young Natalie Wood look-alike, in a pale gold bikini which firmly announced its occupant's intention to beat the high cost of fabric in bathing suits. Clearly, this could not be the Ms. Frosty Jane had talked to—and it wasn't.

"Oh, yes, Mr. MacCardle. You're here to talk to my grandmother. I'm Megan Carter. Come in, please, sit in the living room. I'll go fetch Miss Smithers and she can take you upstairs."

Inside, the house was dark and cool, the air kept circulating by a series of Hunter paddle fans, noiselessly swooshing away overhead. The air was faintly scented, hard to identify . . . ah, that was it—rosewood. The living room was cathedral size, made the more imposing by its tailored understatement. Williamsburg green walls, off-white wainscoting. Ankle-deep rugs of various oriental designs, greens and golds and rusts, showing nicely against the dark wide plank floors. Camelback sofas, Belter chairs, Pembroke end tables. Not out of the catalog either; the rich patina of the well-tended wood indicating age and quality of material. Floor-to-ceiling drapes in a delicate cream brocade, silver-framed prints of various English castles, and an enormous bookcase wall rounded it out. Imposing was exactly the word, but somehow also a comfortable room, assuring the visitor it would be there long after the horrors of angular metal furniture, indoor-outdoor carpeting, and Leroy Neiman lithographs had been mercifully incinerated.

"Ah, you'd be Mr. MacCardle, then? Janice Smithers here. I understand you've already met Miss Megan."

She'd come striding through the door and across the room, head up, shoulders trued, on her way to cope with whatever needed doing. Giving my hand a firm shake, looking me square in the eye all the while. It wasn't that she was mannish, although the square chin and lantern jaw weren't going to help if anyone decided to put her up for Miss British Empire. It was the distinctive aura some Englishwomen have. The approach to horses, crises, and love affairs done with the same hearty sense of involvement and a desire to see it through properly. I'd known one such in New York, before I met the Pearl, spending several summer weekends at a guest house in Quogue. I emerged from each of those encounters amused, bemused, capable of doing a highly credible imitation of a sponge. Eventually, she'd married one of the at-

taches at the British Embassy, returning to England to produce baronets, provided Sir Roger could stand the gaff. Formidable.

"You must understand, Mr. MacCardle, that you mayn't
stay too long with her. Mrs. Donaldson is eighty-one, not at
all too strong these days, particularly the last two years. I
shall accompany you, of course. Miss Megan was about to
have a swim when you arrived. P'raps we three could take a
bit of tea afterwards? Fine, then. Come along, it's just this
way."

I trailed along behind her, up the wide curved staircase to
the second floor, down a long hallway to Mrs. Donaldson's
bedroom suite.

She sat upright in an ancient four-poster, propped up by
an array of pink bolsters, looking every inch an empress. She
was a tiny woman, perhaps made smaller by the passage of
time, but the thin patrician face still made it clear she'd been
a real beauty in her day.

The introductions made, La Smithers retired to a chair in
the corner, working away on some needlepoint, leaving me
standing by the bedside, notebook and list of questions in
hand.

I got absolutely nowhere.

Worse, after ten minutes or so, I realized I wasn't ever
going to get anywhere, not even if I stood there until *my* dot-
age.

She wasn't uncooperative, she simply couldn't stay in one
mental place long enough to understand and reply to a question.

Example. I told her I'd come to ask about her lawyer,
Tom Horton.

"You're quite mistaken, young man. Andrew Philbin is
our lawyer, has been for years. Check with Cyrus, he'll bear
me out."

Corrected gently by Smithers, the old lady had finally remembered Tom.

"Ah, you mean Young Tom. What a thoughtful boy, reminds me so of Cyrus when we first met . . ."

And off we went to a central Florida of sixty years ago, to people, places, and events known only to the imperious figure in the bed.

I finally shrugged my shoulders, said goodbye to Mrs. Donaldson, thank you for all help, collected Smithers, and left, pausing at the top of the stairway.

"Is she always like that? I mean, she's perfectly pleasant but she wasn't in there most of the time."

"It varies, Mr. MacCardle. There are days when she is as lucid as a barrister, giving orders, cracking the whip, totally in command. Then there are times when she's like this, more of them lately, I'm afraid."

"Senility?"

"Too easy a label. She is simply getting old. Her health is excellent, save the arthritis, easy to tend to, none of that horrid incontinence one often encounters. The body is simply wearing down, as it must for all of us. Now—why don't you go down to the pool, I'll be along shortly with tea. Go through the door in the living room; the pool house is just in the back."

"Miss Smithers, if it isn't too much, could I have coffee instead?"

"Of course, though tea is ever so much better for you. Off we go, then, won't be a moment."

I sat in a canvasbacked chair watching Miss Megan finish the last of the backstroke laps, whereupon she climbed out of the pool, took up a towel, came to sit beside me, not even the slightest out of breath.

"Sorry to be rude, Mr. MacCardle, but if I don't do twenty-five lengths every morning, the old tum-tum goes south in a hurry."

The old tum-tum looked fine to me—even splendid—but it seemed inappropriate to start the conversation with lecherous comments.

"Could we drop the Mr. MacCardle thing. People call me Cam, short version of my middle name."

"Sure. People call me May or Megan, I don't much care which."

"Not Meg?"

"Ugh, right out of Louisa May Alcott. Please, no."

"Okay, May or Megan, word of honor. Just the three of you live here?"

"Um hum. Obeliah comes every day to do the major house cleaning, J.R. tends to the lawns and grounds. We get along all right. Janice is superefficient."

"Has she been with your grandmother long?"

"At least ten years. I know she'd been here quite a while when we came to live with Gramma Julie."

"We?"

"My brother, Mark, and I. Mark's two years older. He lives in Key West—in an artist's commune or colony or whatever they set up down there."

"A hint of distaste?"

"It's his life and his lifestyle. Not for me, but he's welcome to it. Writes terribly symbolic poetry—blank verse about love spurned and life in perpetual shadow. Incomprehensible."

"Do you write?"

"Me? Never. Mark's the big intellect. I don't see my life's mission all that seriously. I help take care of Gramma, do some Junior League projects, work one afternoon a week at the church's thrift shop."

"St. Paul's, by any chance?"

"Yes, how did you know?"

"Pure guess. Do you know Reverend Graham?"

"Everyone knows him. I adore that man. He's just so . . . regular about everything, not preachery at all. You know him?"

"My best friend."

"I'll be fried! May be trite, but it really is a small world. I had the biggest crush on him for a while—he probably didn't notice."

"Shall I ask him?"

"You better *not*. Janice, guess what? Cam is Reverend Graham's friend, isn't that wild?"

"I don't know, Miss Megan. He is certainly not one's average vicar, especially with that odd looking mini-lorry he drives about in. Not too surprising he'd have a private investigator among his friends. Cam, is it? Short for Cameron, I'd wager. First name?"

"Middle name."

Went on to explain how the name came about. In the telling of it, particularly my brother's belief it was a hard-hearted world that could saddle him with a brother named Angus, the last reserves melted away and we talked easily over the coffee and tea, May/Megan, Janice, and Cam. Much milder that way.

"My family came out from England early on in the war. They lived in Croydon. When it was destroyed, my father packed it in and took the family to live in Jamaica. He and his brother ran a chain of greengrocers there. I was born in Jamaica. Might well never have left."

"But obviously you did."

"Had to. We were caught in the great unrest of the middle sixties. Government rushing about nationalizing things. Blacks seeking instant retribution for what they considered centuries of exploitation. Killings, burnings, riots. Not healthy at all."

"Then what?"

"St. Petersburg. Daddy had set enough aside to retire by then. My brother Austen had returned to England to accept a posting with Barclays Bank. I had decided I wanted to be a nurse, not go to a four-year college, so we were quite flexible."

"Tell Cam how you came to Gramma, Janice."

"How you natter, child, totally boring story. . . . Very well. I went into the nurses' training program at Judson Memorial, got my cap, stayed on there, aiming at becoming an operating-room nurse. Terribly romantic. White lights, green gowns, dedicated people snatching life from death. Plain bloody hard work it was, and lots of it as well. Then, one Sunday, I read an advertisment Mrs. Donaldson had placed in the newspaper. It sounded intriguing—part nurse, part companion—so I telephoned for more information, gave them the references they requested. I went to see her on my day off, enjoyed the interview thoroughly, accepted the position instantly it was offered. I've been with her ever since—more than a decade now. Janice Smithers, faithful retainer."

"Family member would be closer to it. I can't imagine what it would have been without you."

"Thank you, Miss Megan. It has been like a second family. I only wish Mrs. Donaldson was bearing up better. She is, at least, comfortable—the Lord be praised."

Having zero options, I asked the two women the questions Mrs. Donaldson had been unable to help me with. Yes, Tom had been there Friday, both a morning and an afternoon session, in deference to her limited endurance. No, nothing out of the ordinary they could remember. Megan had talked to him midmorning, then gone grocery shopping. Janice had sat in with him for both meetings—as she had with me.

I told them the diaries indicated Mrs. Donaldson was changing her will, asked them if they knew why. They burst out laughing, together.

"She's always changing her will, then changing it back again. She must drive those people down there nuts. Poor Mr. Horton. She'd give him detailed instructions on what she wanted, then call him two days later and cancel all the new provisions. I bet the records show she still has the will they drew up after Grampa Cy died."

I would look, but I wasn't very encouraged—particularly after my nonmeeting with the old girl this morning. Priority justified.

"Should I talk to your brother?"

"If you have nothing better to do. I doubt he's been out of adorable Key West for three years."

"Gotta look thorough, at least. I work for a real taskmaster. Would you set it up for me? That way it won't be so much like a stranger."

"Sure. Any particular time?"

"Not this week, I'm full up. And not until Tuesday of next week either, I'm out of town for the weekend. Any time after that."

"Do my best. How do we get hold of you?"

"The number on this card. If I'm not there I have a message receiver. While I'm at it, here's one for you, too, Janice. If either of you think of anything that might be helpful, I'd be most obliged."

I left them by the pool, Megan back in the water, Janice with her head tilted backward to pick up the sun coming over the roof line. Two nice people, linked by affection to a dying woman.

In some way it seemed a waste, at least a temporary waste.

*   *   *

Balmy Breezes is one of those housing accidents that are becoming more common as Florida's population soars. At one point, it had been a stand-alone village, a brave little circle of trailers on an outpost of land nobody wanted. Then as big, brash Boca Raton strode confidently north and old-money Ocean Side edged south, each found they'd acquired a common neighbor, an incongruous neighbor at that. It was as if two society dowagers at the wedding supper found that, somehow, a raffish hobo had been seated between them. Too late to do anything, of course, I mean, the man was already seated and eating, no other places available at the table, not to make a scene, my dear. So it was with Balmy Breezes. You could probably make a good case as to who was the most uncomfortable.

The sign at the gate was done in the shape of a giant

ship's rudder—weathered oak with rope trim around it. The words "Balmy Breezes" were deeply carved in the wood, picked out in gold paint. Once inside, it proved a tidy miniature metropolis, streets laid out with grid-line precision, street signs smaller versions of the rudder at the gate; even a pleasant park, dotted with benches and shuffleboard areas, served as the town's core.

In my father's time they called them trailers, any gathering of them a trailer court. Today, courtesy of relentless marketing gluttony, the industry has spawned an offshoot known as "mobile homes." Thus, Balmy Breezes, as the sign so proudly stated, was a "mobile home community"

Not much mobility to most of these, I thought, driving through in search of Cove Lane. Individual boundary lines were demarcated with whitewashed stones. Flower beds, plants, and vines obscured the fact that *any* of these monsters had been born with wheels. Altogether a job well done: good planning, good execution, not what one would expect passing by on A1A.

The nautical motif had been carried out in the street names. Already I'd passed Harbor Drive, Basin View, The Moorings, Gull's Way, and a horrible pun—Tern Around. I realized I would never find Giles's place without help, decided to stop at the first sighting of a local. Found him at the head of Clipper Street, on a small patio he'd made by extending a tarpaulin from one end of the mobile home, sitting in a webbed aluminum armchair. He saw me coming, waved an encouraging arm, knocked down the radio volume so he could hear me.

"Afternoon. Wonder if you could help me?"

"Depends on what you want, son."

"I'm looking for Cove Lane. Eleven Cove Lane."

"Know where it is, know who lives there. Take that other chair and we'll talk on it. Names's Trimble. Bob Trimble. Greenfield, Mass."

"Thanks, Mr. Trimble, but I really . . ."

"Sit, son, nothing's so important it can't wait a while. Found that out too late to make good use of it. Iced tea?"

Well, why not? For sure Giles wasn't going anywhere soon, even surer I wasn't going to find him unaided. So I introduced myself, took the offered tea and chair, sat waiting for Trimble to tell me what I needed to know.

"Damn Red Sox. Find a way to lose every year. Don't know why I stick with them. Little piece of home, I guess."

"Been here long, Mr. Trimble?"

"Bob, son. Been nine years come December. Spent forty making fancy silver for the Lunt people. Decided I couldn't stand one more of them winters. Been here since."

"Nice place, Bob."

"Suits us. Ruth gets to do some gardening, shell collecting for the grandkids, gassing with the other women about the old days. I got my radio, sunshine, peace and quiet. Fair swap."

"Good tea. Tasty."

"Thanks, made it myself. None of them instants, neither. Called sun tea. Fill a clear bottle with water, pop in one of them big tea bags, close it up, set it in the sun. Day later you got the best tea brewed. All natural, too."

I decided to get to the point of the conversation, just as quickly decided not to. My Dad used to say, You can always tell a New Englander, but you can't tell them much. Want something from them, you go at their pace. Maybe a little directional nudge, though.

"This is one of the best kept neighborhoods I've seen in South Florida, Bob."

"Surprised you, eh? I know, looks like hell from the road. Good base plan, though, and we all pitch in to keep it that way. Committee system. Community involvement. Right now, I'm on Parks and Grounds, Ruth helps organize the Bingo Nights, couple of other entertainment projects. Everyone works at it, 'cept for a few do-nothings like your friend Giles."

He was looking at me slyly, half pleased I'd been playing

his game, half disappointed the conversation was developing an ending point.

"You know him, then?"

"I know who he is. All I want to know. Last year I got the job trying to recruit him to serve as assessment clerk—check the income of annual membership dues, make sure the books balance. Hell, he'd been a accountant before he got banged up, and we figured it would be good for him and us both."

"No luck?"

"I'll say. Threw me out, so to speak, never even let me into the house. Said I was a meddlesome, troublemaking old fart. If I came back, he'd put the dog on me. Got one, too, mangy devil, meaner than sin, twice as ugly. Haven't been back since and don't plan to. Sorry if he's a friend of yours."

"Never met the man . . . speaking of which . . ."

"I know. Pardon me goin' on—easy habit to fall into when you don't have much else to do. Go three blocks that way, turn right on Crow's Nest. Cove Lane is the first right off that. He lives to the rear of it, numbers run backwards on the cross streets."

"Bob, I enjoyed it. Thanks for the tea, too."

"Come back anytime, son, chances are I'll be here."

Eleven Cove Lane might once have been attractive. Now it looked as out of place in the neat little community as a coal barge at the Lauderdale Boat Show. The boundary stones had faded to their original gray, in a yard where sparse patches of grass fought for life against the weeds and the gray coral sand soil. No flora to hide the cinder blocks on which the house rested, blocks rust-stained by the hard water of Florida's subsoil reaching the surface. The piles of dog droppings made the approach to the front door a wary thing, an ultimate proof of the owner's lack of concern for neighborhood beautification.

My rap on the side of the screen door produced a thunderous barking, an ominous sound of movement within. Instinctively I edged sideways, out of the way of a frontal attack. The voice was thin and querulous, barely audible over the barking.

"What is it? If you're selling, I'm not buying. If you're leaving something, drop it by the door. You got one minute till the dog comes."

"It's MacCardle, Mr. Giles. Remember you said you'd meet me this afternoon?"

"Come back tomorrow. Ohhh, hell. Long as you're here, let's get it done with. Give me a minute to chain the dog."

More sounds from inside, punctuated by a thud and a yelp. Then Giles appeared, framed in the middle of the screen door, sitting in the wheelchair, a miniature baseball bat in his hand.

"Bastard's getting worse every day. Had to zap him one—remind him who's boss. You got identification? Both hands, please; burglars love the high rent districts. Okay, c'mon in, welcome to Paradise Ranch."

If anything, the inside of the house was a step downward—with an added dimension—it stank, worse than the Giants' locker room at five on a Sunday afternoon. The little air conditioner was laboring away, but it didn't stand a chance of clearing out the combined smells of dog and garbage and unwashed Giles. As if reading my thoughts, he gestured toward a dilapidated sofa against one wall, covered with clothes and newspapers, two bricks replacing a broken front leg.

"Clear away a place on the guest of honor couch. Don't imagine you'll be staying very long anyway."

"You always this hospitable, Mr. Giles, or is this a special effort just for me?"

"Got some teeth to you, huh? Good. Most don't nowadays. Spineless fakes. I'd show them all too, hadn't been for that stupid bus and a worthless legal system."

"I understand you're an accountant."

"Was. No more. Who wants to see the funny cripple run the calculator? I was going for my CPA, too. Nights. Now I'm lucky if some busted-down tailor asks me to look at his books."

"Accounting is a mental activity, Mr. Giles, in all deference . . ."

"What are you, MacCardle, some kind of do-good social worker? You didn't listen. Think I'm going to get hauled around in public like some kind of circus freak? Little kids laughing, rest of the world taking pity on Morton Giles? Forget it. I'll get those bastards yet, every last one of them."

"What bastards?"

"You *are* a dense one. Didn't you read about my crummy settlement? Incompetent bus driver, lousy lawyer, crooked judge, moneygrubbing politicians. You wait. I'll get them all."

"How?"

"I've got my ways. None of your business, anyway. You can see how busy I am. What do you want?"

"You heard about Tom Horton?"

"I heard about Tom Horton, read it in the newspaper, saw it on the television. Tough titty. What's it got to do with me?"

"He *was* your lawyer. That means he fits in with that group of 'bastards' you mentioned."

"You got dung for brains? You can see I'm tied to this trailer like it was my mother. I don't ever leave it. A woman comes by, takes out the dog and the garbage, brings me groceries. Crazy woman. Lost a husband after Korea. Got a thing for guys in wheelchairs. Sick, but helpful. Morton Giles, crazed killer, whipping around on his wheels knocking people off. Keen idea, MacCardle."

"You didn't have to be there physically."

"You mean hire a hit man to do it? On that rajah's ransom the court gave me? Time you were going, mister, you're getting to be a bore."

"I hear they come pretty cheap."

"What's cheap? On my income I couldn't hire a seven-year-old kid with a slingshot, unless he took food stamps. I got a lot of those. Let's quit crapping around. If the cops got a

warrant let them arrest me. Want to put me on the poly-
graph? Bring it out here. Otherwise don't waste my time."

"Well, Mr. Giles, I'd like to say it's been fun, thanks for
all your help, that sort of thing, but you make it kind of
hard."

"We all have our problems. You won't mind if I don't
show you to the door, I'm sure. Do keep in touch."

I went out through the ravaged front yard, picked my
way back to the main gate of Balmy Breezes, and turned
south for home, realizing I was banging the hell out of the
center armrest with my fist. Poor substitute for wringing his
neck, for stifling the whining voice and the endless stream of
venom.

A sad, broken clown. Unable to distinguish concern from
pity, solicitude from scorn, an unwarranted settlement from a
political buyout. Chained to a chair in a grimy cabin, attended
by a dog and a madwoman. All of his own doing, which—in
his self of selves—even he had to recognize. A bleak existence with little prospect. I wondered if his hatred would sustain him or consume him. The long remembered Robert
Burns words came to mind, "Oh wad some power the giftie
gie us, To see oursels as ithers see us." For Morton Giles it
could mean waking one morning to a pitiless light of self-ex-
amination, a final acceptance of all the truths, a gun to the
head, and eternal release from the self-made prison.

*   *   *

I changed into swimming trunks when I got home, jump-
ing into the pool and plowing back and forth until I got tired
of it. Not for the old tum-tum, I thought—more a spiritual
kind of cleansing.

I went inside and built myself a Screw-Up, a concoction
I'd first been introduced to one afternoon in the bar of a golf
club in Connecticut. A big glass, plenty of ice, then a third
vodka, a third orange juice, a third Seven-Up. Nice taste,
plenty of vitamins, enough booze to make you quit after two
unless you enjoy falling down a lot. I listened to my telephone

messages over number two, using the fast forward lever to get rid of the junk calls. Only two messages of interest. Call Megan Carter, call Chip Ordonez. I'd have to wait until eight for Ordonez. Megan I could call now, and did.

"Hi, Cam, how was the rest of your day?"

"About as many laughs as the Johnstown Flood."

"How awful! Well, cheer up. The Poet Laureate will receive you. Next Tuesday, at two. At his 'ah-tell-yay.' Can you stand it? I mean I was *there* once—a beat-up apartment with no furniture and cheap copies of Diego Rivera murals on the wall. His atelier. Really!"

Despite my mood, the tone of her voice, the enthusiasm, and the word pictures got me, like an injection of optimism. I took down the instructions on getting to Mark's "atelier," thanked her for the quick contact job, promised I'd tell her what transpired.

"Any messages for him, Megan?"

"None I didn't give him this afternoon. Gotta run, Cam. Take care, let me know how you do with the P.L."

The schedule was filling in quickly; at least that part was going well. But no Paul Goodman yet, and he was tops on the priority list. Typical MacCardle, do everything backwards. Chip had said last night that Goodman lived in Coral Gables. With any kind of luck I could wire him into my trip to Key West, see him on the way back. Kill two birds with one stone—a singularly inappropriate choice of metaphor, I thought. Maybe it all ends there, too. Wouldn't that be nice. I picked up the phone, dialed the Coral Gables number, let it ring, hung up. Tried again half an hour later, with the same result. Kept at it on the half hour, eventually moving into the kitchen to scrape together a sort of supper. No help.

I was reaching for the phone one more time, when it suddenly rang, startling the hell out of me. Ordonez.

"Nice of you to return my call, *companero*. Too busy running around playing Rockford?"

"I was waiting for you to come on duty, plus trying to get

hold of Paul Goodman in Coral Gables. You sure you gave me the right number?"

"Read me the one you're using."

"Hold it. Here, eight–five–six seventy thirty-six."

"That's the one. You remember to dial 'one' before?"

"Give me a little credit, would you; I'm not *that* dim. Wonder where he is?"

"Could be any number of places. This ain't the movies, Cam, people aren't sitting around waiting just for you. How was your day otherwise?"

I reviewed the two visits with him, brought him up to date on the balance of the scheduling, needing only Goodman to round out the lot.

"Think we should bring Giles down here for more questioning?"

"Let's hold off for a while. Like the man says, he isn't going anywhere. Let me get the rest of the preliminary stuff out of the way first. What did your guys come up with on Diaz?"

"A bunch. That guy goes to court more than your friend Ellis. Always gets off, too. He's got a lawyer named David Bonner, very slick character."

"The one the media calls the 'poor man's Melvin Belli'?"

"Very same. Champion of the Oppressed, big with the ACLU. The patter says the Sparrow's going big time. Purchase, possession, and resale of mind-altering substances—cocaine in this case."

"And?"

"And the two key witnesses for the state just vanished. Poof, into nowhere. *Finito*. Haven't found them yet. They're probably fish food or twenty miles of Interstate highway. 'Course, the Sparrow doesn't know anything about them, right? Law-abiding pillar of the community that he is."

"So Horton is right."

"Very right. Look, keep your appointment with the mayor tomorrow. See what the Commission has dug up. I'll have Diaz picked up for questioning, say one o'clock Thursday. Can you make that?"

"Sure. But isn't that just a tad illegal?"

"We got enough unsolveds kicking around to choke a hippo. More than enough for me to find a possible link to such a sterling citizen. My show, though. On this one you're an interested listener."

"So how do we get around to Horton?"

"Trust me. See you at one."

I watched as the Mets absorbed yet another loss, this one to the Cubs, on a wild pitch in the fourteenth inning—a game very few people would ever recall. Kept dialing the Goodman number every half hour, finally gave up at eleven thirty, went off to bed mumbling.

Patience is not one of my long suits.

10

"Not bad for a Pontiac dealer, eh, Cam? Only wish my mother could have seen this. She always said I'd wind up on the wrong end of a rope. 'Course I think she was only teasing."

Osgood Peters, mayor of Cypress Beach. Osgood Peters, high school classmate of Dick Ellis, known as "Oz" to his friends, of which there apparently were legions. Used car salesman, boss's-daughter marrier, franchise inheritor, Rotary, Elks, VFW member. School board, church vestry, alderman, now mayor.

He looked like a mayor, too. Right out of central casting. A compact bowling ball of energy, from the prematurely gray hair to the polished loafers. Unhappy deprived of constant people contact, unfulfilled unless involved in dozens of projects at once. A man with the rare ability to make you believe he thought you were the most important thing in his life at the moment, without being the least bit phony about it.

"I'm so glad you're helping Dick look into this terrible affair. I was really fond of that young man. Taken away in his prime, leaving Linda and those two swell kids. A tragedy, no other word for it. Well, you can count on us for every bit of help we can give you."

"Thank you Mr. Mayor . . ."

"Please. In here it's Oz. This isn't an official function, just a bunch of worker bees trying to get a job done. Okay?"

"Fine. Mind if I take my coat off—little warm in here."

"Not at all, I'll join you. Around here we keep the air conditioning set at 78 degrees. You know, energy conservation, set a good example and all. It does get warm, though, particularly when the sun's right on us . . . Dick said you were interested in knowing more about Tom's work on my Commission on Pornography."

"Yessir. With special emphasis on a man named Angel Diaz."

"A pernicious man. Unfortunately, you'll find he's not the only one. I've taken some steps that I hope will prove helpful to you. Number one, I have file copy for you of all the minutes of the Commission meetings since it began. Floey will give it to you when you leave. More importantly, I've invited the six ranking members of the Commission to lunch with us. We'll have some sandwiches sent in—you can get to know them all. Obviously, ask any questions you want. Let me just check and see if they'll all be here."

He bounced out of the big chair on the run, disappearing into the anteroom for a few minutes, undoubtedly pausing to cope with several other fires along the way. The file sounded like something we could really get our teeth into, particularly Chip and his people. Smart of Peters to have thought of that one, looked like we came to the right man. He'd said Diaz wasn't the only baddy they were looking into, the implication being there were several. More work for Mother, but more potential leads, too. Worth the trip for sure.

The mayor came bustling back in, scanning a typewritten sheet of paper on the way.

"Hmmm . . . pretty good turnout. Let's see. Tip Atkeson, Jim Palizzi, Stuart Davis, Rabbi Udell, and Dick Hauser. Only one's missing . . . Tom Lincoln. Well, still, five out of six ain't all bad, right?"

"I'll say, particularly on short notice. You must have a fair amount of clout with them Mr. May . . . Oz."

"It's not that. They're just as shocked as I am. I mean Tom was one of them. They're probably all wondering who's next. You'll find them more than cooperative, all right. That I guarantee you."

"How did this whole Commission thing get started?"

"Oh, it started right after I took office, almost two years ago. A bunch of people came at me, all wanting the same thing, how to stop the growth of pornography in the city—eliminate it altogether, if possible. I told them what they needed was an organized effort, that individuals running around willy-nilly weren't going to solve it."

"Then what?"

"Then they put together a coalition—did a good job of it too. They have representatives from the homeowners, business sector, church, and a couple of academics for good measure. Once they did that, I told them they needed a plan—a well-thought-out, written-down plan. Objectives for what they wanted to do, strategies on how to achieve them, a time frame for each step. They've stuck to it quite well; we're starting to see some real progress—though there's still an awful lot to be done."

"Give me an example."

"Sure. Give you one that happened last week. Ever been in what they call an adult bookstore? No? You really ought to, at least see what we're up against.

"Don't get me wrong. I'm no burn everything but *Peter Rabbit* prude. I read *Playboy* every month at the barber shop, don't mind admitting it. I like girls. I too, like old Jimmy Carter, lust after them in my heart. These days that's about all I have time for—even if my wife would let me do more.

"Anyway, this new wave has simply gotten out of hand. Rabbi Udell took me to one early on, 'course not in our solid citizen clothing, you know? I tell you it's enough to turn your stomach. Every kind of twist: interracial, homosexual, whips and chains, bestiality, the works. The worst is what they call "kiddie porn." I mean, real children . . . like my own—only younger. Just awful."

"How do you go about closing them down?"

"Harder than you think. You can't legislate morality or taste. Start making enough subjective judgments and you get labeled Nazis. The First Amendment and a crew of sleazy lawyers aren't any help, either.

"In last week's case we got lucky. Guy was running a big operation considering it was just two stores. Last year he reported gross sales of over half a million and that was just what he reported—God knows what his total income was. Anyway, a high school kid heard the guy was running live sex shows in a little theater in the back of one of his stores. Went over, paid his money, watched the show with four or five others. Told his father about it, his father called the police. They sent out a plainclothes guy and, whammo, instant shutdown."

"What happened next, Oz, to this owner, I mean?"

"That's the sad part. Unless he has a record, he'll get off with a fine and either a suspended sentence or some kind of probation. Be open for business again in no time. Different location, different store name, maybe a dummy owner, but he'll be back. The money's just too good for that kind not to take the risks."

"So how do you stop it?"

"I wish I knew. Some hold with stricter zoning laws, but I don't think that's the total answer. Some want to go after the publishers, make it illegal to sell any way but by mail. Problem there is definition. What is or isn't pornography and who makes that judgment stick in today's legal climate. Still others, Tom Horton was one of them, want to shut down the distributors, cut off the supply sources to the stores.

"Meanwhile we'll just have to take it on a case by case basis, like that Lotus Valley store last week."

"Lotus Valley?"

"Nice, huh? Anything but, let me tell you. You really should go see for yourself. Yessir, a real education."

The intercom buzzer on his telephone rang. He picked up, listened for a moment, told Floey to send the Commission members in as they arrived. Atkeson and Hauser came in together, followed shortly by Davis, then the rabbi, finally Palizzi—apologizing for being late; caught in the noon-hour traffic. The introductions were made, Floey and one of the other secretaries brought in a tray of sandwiches, soft drinks were handed around, and the discussion began.

It started with me telling them who I was and why I was involved. They all knew Ellis, of course, so that part was quick and easy. Peters told them he had a file on the meeting minutes, so we didn't have to cover that ground twice unless someone had something outstanding he wanted to mention.

For the balance of the meeting, they took turns outlining what they hoped to do, progress so far, directions that had been recommended. Helpfully, they concentrated on the areas most deeply involving Tom Horton, although taking pains to ensure I also got an extremely comprehensive overview of the Commission's activities.

A very impressive group, I concluded. Not zealots, not witch hunters, certainly not publicity seekers. Just hard-working men, successful in their own fields, giving time and brain power to fight something they regarded as a serious threat to Cypress Beach. A refreshing change of pace from a world where involvement and responsibility were postures to be avoided at all costs.

I gave them each one of my cards as the meeting broke up, telling them to call me if they thought of anything even potentially relevant, assuring them I would have no inhibitions whatever about calling *them*. I stayed behind until they'd gone, reclaimed by the pressures of students, business, and temple members.

"Thanks a million, Oz. Good people, most helpful meeting, and a marvelous thought of yours, putting that file together for me. Wish I could vote for you."

"Our pleasure. Check with Floey when you leave. Good luck and, to steal a line from Rabbi Udell, God Bless. We're all pulling for you."

I went home, chucked off the trappings of civilization, got back into normal-for-me-wear—faded khakis, comfortable polo shirt, bare feet. I had just opened the file when the telephone rang.

"Buy you a meal, sailor?"

"What are you . . . Oh, right, Wednesday . . . the lady's day off. What did you have in mind, honey?"

"I have a terrific quiche I read about in *Southern Living*. You'll love it."

"Yeah . . . well, Carole . . ."

"It's cunningly disguised as a sirloin; I think we can grill it on the balcony without burning down the joint. Sevenish?"

"*Si, Senorita. Con mucho gusto.*"

"Been watching 'I Love Lucy' reruns?"

"Influence of my new associate, Sergeant Ordonez."

"I expect it'll be a lot better when you don't sound like you're gargling. Oh . . . Cam, *por favor* in your tongue, please pick up some wine on the way. I forgot to and it's too hot to go out again."

"*Avec plaisir*. See you later, luv."

"I think you better stick to Spanish."

*   *   *

I plunged back into the file, pausing every so often to call Paul Goodman's number, each time getting the same negative results.

The file started off slowly, being mainly concerned with what the Commission's organization should be, who should be doing what, and the creation of the grand-design plan Oz had mentioned. As they gained experience and confidence, the pace of activity increased, showing them close to several breakthroughs on their original objectives.

There were three new names to add to the list—Emilio Vasquez, Darvan Williams, and Michael Lucchese—a veritable United Nations. Apparently, everybody was getting into the pornography racket in the finest American tradition— without regard to race, creed, or national origin.

The unquestioned star of the show was Angel Diaz, both in terms of numbers of mention and the scope of activity tied to him. As the records pieced his operation together, they found he began some four years back with a Quonset-hut theater, showing eight-millimeter shorts. It had now grown to direct ownership of five theaters, three adult bookstores, a head shop, a tavern, and a pawnshop—the majority located in Action Junction. Additionally, he was suspected of at least minority ownership in more than a dozen similar outlets, plus controlling interest in at least one film distribution company. The tavern, with the somewhat unlikely name of Flanagan's, would purportedly sell its clientele any number of ways to warp the head. *It* was the operation that had earned him his most recent court appearance, which, per the records, didn't seem to have slowed Flanagan's down one iota. Might have to drop by there one of these days, making sure I *didn't* bring Carole.

Which reminded me it was time to be getting ready for dinner. I put the file in my desk with the rest of the paperwork, shaved for a second time, climbed into the shower, thinking our little Sparrow had done all right for himself in a not very long period. I suspected he would not take it kindly if someone was trying to upset the nest he'd built so carefully.

*   *   *

I got a huge smile and a wave through from George, the jolly black giant who spells Nick the Surly on the the nights they let Nick out. Apparently, George doesn't have a last name. If he does, nobody knows it. Then, again, if you're that large and you want to be known only as George, you certainly won't get an argument from me.

Toby met me at the elevator, marched me down the corridor, looking over his shoulder periodically to ensure I wasn't getting lost. His final look, as he pushed through the slightly open door, was an invitation to enter, which I accepted. His owner was making a fearful clatter in the little kitchen, giving a gasp of surprise when pinned to the counter from behind, turning in my arms for a happy-hour kiss.

"That's some trick you taught him, madame."

"Trick? Who?"

"Toby. He met me at the elevator."

"Pure accident. I must have left the door open. What did you bring to go with the quiche?"

"Bordeaux. Château Beychevelle, says here. Nineteen Seventy-five. Good year, the man told me."

"What's the celebration for? You solve the murder?

"Figured you must be getting tired of Ripple. And the murder is a very long way from being solved."

The man had also said to open the wine some time before dinner. Did that, made a getting-supper-ready drink for the cook, passed myself, settled onto the couch to read the paper. Picture of domestic bliss. A picture shattered when a cannon-ball came screaming past my ear, knocking the newspaper out of my hands.

"He hates it when you don't pay attention to him, Cam. A bottomless well for affection—on his terms, naturally. I have to go into the bathroom if I want to read the paper. You haven't got a chance. Anyway, come help me with the steak. Everything else is ready."

As we were finishing dinner, one of those vicious line squalls came blasting through—sheets of rain, jagged lightning streaks, the heavy artillery of thunder. The lights went out, catching Carole in midflight to close the balcony doors.

"Cam!"

"Probably a power line down, honey. Stay where you are—you'll get your night vision in a minute or so."

When *I* could see, I got the second bottle of wine and the glasses, put them on the table near the couch, went to retrieve her, still frozen in the middle of the room.

"Hold me, Cam, these things scare me to death."

"I'll have to remember that. Not to worry—they move through fast."

"But what if lightning comes into the apartment?"

"What if Ronald Reagan turns Communist? About the same odds. C'mon over to the couch, we're all set up. Take my hand, just follow me. That's it."

We sat on the couch, holding hands like teenagers, sipping the excellent claret, watching nature's free fireworks. After one particularly blinding flash, I heard a clink of glass on the table, felt Carole doing her best to burrow under my skin.

"I don't mind telling you, Mighty Hunter, this is one scared squaw."

In my nation it is a sacred duty for the hunter to protect the frightened. This may require the removal of certain restrictive clothing—to maintain proper respiration and circulation levels. In extreme cases, the ancient ritual of the laying on of hands is needed. Clearly this was one such case. Carefully, diligently, the hunter carried out the sacred rite, softly, slowly, entirely, ceasing only when the even breathing assured him the calming process had been properly accomplished.

"Good thing the squaw is on the pill, Mighty Hunter, you move fast for an old Seminole."

"You forgot sly and wily. You think I *caused* that thunderstorm."

"I wouldn't put it past you. Anyway, storm's gone. What do you say we put the breechcloths on, 'case we get the lights back?"

"You do mine and I'll do yours."

"No chance, Chief Many Hands. If I get any calmer I won't be able to stand up."

The lights caught Carole in brassiere and bikini panties, causing her to bolt into the bedroom, returning in a minute wearing a long green dressing gown.

"You are the most modest woman in Florida, honey, with absolutely nothing to be modest about."

"Climb into your pants, Mighty Hunter, I'm off to make coffee and rescue Toby. He hides behind the refrigerator."

Later, we sat on the couch, close together, Carole curled up, head on my outstretched arm. She spoke what I was thinking.

"Wish I could go to Charlotte with you, but I can't . . . you know that."

"I know, sweetheart. Not to worry, there'll be other times."

"Call me when you get there? First thing?"

"Count on it, lady."

I drove home through the now clear night, looking at the stars, whistling, totally at peace. A thoroughly enjoyable evening.

Wonder how you do start thunderstorms.

*   *   *

"I may have to bail out of this meeting early, Chip. Got a three o'clock flight—blow that and I won't get to Charlotte until after midnight."

We were sitting in Interrogation Room 3, a larger version of the room next door, where I had first met Ralph Morgan. Five minutes to one, waiting for Angel Diaz.

"I'll run you out. We can flip on the siren, so you won't need to bother with the parking, either. Give us a chance to talk."

"How about my car?"

"I'll get one of the guys to drive it home for you. You can take a cab back from the airport. I'm sure Mr. Ellis can afford it. You got your ticket? Good, that's settled. Ah . . . here's our Sparrow, right on time—probably knows he'd get bounced if he wasn't."

Diaz came into the room like a gunfighter in an old western—poised on the balls of his feet, ready for retaliation to an attack from any quarter. Black, raw-silk suit, white-on-white shirt with ruby links in the French cuffs, Countess Mara tie with a matching handkerchief arranged in the breast pocket. Mr. Cool. A handsome man, like a younger Cesar Romero, complete to the macho mustache.

"Diaz? I am Sergeant Ordonez. This man is my associate, Mr. MacCardle. Take that seat there. Keep your hands on the table where I can see them. Let's get this meeting under way."

The voice surprised me when Diaz replied. An even,

modulated tone, virtually devoid of accent, almost an actor's voice.

"In the first place, gentlemen, the name is *Mister* Diaz. Secondly, it would seem to me a small act of courtesy if you would offer coffee, even for such a brief meeting. Which brings me to point three—this will be a brief meeting because I have never heard such silly . . ."

A whipcrack of Spanish exploded from beside me. "*Silencio, Senor Grano!*" Then more rapid-fire delivery. Diaz looked as if he'd been struck, shrinking back in the chair, trying to avoid the torrent aimed at him. I looked over at Chip. This was an Ordonez I hadn't yet seen, chin thrust forward, eyes slitted, fists knotted, looking like a finely tuned welterweight about to let the big left hand go.

The verbal onslaught went on without a letup, all in Spanish that eluded my high school brand, now so little remembered. Every attempt by Diaz to speak in English was rebuffed harshly, generally with three- and four-word phrases that seemed to hit like bricks. I realized there was little I could contribute in these circumstances, reconciled myself to watching Diaz and taking notes that Chip could amplify on later in the car.

Harsh, stinging words. *Puerca. Topo. Amenaza. Olfato. Muchedumbre. Desecho. Sucio. Encanijabo. Rufian.*

Diaz began to wilt physically as the tirade ran on. The expensive handkerchief was no longer a stylish ornament, but instead was used periodically to mop the face grown drawn and sweaty. The shaking hands reached for cigarettes and lighter, dropping both under yet another explosion when Chip evidently told him there would be no smoking. Deprived of even that slight comfort, he sat sullenly, slumped in the chair, making small attempts at reply which were immediately cut off as Chip continued to wade in.

Finally I heard some words I could recognize, as Chip nodded at me while throwing the last bomb. Horton, *abogado, Comision del Alcalde Sobre la Pornografia, homicidio, investigacion,* MacCardle, *excusa.*

I thought Diaz was going to have a heart attack. His eyes bulged, cords worked in his throat. The words of reply were stammered and nervous. Chip kept boring in, cutting him off, slamming away at every opportunity.

He had just finished a long passage containing the recognizable word *confesion* when the door opened and a uniformed patrolman came in, spotted Chip, whispered something to him. Chip sighed, nodded to the patrolman, sat back in the chair as the officer left.

"Well, *Senor Grano,* your luck is running high. It seems your estimable attorney, Mr. Bonner, is finally here. He is on his way to join us even now."

A whirlwind burst into the room, a long-haired whirlwind in mod clothes, down to the gold chain bouncing against the exposed chest.

"What are you trying to do to my client, Sergeant? You have no right. Worst kind of harassment. You have a warrant? If not, we walk out of here right now."

"Calm down, Mr. Bonner. We're simply talking with this public-spirited citizen about the moral climate of Cypress Beach. Nothing to get excited about."

"Sergeant, you've been around long enough to know you can't pull this kind of stuff. My client has rights. What did you talk about? What, specifically, is he accused of?"

"Right now he is only accused of being a piece of filth, Mr. Bonner, which even you would be hard put to deny. As to our discussion, talk to him about it. We're done for the time being."

Diaz pulled himself out of the chair gingerly, as if another Ordonez blast was on the way, one that would destroy little Mr. Bonner as well. But as they walked out he looked directly at us for the first time since the meeting started. It was a look of pure, naked hatred, of a man publicly humiliated. It was not a look that encouraged you to put all the money in annuities.

"What did you say to him, Chip? You sure busted his balloon in one helluva hurry."

"Tell you in the car. Let's go—we're cutting it fairly thin as it is. Don't forget we have to pick up your bags."

I walked with him back to his cubicle, waited while he stowed his gear, went over with him to greet the slim, gray-haired patrolman he had summoned.

"Cam MacCardle, meet Steve Dorn. Steve's in my section. Cam's working with me on the Horton thing. Do me a favor, Steve. After you get off, take Cam's car home for him would you?"

"Sure, Sarge. What kind of car and where does it go, Mr. MacCardle?"

"Copper-colored Olds Toronado, with a black vinyl roof. It's in the covered part of the municipal lot, third deck. Here's the keys and the ticket stub, registration's in the glove compartment. I live at 23 Areca Way in Lighthouse Point. The numbers over the garage doors. Need directions?"

"I'm a native, Mr. MacCardle. I remember Lighthouse Point when it started thirty years ago. No sweat. Leave the car in the garage?"

"No way. I use the garage as a storeroom. Right now you couldn't get a bicycle in there. Driveway's fine. Just shove the keys in the ashtray and thanks, Steve."

"C'mon, Cam, quit gabbing. We gotta make tracks if you want to catch your flight."

*   *   *

"Isn't he a little long in the tooth to still be a patrolman?"

"Dorn? Yeah, guess so. Probably stay a patrolman the rest of his career, too."

"What's his problem?"

"Attitude. He's smart enough, but Steve's one of those guy's who really, truly, doesn't give a rat's ass. Bachelor, no family pressures on him. Just drifts along. Good enough cop, but no ambition. Only thing he really cares about is horses."

"Raising them?"

"Betting on them. The man's really into it. Gulfstream, Hialeah, Calder, even Pompano for the trotters. Claims he does well; maybe he does. I went with him to Hialeah once, came out twenty ahead. Steve won a couple of hundred, bought me a Class A dinner. Whoops—almost missed the turn."

We swung onto the big cloverleaf that would bring us up to I95, accelerating at the top of the ramp, the blaring siren helping us ease into the traffic flow.

"I make it about a twenty-minute run, Cam, plenty of time. Tell me about your Mayor's Commission meeting."

"Very useful. Peters is a checked-out guy. Made us a file of the minutes of all their meetings. Fascinating reading. I'll leave it with you."

"Top line?"

"Diaz is the hero, if that's the word for it. Three other people I think we should check out. Let me get out the file. Okay . . . Emilio Vasquez, Darvan Williams, Michael Lucchese. Vasquez and Lucchese are independents, Williams works for Diaz. Evidently muscle. Raiford graduate, attempted manslaughter; threw some chap through a plate glass window for missing a loan payment, busted up one of your people pretty good until they got the cuffs on him."

"What kind of name is Darvan?"

"Look who's talking. What kind of name is Cipriano, or Angus, even?"

"I guess. Lucchese I know. The other two names are blanks. Lucchese's father was with the Genovese family in New York, came down here for his health. Looks like little Michael plans to take after Daddy."

"Mob?"

"As in Mafia, Cosa Nostra? Maybe, we'll sure find out in a hurry. That's good, Cam, I'll get somebody on it first thing tomorrow."

I swung the conversation back to Angel Diaz, asking Ordonez what he'd said to produce that kind of reaction. Chip was smiling.

"All punk, amigo. I knew it the minute I saw him. Hides

behind the fancy suits and the big cars. But all punk at heart. Whoever named him Sparrow was dead on."

"What did you mean by *Senor Grano*?"

"A tone setter. It means pimple. Only thing that kind understands is bullying. That's why I wouldn't let him speak English, as if *I* thought *he* couldn't. Also why I used Castilian Spanish instead of the colloquial—make him feel he was being talked down to, which he deserves, of course."

"I got the part about the Horton murder, but the rest of it blew right on by. I took some notes though. *Puerca, olfato, desecho,* so on. What's that all about?"

"Total abuse. *Puerca* means sow, I was referring to his mother. Went downhill from there. *Olfato* means stench, *desecho* is garbage. You get the idea."

"*Excusa?*"

"Means alibi. I told him his better be watertight the night of the fifteenth or he'd find my *zapato*—shoe—right on his throat. That's when he looked so sick."

"Think it will be watertight?"

"On the surface. He'll have thirty-seven assorted hoods and honeys claiming he spent the whole night saying a novena. We'll stay after him, though."

"I can't say I'm in love with that ten-pound glare he hung on us."

"His pride's hurt. Comes in looking like Mister Macho himself, leaves like the punk he knows he is. But we watch him carefully. I may have done too good a job trying to castrate him."

"That lawyer make trouble for you?"

"Bonner? No, he's all mouth and no action. Put up a show to earn his money, impress Diaz with how he stood up to the big, bad police. Another punk—educated division."

We were on the back road approach to the Ft. Lauderdale Hollywood Airport when Chip cut off the siren. Pulled up at the Eastern terminal with fifteen minutes left, plenty of time. I got my garment bag out, left the file with Chip, was turning to go when I remembered.

"Do me a favor? I haven't gotten hold of Goodman yet. Maybe you'll have better luck. I can see him anytime after Tuesday. I'll check with you Saturday."

"Will do. You better scoot, *compadre.*"

I scooted. Made it with three minutes to go, too. No smoking, please, aisle if you got one left. You do? Dynamite.

Clean living pays off.

*   *   *

"The whole row to yourself. How nice. May I get you a beverage, sir?"

Five-three, jet-black hair, pug nose, freckles, a figure even the baggy airline uniform couldn't disguise. The name plate pinned on the apron said "Sharon."

"Two beverages, please. Gin and tonic, if you would. Hard day at the mine."

For a long time I was convinced Eastern was trying for the *Guinness Book of Records*—World's Oldest Stew category. I remembered one flight to New York when all three of them had been older than my mother and not nearly as solicitous. Lately, things had taken a decided turn for the better, Ms. Sharon being a prime example. Well done, Mr. Borman, you earned your wings with this one.

"No lime aboard, sir, sorry. Settle for a lemon?"

"Settle for plain, thanks, Ms. Sharon."

"It's Miss. Can't afford to have some attractive hard-of-hearing person think I wouldn't consider a date."

"Through for the day in Atlanta?"

"No, sir, really just starting. On to New York, then to Boston."

"Going home, eh?"

"There goes three hundred dollars worth of voice lessons. Actually, I live in Framingham. How did you guess?"

"Two words. 'Hard' and 'starting'—you forgot the R's. I wouldn't work too hard to change it, Sharon. It's a nice accent and a great city."

"Thank you on both counts. Wave if you need anything more. Enjoy your trip, sir."

Two hours plus to Atlanta, hour-and-a-half layover there, a little less than an hour to Charlotte. Use the layover to get something to eat, one way to kill the time, they certainly aren't going to feed you on the hop to Charlotte. What with air traffic delays and going through the rental-car procedure, I got to the Radisson shortly before nine.

*   *   *

"Yes, Mr. MacCardle, we've been expecting you. You're preregistered. Room four-oh-six. There's an envelope for you and a message. The boy will take your bag up. Enjoy your stay with us. Front!"

I read the message on the way up in the elevator. It was from Ben Reed, saying they'd gone to dinner, should be back around nine, look for them in the NASCAR hospitality suite, 810–812.

I tipped the bellman, unpacked, laid out the shaving gear on a towel at the side of the left hand sink, called Carole. So domesticated.

The Reeds weren't there when I got to the suite but lots of other familiar faces were. Owners, drivers, sponsors, broadcasters. I spotted Ned Jarret, himself a former Grand National champion, evidently assigned to doing the color for the CBS telecast, from the emblem on his blazer. Hoss Ellinton, Buddy Baker, Bobby Allison, young Tim Richmond. Ron Bouchard, the driver from Massachusetts who they all tease about his Yankee accent. He'd told the press how pleased he was to get his first win at "Talla-day-ger," and they hadn't let up on him since. The Reeds came by, Ben looking like a general, graying and distinctive, Sally as pretty and charming as ever. Waved off my thanks for the tickets and credentials, told me the STP/Champion people were holding a place for me at dinner Saturday. Why had I been such a stranger? What could he do to make up? This last with tongue planted securely in cheek.

Nothing like the NASCAR folks to make you feel at home in a hurry.

"Cale, how you doin? Hey there, Richard, still wearing the slash glasses, huh. Good to see *you* again, Hoss. Has been a while."

Too long, I thought, won't let that happen again.

11

I love hotel living, always have. To me a hotel room is like an island of irresponsibility. If the faucet drips, it's *their* faucet and *their* plumbing bill. Fresh linen every day, an unseen elf to tidy up and do the dusting. If you get hungry, the telephone produces your choice of food somebody else cooked—on dishes somebody else will remove and wash. Probably a serious character flaw, one I have no intention of working on.

The room service menu featured an item called the Plantation Breakfast. Juice, cereal, three eggs, sausage, grits, biscuits, and a pot of coffee. That should hold me until lunch, I thought, ordered it and a copy of the *Charlotte Observer* to keep me company.

The sports section was dominated by news of the National 500. Interviews, sidebar stories on the drivers, expert prognostications on the outcome. The consensus favorites were the three old veterans, Allison, Petty, and Yarborough, plus the young veteran Waltrip—with an outside chance given to Terry Labonte, the current points leader, who hadn't won yet this year but was consistently finishing in the top five. Everything pointed to the usual NASCAR heart-stopper finish. Sunday would be a day to savor.

But today was a Friday, definitely not a play day. Four

hours from now we'd see what Mr. Alden had to contribute. Tied up like a trussed steer financially, bitter about the settle- ment and its future restrictions, in a job that gave him un- limited traveling flexibility. All the right elements for a prime prospect. Meanwhile, Ordonez was running down the elusive Mr. Goodman. Once we had him lined up, the first phase would be complete, and we could start playing hardball, al- though that wasn't exactly a lollipop Chip had thrown at An- gel Diaz yesterday.

The telephone caught me in the shower. I hustled out wrapping a big bath towel around me, sat on the bed in a gathering pool. *Their* problem.

"Mr. MacCardle?"

"Yes."

"This is Boomer Mays. Heard you was in town from Mr. Reed. You been doin' all right?"

"Fine, Boomer, just fine. Great to hear from you. What are you doing these days?"

"Take too long to tell you on the phone. Got me a new driver, Wayne Rollins, don't think you met him down to Day- tona."

"No, I didn't."

"Well, him and me gonna have supper tonight, you wel- come to join us if it fits."

"Fits fine. Where and when?"

"We be done here around five, everthin' goes good. Say six thirty, place called Slug's Rib, around the corner from you, top a one of them bank buildings. I'll get Miz Bonnie to make us a reservation. I 'spect it'll be right crowded."

"Six thirty it is, Boomer. Looking forward to it."

"Me too, Mr. MacCardle."

I hung up smiling. They must have had Boomer in mind when they coined the phrase "good ole boy." A monolith of a man with a great rumbling drawl and an encyclopedic knowl- edge of NASCAR racing, having been involved with it almost from its inception, he'd been part caretaker, part teacher, and instant friend at Daytona. I know I wouldn't have met nearly as many people, or learned so much so quickly without his help. A good ole boy, indeed, in the best sense of the words.

* * *

The Regency Room was jammed when I got there, a little after one. Every table taken, waiters scurrying around, a low roar of conversation going on, apparently *the* place in Charlotte for the business community to hold luncheon meetings. A somewhat harried maitre d' acknowledged me, steered me over to a table in the corner where a dapper man in a blue and white seersucker jacket was sitting, idly twirling a water glass on the tablecloth.

"Mr. Alden?"

"Ned, please, call me Ned. Everybody does, 'cept my ex-wife, Earline, but then you'd know that."

"Sorry, never met the lady."

"The better for you. You're *Cam* MacCardle, right? Why didn't I put that together sooner? Saw you play in the Orange Bowl once when they called you out of bounds on a touchdown pass. You seemed a little upset at the time."

"That nearsighted robber. I was pushed out of bounds by one of your safety guys, in the air, never had a chance to get my feet in. Film showed it all clearly—by then it was too late. Only reason I didn't get thrown out was because the official knew he was wrong."

What was I doing? I'd come here to talk to a potential murder suspect and here I was babbling away about a piece of ancient history. The slightest mention of my former occupation and there I went, bounding along, back to Nostalgia Land. Some investigator you are, laddie. Hampton, Ordonez, et al should only see your keen little mind at work.

"How about we order a drink and menu, not that I'm in any big hurry. Sponsor's plane doesn't get in 'til five, might as well take it easy meantime. Is it true what they say about the race problem in the NFL? Teams with quota systems and all? Not to bore you, but I don't often get a chance like this—as in *never*, to date."

Despite myself and my errand, I wound up liking Ned Alden. Not simply because he was talking football. As the conversation went on to other avenues, he stayed the same—open, candid, good questioner, a better listener. It wasn't just the good looks that got him into all that trouble, I thought; he has the flair all the great salespeople have. Eye contact, a willingness to help, a sense of wanting you to approve of him. Example:

"I said that?"

"That's what the records indicate."

"Records don't lie. I must have. I don't remember too much about that day. Except wondering why Earline was being so vindictive. I was guilty and she was bound on getting her pound of flesh. More like my whole body, as it happened. Maybe I shouldn't be so surprised; I could have said anything that day."

Another example:

"Murder? Me? Sorry, Cam, that's a little out of my line. Look, there won't ever be the Ned Alden medal for most merit badges earned in the troop. I drink too much, lose a little at poker, can't stop chasing the ladies, probably never will. But murder? No way. Besides," he said, smiling at me for the first time in this part of our talk, "if it had ever crossed my mind, you can bet I wouldn't have started with Earline's lawyer. Go straight to the source, I always say."

On where he had been that night:

"This time the records are on my team. I was in Baltimore and Philadelphia the whole time, talking to the agency people there. Our accountants are tough on expense vouchers. They'll have all the hotel bills, resturant receipts, airplane coupons, rental car papers, the works. Those will pinpoint where I was every second except when I was sleeping. Which wasn't often—not with the advertising agency folks. They do love to party, particularly when it's the station's money."

And finally:

"Hire someone to kill him? Sure, I could have, but I didn't. I can get you anything you want, especially around here, but I wouldn't know how to begin to rent a killer. Do you? No, don't tell me, just think about it for a minute. Sure, you read about hit men all the time in the papers, see it on TV—got to be an easy thing to do, right? Okay, now tell me how you'd do it, and better yet, how you'd ensure it couldn't ever be traced to you?"

Damned if I could, either.

"I'm sorry the man's dead. I didn't know him at all, except as Earline's legal brains in the settlement. He had nothing personal against me, just doing his job for the aggrieved party. And he did a job, no two ways about it. But I still earn a living, and a good one. Still got the travel, the good restaurants, the young lovelies. No matter what, nobody can take those away. I'm going to give all that up to kill a man I didn't know? Be honest. How much sense does that make to you?"

Not a whole helluva lot, I had to admit.

"Sure you should keep digging at me. That's your job. I'll be right here, too. If not, the station will know where you can get me. But I'll bet you all the money Earline didn't get yet, you won't find a thing, Cam. There isn't anything to find—believe me."

I went back to the room, lay down on the bed, reviewed the conversation with Alden once more. No matter how much I wanted to keep him on the possibles list, my gut reaction was to eliminate him. Either he was innocent or a first-rate actor. Even there, his comment on being a loser at poker made me feel even surer he wasn't our man. My hunch told me we'd find a Wednesday night American Express receipt from some expensive nightclub in Philadelphia with the notation Mr. and Mrs. Jones of the Whap, Bap and Bop Advertising Agency on the back, and a waiter the big tip had impressed enough to remember. So, scratch Ned Alden, television time salesman, philanderer, divorced person. Tell Ordonez the story tomorrow. See how he feels. See if he thinks we should push any further. For my money, we'd come to the end of this particular line.

No sense in getting all gloomy about it—we'd only just

started. One lead down but three more picked up Wednesday. Goodman, my own pet, still to come. Too early to worry. Relax and enjoy the race weekend. Or, as some tanglebrained sportscaster once said, "Your future's all ahead of you."

Easy for him to say.

* * *

Boomer's bulk dwarfed the man sitting at the table with him, not too difficult granted Boomer's size, but telling me Wayne Rollins wasn't the Large Economy size most NASCAR drivers seem to come in. More like Cale Yarborough or Bobby Evans, I thought. Not tall, but with enormous upper body strength, a must to keep the snarling racers inside the fence and right side up as the speeds climbed into the upper one hundreds—even past two hundred at Daytona and Talladega.

Boomer stood up as I got to the table, shaking my hand with one awesome-sized paw, introducing me to Rollins at the sound level that earned him his nickname. Evans had told me that years of working on the high performance engines had cost Boomer the better part of his hearing. But Boomer was too vain to wear a hearing aid, compensating with a voice to shatter glass.

"Wayne, this here's Mr. MacCardle. Mr. MacCardle, Wayne Rollins."

"Last time it was Cam, Boomer. How come so stiff, getting formal now you're a real life crew chief?"

"Mr. Reed tell you about that?"

"He did. About time, too. Wayne, my name's Cam, that is if Mr. Management here can stand it."

"We'll work him over together, Cam."

"So, Mr. Crew Chief Mays, sir, tell me what's happened since Daytona."

"Real nervous-makin' time. When the gang split up after Bobby was killed, they was many a night I just knew it was goin' back to tobacco growin', hadn't done that in twenty-five years. Real nervous-makin'. Could've threaded a sewin' machine while it was runnin'."

Same old Boomer, country humor and all.

"So what saved you from a life of agriculture?"

The old boy network, apparently. Some marketing biggie at Universal Moving and Storage decided sales in the South weren't what they should be, picked NASCAR sponsorship as the major image-building vehicle in their promotion program. Knowing next to nothing about racing, he did the smart thing, contacted the long-established, successful teams to see what they recommended. The consensus was to hire Bub Stokes, a Junior Johnson graduate whose sponsor had decided to get out of the sport. Stokes had picked Wayne Rollins and Wayne and Boomer were old friends.

"So Bub runs the program, but I run the pits. Got Big John and Maynard with me—you'll see them tomorrow. Good sponsor too, hands off and no cuttin' corners on expenses. First class deal, huh, Wayne?"

"You won't hear me complaining. Ten years running independent, difference is unbelievable. That Darrell blows up an engine, they just say, 'well durn.' With me, was sometimes a month before we could get back. Used to run on used tires the Pettys sold me. Those days are gone, least as long as Universal stays with it."

"Wayne, you guys run all over the country. Do you develop favorite tracks or are they pretty much the same?"

"Well . . . good question. Got to answer it conditionally, though. When I was running independent, I liked the short tracks, Martinsville, Bristol, Nashville, the half milers—only way I had a fighting chance with the big teams. Now I like the super speedways best."

"I guess I always thought a car was a car was a car."

"Only up to a point. After that, money takes over. Take Junior—Johnson—for example. That team has five different car setups off the basic Chevy Monte Carlo Darrell runs. Junior's so smart and so good, he'd have thirty-one different setups if he could, one for every race."

"Why so many? Don't you run twice a year on most tracks?"

"Yeah, but conditions change. Daytona for the Five Hundred in the winter is very different from the same Speedway at the Firecracker Four Hundred in July. Week in, week out, you never know until you get there what setup is best for what track on what day."

"I had no idea it was so complicated."

"Most don't. They think it's a sport where forty guys go round and round in the same kind of cars. Once upon a time, it was like that—but no more. Now you hear about slipperiness quotients, wind-tunnel testing, spoiler engineering— sometimes think you're at an MIT seminar 'stead of a race track. That's why the big teams dominate. You combine know-how, money, and a top driver, the independents really don't have a chance."

"Why do they hang in?"

"Some for the love of it. Others, like Boomer here, 'cause they don't want to go back tobacco farming or wherever they come from. In my case, I kept hoping to hook up with a major sponsor, which finally happened, the Good Lord be praised."

"What if everybody had the same equipment?"

"There'd be some changes, but not revolutionary. James Hylton would do better. Bill Rains, Carnie Lyle. I mean the driver's still a critical part of the deal, high technology or not. You'd still see the superstars do well. But even if the equipment was equal, you can't equalize for a Junior Johnson. That man would find a way to beat you if we were running bicycles—he's that good. That's why I'm so pleased Bub Stokes is running our team. He spent seven years with Junior, you can't beat that kind of education."

"How do you think you'll do Sunday?"

"We'll be competitive. Qualified fourteenth Wednesday, in the low thirty-three seconds—a hundred sixty three and change. That gives us two days to keep dialing in the car."

"Dialing in?"

"Little modifications. Gear-ratio adjustments, spoiler changes, rear end, chassis pressure points—those things. Don't sound like much but they add up. By two o'clock today, between Bub and Boomer, we had it running the upper end of a hundred sixty four. We'll be up there all day—couple of breaks, we could walk away with the whole thing."

"Track in good shape?"

"Always is—they do a nice job here. Again, money. The big tracks get the big crowds, get the television money, just *keep* getting better. Talladega, Michigan, Daytona, Atlanta, here—all top-notch conditions."

"What will you guys be doing tomorrow, Boomer?"

"Not much left we kin do. Right now, it's runnin' as good as I know how. We'll watch the Miller Three Hundred—late model Sportsman race-recheck on the good grooves in the turns. Final practice session at three thirty, after the race. Hope the gremlins ain't bit us. C'mon by and watch with us, might learn somethin'."

"No doubt about it. Here, let me get that. Small enough price to pay for all that background. Got a couple of little things I have to do in the morning. Probably wander over around eleven."

"We'll be there. Either in the garage area or the drivers' lounge just around the corner. Ask anyone."

*   *   *

One of the "little things" I had to do was call Chip. Post him on my meeting with Alden, find out if he'd succeeded in reaching Paul Goodman. I set the alarm for seven thirty, put in a wake-up call for backup insurance, called, and just missed him. Terrific.

I left the message and number with the desk sergeant, ordered up a repeat of yesterday's breakfast, again with the paper to give me something to do while waiting.

At eleven thirty, I gave up, got dressed, drove over to the Speedway. The day was cool and gray, overcast, with more than a hint of rain. I found Wayne in the drivers' lounge, bitching about the weather.

"See what I mean, Cam? All week long it's hot and dry. So you set the car up for those conditions and look what happens. This keeps up, mean some major changes. The hell of it is, we just don't know about tomorrow's weather. They say it's a front coming through. May be gone tomorrow, maybe not. Lousy guessing game, for pretty high stakes."

I left him cursing the weather gods, walked through the garage area, stopping here and there to chat with various people I'd met at Daytona. Ran into Ben Reed again, agreed to meet them in the hotel lobby at six thirty, go with them to the STP/Champion dinner. Ben told me a delightful Martha Jarret story.

"You've met Martha, Ned's wife, haven't you, I thought so. Pleasant, soft spoken, one of the real great ladies in our business. Funny, too, which I didn't really appreciate until the banquet here at Charlotte last year. I forget who put it on, but the feature attraction was a female singer who'd once been a Playmate or a Bunny—one of the two. Anyway, here we are, at an upfront table, Sally and me, Martha and Ned, a sponsor and his wife, two empty chairs. We'd just finished the fruit cup when La Bunny and her husband made their grand entrance—her in an outfit that was more girl than material. Like all black shoelaces. A real head-turner. Here she comes across the room, raising all the male temperatures a couple of degrees, plunks down next to Ned, whose face promptly turns the color of Labonte's car. I mean, *fire-engine* red. La Bunny's husband apologized for their being late, that it had taken her a half hour to get into her outfit. Dead silence at the table . . . then Martha's low gentle voice, "I think she should have taken another twenty minutes to finish the job." I didn't know whether to laugh or chew the spoon in half. Sally kept kicking me under the table. And I think it went right over La Bunny's pretty little head. A shot to remember, all right."

I watched the Sportsman's race with Boomer, including two spectacular wrecks in the number-four turn that Boomer filed away for use in the big race. Decided to skip watching the practice, told Boomer I'd be there by ten tomorrow, went back to the hotel and found Ordonez had called, wanted me to reach him at home, the number at the bottom of the message slip.

He answered somewhere around the eighth or ninth ring, obviously still half asleep. I gave him time to clear his head, told him about my lunch with Ned Alden and my feelings on any further follow-up.

"Swell, that makes it a clean sweep for the day."

"You couldn't find Goodman?"

"Worse. Much worse. He's dead."

"Goddammit, Chip. How?"

"Apparently natural causes, specifically a heart attack. We tried getting him Thursday afternoon and all day Friday. Nothing. This morning I called the Coral Gables people, asked them to go see if he was still living there. The super went up with them, unlocked the door, and there he was. In his pajamas, in bed, cold as a mullet. No signs of a struggle, nothing to indicate he wasn't alone when he died."

"Any feeling for when?"

"Preliminary report says five days to a week, no more. The boys said it was *very* fragrant in there."

"That was my number-one man."

"I remember. You realize the real hell of it, I assume?"

"What could be worse?"

"Goodman could have killed Tom Horton. One way or the other, we'll never know—at least from him. It's worse than just a dead end, it's a dead end wrapped in a puzzle."

"So, now what?"

"Partly your call, *compadre*. When are you coming back?"

"Planned to be there Monday around noon. Then to Key West Tuesday to talk to Megan Carter's brother. With Goodman gone, that finishes up the contacts I had lined up. Maybe I ought to come home now and start digging some more."

"Your choice. If I were you, I'd stay up there, try to enjoy the rest of the weekend. There isn't all that much for you to do here. Monday, we'll start looking at those three guys you turned up, start putting a full court press on Diaz."

"Shouldn't I be along?"

"That's what we get paid for. Go see the brother, then maybe we get together for lunch on Wednesday, on where we are."

In the end that's what I did, but my heart really wasn't in it. I went through the motions of what should have been a most enjoyable dinner, disregarding the looks of concern from Sally and Ben, managing to stay just this side of civil.

The race the next day was an anticlimax, virtually a non-event for me and anybody else cheering for Wayne Rollins. He'd done well in the early going, moving up through the pack, running a strong number four in a tight pack of cars at the front. On the eighty-first lap, less than a quarter of the way through the race, he came flashing through the four turn, door handle to door handle with Ricky Rudd, accelerating toward the start/finish line. I saw a puff of bluish white smoke from the exhaust pipe, assumed it was back pressure, looked around to see the pit crew disgustedly beginning to pack up all their gear.

"What's wrong, Boomer?"

"Be some kind of valve problem. Dropped, burned, or cracked, find out in a minute. Any case we all done for the day."

Sure enough the car was running at the bottom of the track, crawling along slowly, trailing a light wisp of smoke as the yellow caution lights and flags came out. Boomer left the crew to put the equipment away, I walked with him back to the garage area behind the pits. Wayne was there when we arrived, whacking his helmet against his thigh in frustration.

"Damn it all, Boomer . . . lousy two-bit valve. The car

was going like a scalded cat, everything right—then—blooey, no warning, no warning at all. I thought we had 'em today."

"Racin' luck, son. You been around to know that. Let's go buy you a shower and a beer 'fore we leave."

There wasn't much I could say, so I promised I'd try to catch up with them in Atlanta, wished them all well, watched them walk away, the giant's arm consolingly wrapped around the angry shape in the brightly colored flame-retardant driver's suit.

Some things just aren't meant to be.

*   *   *

"Turn here, Mister?"

"What? Oh, sorry, yes, a right. Eighth house down on the left."

The cab driver had caught me in the train of thought begun on the plane ride home, a confused train of what ifs, what nows, and one huge what might have been. Nothing ever comes easy, my father used to say, and if it does, be on your guard because it wasn't supposed to. Square on, dear old Dad.

"Phew, something sure stinks. Must be low tide. That's twelve-fifty, Mister."

I paid him, collected my bags, walked up to the front door. Something stank all right, but it wasn't low tide. Someone had left a very large fish on the last flagstone. Grouper by the look of it. Very large, very dead, very redolent. Just what I need, a practical joke, catch that wise guy and I'll make his life miserable. I stepped around the corpse, went into the house, unpacked, changed into my least favorite chinos. Got a garbage bag to stuff the fish into, thinking how pleased the trash man would be, probably skip my house for a month after this.

As I was wrestling the fish into the bag, I noticed something under it—an envelope, wrapped in a plastic bag for protection. Carted the fish over and slung it into a trash barrel, took the envelope into the house for a closer look.

Inside was a single sheet of lined notebook paper, folded in half, words cut out from a newspaper and pasted on. A very simple message:

STOP INVESTIGATION now extreme DANGER otherwise FINAL/WARNING

It wasn't signed.

*   *   *

"Thought you weren't going to call 'til Wednesday, Cam, get lonesome?"

"Got a homecoming present I'm not real fond of. Maybe you can tell me what it means."

I described the fish and the message to Chip, caught the sharp grunt of surprise, listened with mounting concern to the answer.

"May be a practical joke, but it sure doesn't sound like it. The fish is an old practice, started with the Unione Siciliano crowd. They used to deal with informers that way. A 'say one word and you're dead' gesture. The cutout device makes tracing impossible, unlike handwriting or even typewriting. Somebody wants you to find another line of work."

"I don't like dead fish and I don't like threats. Put it down to stubborness, Chip, but I'm staying in the hand. Have to."

"Okay, but play it cool, *companero*. On your trip to Key West, keep a sharp eye out. If you think you're being tailed, pull over to the first public place and call in."

"It still may be just a gag."

"If it is, you got a friend with one weird sense of humor. Take care, Cam. Hope I don't hear from you until Wednesday."

I hung up, sat back in the chair, thinking hard. Who had known I'd be out of town? Began ticking them off and realized I was overthinking the thing, as usual. The way I sleep, someone could leave a dead elephant in the front yard at night and I'd never know it.

But I would keep a close watch on the way to see Mark Carter.

12

"Key West? You'll adore it, Cam, you romantic devil. Who's the lucky lady?"

"Business, Max, strictly business. Believe me."

"Implicitly. Santa, the Easter Bunny, and MacCardle go to Key West stag."

A late afternoon telephone conversation with my friendly travel agent, Maxine Kyle, of MIP Tours, Lighthouse Point. When I was shopping for a local agent a couple of years ago, I'd noted the MIP ad in the Yellow Pages, saw how close by they were, walked in, and met Max. One of the last of the great free spirits, inventor of a game called Strip Authors, which she introduced one night at a party at my house. A simple game—each player in turn gives a famous book title. Guess the author and the player has to shed an article of clothing. Stump the panel, and each member of the group contributes a piece. I declined to play, not out of modesty or inhibition but because I was aware that behind that cover-girl face and chorine's figure dwelt a mind that had earned an honors degree in English from Vassar. The lecherous were virtually *shtarkers* when I cut them in on that bit of background information. In retaliation, they threw her in the pool, still fully clothed, laughing like a maniac the while.

"No, you don't need a map, dimbulb; even you can find

Key West. Run down I Ninety-five to the end, you'll start picking up signs for the Ocean Highway—stay on it straight through to Key West.

"How long?"

"A good four hours, closer to five if the traffic gets dicey or you want an occasional peek at the scenery."

"Ten hours . . . kinda shoots my down-and-back-in-one-day plot. Any decent motels there, Max?"

"Come now, my man. A little class, if you please. Stay at the Casa Marina. Reynolds Street, right on the ocean. Wonderful old pile of a place—built in the twenties, completely restored by the Marriott people. Posh, but not nouveau."

"Expensive?"

"Definitely not the YMCA range you keep insisting on. Live a little, Cam. If it really is on business, you can write off the cost. Single or double?"

"Single."

"Why must I spend my day dealing with the narrow minded? Very well, I'll instruct them to guarantee the reservation. That way, you can show up anytime tomorrow."

"Always looking after my welfare, Max."

"Bon voyage, Pilgrim."

Whatever else she was, Max was an excellent travel agent, as I'd discovered while running all over Mexico trying to track down Lisa Wentworth. So the Casa Marina would be up to its ears in what Max calls "panache," with a bill that would no doubt make Dick's fussy accountant wince when I sent it in. Might as well be shot for a sheep as a lamb. Gotta be a Big Kid once in a while.

* * *

What Max hadn't prepared me for was the sweep of the Florida Keys and the incredible Ocean Highway. A hundred and thirteen miles worth, running on land where there was land, otherwise flinging itself over the blue-green water on elevated pilings, including an unbelievable seven miles of bridge between Marathon and Bahia Honda Key. The Atlantic Ocean on the left, Gulf of Mexico off to my right, like going to sea in a car. Many of the Keys looked well worth stopping for; store that away for futures. One by one they rolled on, Largo, Tavernier, Plantation, Islamorada, the Matecumbes. Long Key, then Duck, Grassy, Marathon, and the breathtaking bridge. Big Pine Key, the Torches, Ramrod, Summerland, Curjoe. The Sugarloaves, Coppit, and Boca Chica, finally into Key West. I wanted to turn around immediately and do it all over again. A whole entire trip, in and of itself. Fantastic.

Megan had said her brother lived in Old Town, in a little court that ran off Duval Street. So I started poking around looking for it, got lost several times, finally swallowed my pride and asked for directions. Found a parking lot three blocks away from the court's entryway, dropped off the car and backtracked. Once inside, off the noisy street, it was very well laid out. A three story, square cul-de-sac, brick paved, with palm trees shading the interior. First floor—all stores and an ice cream parlor, with small tables and bentwood chairs in front. The second and third stories were accessed by winding wrought-iron staircases leading up to the U-shaped veranda that ringed the court. Presumably the apartments would be off the verandas. Only one way to find out. I'd been prepared for the worst. So far this looked like pretty nice living.

A startling version of Megan answered the door. As if she had grown her hair waist length and adopted a beard. Rope-soled sandals, white duck trousers with a yellow knitted tie serving as a belt. A wine colored, short-sleeve shirt, entirely open at the front, a necklace of tiny shells contrasting against the tanned chest. Hmmmm.

"You must be Mark Carter. Your sister looks exactly like you. I'm MacCardle, sorry I'm late—got lost looking for your place."

"Time is not worthy of measurement. When we are ultimately called it will not matter how long we endured, rather who we were and what we meant—those alone will be the yardsticks of evaluation."

Whatever you say, Sporting Blood. This may be a *very* long afternoon. Let's give it another try.

"Megan did mention I was coming, didn't she? MacCardle?"

"In this house we do not use last names. No temporal relationship is meant to be permanent. She said your name was Cam. I'm Mark. That is all we shall need."

"Yeah, well, right . . ."

"May I offer you a hit?"

"A what?"

"Ah. Askers are never users. Perhaps a glass of wine?"

"Beer maybe?"

"Excellent. Earthy. Of the earth . . . hold, back in a nonce."

Oh my.

I looked around the main room while he was gone. Again, it wasn't nearly as bad as Megan had said. Extremely high ceiling, tiled floor, whitewashed walls with exposed, weathered gray timber framing. Hanging plants suspended at various heights from overhead. In one corner of the room stood a slanting draftsman's table, a grasshopper lamp clutching the upper left-hand corner. The wall behind was a sea of corkboard with sheaves of paper pinned to it, presumably work done and work in progress. Megan had been right about one thing, though: there wasn't a whole helluva lot of furniture. Cushions everywhere, outsized cushions in various motifs, obviously used for seating stacks. The Mexican rugs lent patches of blazing colors throught the room. In the far corner the only table, a flush-door conversion number, with early Salvation Army chairs at either end. Battered bridge lamps were scattered all around; evidently they and the big lunette windows set high in the fireplace wall provided all the room's illumination. Weird, I thought, but not as weird as Gracious Host.

"Fetter not the Muse with possession's bonds/Nor mew

her in a silken prison./She thrives on severity, austerity,/Her soul her own, unclaimed, arisen."

Return of the poet, bearing beer.

"William Blake?" I asked.

"Mark Carter. A good attempt, nonetheless, I was strongly influenced by Blake at the time. Don't you find it descriptive of the ambiance?"

"Highly."

"Megan detests it. She gobbles on about proper accommodations, responsible lifestyles, the deplorable new morality—all that bleak, bourgeois claptrap."

"You don't get along?"

"*Au contraire.* I love Megan. We simply inhabit different planets. She cannot understand mine and I will not accept hers. Megan's life is driven by materialism and a slavish orthodoxy. I prefer, like the lioness, to remain born free."

A door opened behind me, welcome interruption to the cosmic discussion. She waddled slowly across the room to where we sat, the distended belly leading like a cowcatcher on the old-time steam locomotives. Very blonde, very pretty; very, very pregnant. She stood in the circle of Mark's arms, his face pressed gently against the enormous mound, looked at me placidly.

"Hello, Stranger Man. I'm Columbine. Don't get up, please . . . Off to the doctor, darling. I should be back by five. Tacos and enchiladas for supper. Welcome to join us, Stranger Man, be you still here by then."

And she was gone.

"Pretty lady. Interesting name, too."

"She comes from Colorado. Her mother named her after the state flower. She writes country and western song lyrics. Crystal Gayle bought two so far this year. We are living off the proceeds."

"Your wife?"

"You sound like Megan. Columbine is my sharer. My fellow celebrant. We are joined by stronger ties than arid words or trivial paper."

"As in baby?"

"Merely physical evidence of our communion, a logical, enduring statement jointly made, reaffirmation of reality in a plastic world."

If we keep on like this, I thought, we'll be here until next Michaelmas. And I will come away gibbering like an ape. This character's definitely collectable. But it isn't your job to make value judgments—you came to ask the man some questions. So get asking, before the metaphysics covers you up like leaves.

I started by telling Mark about Tom Horton's murder, his connections with Mrs. Donaldson, and his notes regarding a proposed change of wills. Then I began to question him—getting what I had half expected, namely nothing of value. He didn't know Tom Horton, never met him, was unaware that Tom Horton was his grandmother's attorney. He'd been home the night Tom was killed; Columbine would support that. The last time he'd been out of Key West was seven months ago, to see an ophthalmologist in Miami. Again, Columbine would verify. He didn't know his grandmother was changing her will, and could not be less concerned. His standard of living was of his own choosing, had been long before Tom and his grandmother had ever met, would continue irrespective of any changes in her will. I sighed, put away the notebook, shook hands, and started to leave.

One last canto at the door.

"Cam, I am the antithesis of murder. I am a giver of life, both physically and in my work. Creation is the foundation stone of our existence. Destruction is the negation of creation. Go in search of peace and understanding."

I went. In search of a very dry martini and people who spoke the mother tongue.

*   *   *

I found both at the Casa Marina, plus confirmation that Max was truly a major league travel agent. I read the four-color brochure over my martini. Built in 1921, by Henry

Flagler, the railroad tycoon, solely for vacationing socialites. Two hundred fifty-one rooms. Many, like mine, with balconies overlooking the ocean; 1,100 feet of private beach. Health club, sauna, tennis courts, swimming pool, all neatly tucked into an enclosed estate not accessible to the unwashed. Nice shot, Max, too bad I'm here to work. Which reminded me.

"Chip, it's Cam."

"What's the matter? Where are you? Anybody close by?"

I'd *completely* forgotten our deal. Probably scared him out of his wits, you dummy.

"Sorry, pal. Not to worry. I'm all by myself in my hotel room. Casa Marina. Incredible place, straight out of Gatsby."

"Spare me the travelogue. What's up?"

"I want to postpone our lunch meeting until Thursday. Same time, same place, if you can."

"Sure. How come? You on to something down there?"

"I only wish. The reason is pure cowardice. It's about a five-hour drive home. I'd just as soon do it all in daylight. Just in case my dead-fish friend is for real."

"*Estar seguro,* for sure. Gives us another day to work on our three new players. Nothing down there, huh?"

"Nothing. More when I see you. S'long."

"One favor, *compadre,* no more unexpected phone calls, okay?"

"I'll work on it."

The little man at the tourism desk in the lobby was a mine of information. I must go to Mallory Square for the Street Celebration, especially since this was my first time in Key West. They hold it every day, street musicians, entertainers, jugglers, dancers, colorful costumes. Capped by a sunset so spectacular it'll knock you off the dock—his words, not mine. Then to Sloppy Joe's for one and only one *Bomba Atomica Ernesto,* the rum drink they named for their most famous customer. I did know who that was, did I not? Yes, truly and well. Dinner. Any number of good places in town, but he recommended Henry's, right here at the Casa Marina, not because he worked here either. Try the *lechon*—roast pork with a garlic and orange flavoring. Have the *bollas* with it, Bahamian version of hush puppies. Key Lime pie for dessert, no question about that. Wrote the whole thing down, with pertinent directions, on a piece of the hotel's stationery. Don't mention it, a happy guest was his *job*.

So, Happy Guest wandered off, followed the orders precisely, and had a marvelous time, or at least as marvelous as you can have by yourself. Next time, Mighty Hunter brings squaw. Before many moons, too.

* * *

I got a terrible scare on the way home.

I was breezing along, enjoying the view, when a green four-door Ford showed up in the rear view mirror, the boxy, Mercedes-Benz knockoff, Granada model. At first I thought it was an overwrought imagination. But when I slowed down, so did the Ford. When I accelerated, it kept pace, always in the same lane, maintaining the interval. I made an unnecessary stop for gas at Marathon, watched the Ford pull away as I went down the exit ramp. End of that chapter, I thought, wondering if it was only coincidence but glad to be rid of the problem. I debated calling Ordonez, decided not to. This year's Nervous Nellie Award could wait for someone else.

An almost clear road as I headed north, still too early in the year for the tourist swarm. Fishermen of various ages and degree of equipment sophistication were hard at work along the highway. An old coot at Sloppy Joe's last night called it the World's Longest Fishing Pier, told me an eight-hour day was enough to keep him in food for a month. Clear sailing, almost halfway home.

I'd just left Long Key, heading for the Matecumbes when I picked him up again. No question: same dark green car, same position. Speed up, slow down, faithful shadow remained astern. Stayed with me all the way to South Miami, where we began to pick up heavy traffic. On an impulse, I suddenly swung hard right into some curb space made by an exiting bus. The Ford had no chance to stop, rolling quickly by me, eaten up in the mass of cars heading for I95.

The big fisherman hat and the dark glasses made it impossible to see the driver's face. The size of the shoulders and arms said male—or else the biggest woman in Florida. I did get the license number, though, TWS930, wrote it down with a nervous hand. Get Ordonez to check that first thing, see who my unwanted escort was, why it had tailed me twice.

I got home without any further incident, but with the inescapable feeling there were eyes on my back. Eyes that made me feel highly uncomfortable.

*　　　*　　　*

"You don't look so bad for a guy who got tailed for a hundred miles. Sure hasn't affected your appetite, either."

"Ho ho to you, too. I'm telling you Chip, it was spooky, particularly when he picked me up the second time. Who is Mr. TWS Nine-thirty, or didn't you get a chance to check on . . . why are you grinning, nothing funny about it at all!"

"I didn't have to check on it. Departmental vehicle, plainclothes guy from my section. I sent it. Finn's a little pissed at you for losing him. Backup car caught you just as you got on I Ninety-five. Guess you didn't see her."

"Guess not, Mother. But you forgot to sew my name in my mittens."

"Don't get uptight, *compadre*. I don't like what I'm hearing on the street. After the fish trick, I decided not to take any chances. Jure welcome, joo ongrateful slob."

"Scare me half to death, then knock out what I hoped was a lead for us and I'm supposed to be grateful?"

"Try relieved."

"Relieved, yes. But disappointed, too. I thought we might have something. What did you hear to trigger the convoy service?"

"Things are starting to heat up, Cam. The Mayor's-Commission people are furnishing the liaison vice officers with some solid evidence. The word is the crackdown's soon—on Action Junction mostly, but really all over the city."

"So?"

"So, they know we talked to Diaz, they figure you're involved somehow in trying to put them out of business. You even have a nickname. *El Cojo,* 'the man with the limp.'"

"They?"

"The Lucchese people. The Marielito Seven. The Vasquez operation, which looks even bigger than the Sparrow's. For someone who hasn't done anything, you're picking up a very unsavory rep, *El Cojo.* Tell me about Key West."

"A disaster. Screwball poet and his sort-of-wife, pregnant and then some, looks like she swallowed a beachball. If he's a killer, I'm the Queen of the May."

"You didn't expect much there."

"And that's just what I got. The only one who looks even remotely possible is Morton Giles—for my dough we can heave the others. Damn Goodman, anyway, that was the horse I had the money on."

"Quit kicking yourself. All you can do is keep plowing ahead, keep working at it. Otherwise you'll drive yourself nuts."

"I know, I know—just gets frustrating, that's all. Where do we go from here?"

"I vote for a division of labor. We'll start putting some juice to Diaz and the rest of them. We got enough snitches out there to start a battalion. Sooner or later, something will give way.

"But just in case it doesn't, I think you better go back to the paperwork. Use the same process you did the first time, hours versus type of work. You may have overlooked a couple, or maybe it *was* one of the second-stringers."

"How about Giles?"

"We'll bring him in and put him on the box. Inadmissable as evidence, but it might scare him enough to level with us, if he had anything to do with it. I'll get the Coral Gables guys to poke into the late Mr. Goodman's life. Find out what he was doing for a living, talk to any known associates, so on. I'm not all that hopeful but it's an easy base to cover."

"I'd rather be working with you."

"You *are*—oh, you mean Diaz and friends. No, thanks. Look, Cam, I don't like the fish and I don't like the *El Cojo* number. You're not really involved with these people and that's the way I want to keep it. You signed on as a leg man, not the fastest gun in town. Remember that."

"I hear you. Okay, back to the paperwork. I'll get the tab for lunch—it's my turn. But keep me posted, would you, Chip?"

"It's a deal, *El Cojo*."

*　　*　　*

I unearthed all the records again. Reviewed my work sheets, detailed the next twenty names that had the most hours against them, reread the diaries, cross matching. Dreary, dreary, dreary.

Finally quit around seven when my eyeballs were starting to fall out, decided I'd put off the review until tomorrow.

I called Megan to tell her about her brother, got Janice Smithers instead.

"Sorry, Cam, she's not here. She went to an art auction in Atlanta. Should be home tomorrow morning. Any message?"

"Thanks, Janice, I'll just call her then."

"Why not come over here. Lord knows we could stand the company, just the two of us bashing about in this great ark. Say, two o'clock?"

"Two sounds fine. I'll see you both then."

"Was Key West exciting?"

"About like watching grass grow."

"Oh, dear . . . Tomorrow, then. Ta."

"Okay, Janice."

* * *

Slept late the next morning. No special reason; it just happened. Had breakfast at eleven, cleaned up, took one look at the stack of paper on the coffee table and knew I wasn't up to the thought of plowing through the reviews today. They'd keep until Monday—didn't look too promising anyway.

I called Ellis to give him the latest news, including my lunch yesterday with Ordonez and the next steps we'd agreed upon. I tried to sound as optimistic as I could, ignoring the disappointment in his voice at the gloomy results so far. Even gave him the part about my new nickname, hoping to cheer him up, at least a little. Hung up, hoping I hadn't sounded too much like a chapter from *The Power of Positive Thinking*.

Telling Dick about the lunch reminded me of something Chip had said.

"Office of the mayor, Miss Richards speaking."

"Floey, it's Cam MacCardle. Is he in?"

"Yes, sir, one moment, please."

"Hello, Cam, my boy. What can we do for you today?"

"I hear your pornography commission is swinging right along, Oz."

"Yes, yes. I'm very pleased, Not over by a long shot, though."

"Oh?"

"We're getting the little fish. That's good, must start somewhere, but we need to get at the networks, the people who supply the individual retailers. Only way we can make real headway. If we could crack just one of them, it might just be enough to smoke them all out, get rid of this thing for keeps. How goes the Horton investigation?"

"Just fair. That's about all I can say for it. Anything come up over there that might help?"

"If it had, you know we would have called you."

"I know. Just thought I'd ask."

"No offense—I know you're working hard. Have a nice weekend, Cam."

"You too, Mr. Mayor."

Damn.

*　　*　　*

Janice answered the door, brought me around back to a shaded porch overlooking the big garden, told me to sit and relax while she went to get Megan and some refreshments.

No canvas director's chairs or webbed loungers for this lot, I noted. A gigantic bamboo sofa, with matching armchairs, all padded with yellow floral design cushions. A coffee table and end tables, each with smoked glass tops, fitted into intricate bamboo inlays. They must have poured the floor, then dropped in the bits of colored glass and seashells, finally poured some clear substance over it to produce the smooth finish. It felt like walking on water; very curious effect.

"Hi, Cam."

"Hello, Aunt Megan."

"Aunt Megan?"

"Well . . . about to be Aunt Megan, more properly."

"That's wild! Can you imagine, Janice? Doddering Aunt Megan, the old maid of Playa Lago. Wild! Tell all, Cam."

I did some hopefully judicious editing in the narration, deciding to spare Megan my reactions to her brother, reporting the whole thing straight. Either I failed or she found the situation absurd. In any case, it was several minutes after I'd finished before she could stop giggling.

"Columbine? 'Stranger Man'? She sounds more spaced out than he is. A match made in heaven. God only knows what they'll name that child. Probably something catchy like Xantippe, or maybe Polonius if it's a boy. Far, far out. Did they seem happy?"

"I only saw her for a minute. She was going to the doctor's. Still gone when I left. But I'd say they seemed happy."

"Janice, I must get down there. Those two lunatics won't even have thought about mundane things like baby clothes or cribs or how the poor little tyke will eat. Probably put it on one of those awful rugs, in the middle of the room, while they're communing with the muses. Help me make a list of necessities—I'll go down next week and get them organized."

"Certainly, Miss Megan. I'm rather an old hand at that sort of thing. Shouldn't take any time at all."

"Columbine. I mean, really. Cam, you've made my day. I only wish it had turned out better for you. Any progress on poor Mr. Horton?"

"Some, not as much as I'd like. Interviewed a couple of real dead ends, like your brother. One prospect died, my favorite one, at that. Heart attack, days after Tom was killed. For all I know, or ever may know, he was the murderer."

"What do you do now?"

"Keep looking, stay with it. A few things we've uncovered since we started are beginning to look promising. We'll be pushing after them hard. Might get lucky, who knows? But we're not about to quit."

"I'll bet you could stand a break, though. We're having a pool party tomorrow afternoon. Very informal. Bathing suits, hamburgers and hot dogs, mellow city. You're invited. Bring a date or come by yourself—mostly singles anyway. C'mon."

"Megan, I'd love it, but I'll have to ask for a rain check this time. Promised a friend I'd take her up to Galleon Reef snorkeling, maybe some spearfishing if the barracudas are working somewhere else. We've had it planned for a while and the long-range weather forecast—as much as you can rely on those dimmies, says light winds and two- to three-foot waves. We'll pass this time but thanks anyway."

I looked at my watch. Time to get going if I wanted to pick up Carole and have the *Folly* safely anchored offshore before dark. Christopher Columbus you ain't—better allow plenty of time.

Finished off the iced tea, said my goodbyes and thanks, and went off to the Cypress Beach Racquet Club to claim the faithful crew.

14

Conversation on the *Folly*, outward bound for Galleon Reef.

"How did you wangle a Saturday off, honey?"

"Blackmail."

"*There's* an ugly word."

"Dear Dana's covering for me. I told him if he didn't I'd spread the word about his bikini panties. After that he was putty in me hands."

"A tennis pro who wears bikini panties?"

"In colors, yet. My fave is lime green."

"How in the world would you know that? Peering into the men's locker room again?"

"No need. He has an old pair of shorts that have been washed so many times they're paper thin. They appear every other week, along with the underwear of the day."

"How did he take it?"

"A towering snit. He'll recover. Cam, why are we going around in circles?"

"Waiting for that bridge to open. We'll just slooch around here for a while. Won't be long."

"Slooch?"

"What would you call it?"

"Slooch, I guess. What then?"

"Go through the inlet, out for a couple of miles, then we turn north. Run for about an hour and a half. We should get there around sundown."

"Can I drive?"

"Technically, the word is steer, but the answer's yes. Let me get her set up for you first."

"Does my standing here bother your driv . . . steering the boat?"

"Bother me a lot more if you weren't."

Bells started ringing, signaling the opening of the Hillsboro Inlet bridge. We fell in line behind a gorgeous blue ketch named *Aphrodite*, trudged through the inlet out into the gentle seas Marine Weather had promised. For once, they had been right, hope it stays that way. I swung to port, boosted the RPM level to three thousand, adjusted the levelers to bring the *Folly* to plane, synched the engines until they sounded like one. I have an electronic gadget to do that job, but I don't use it much anymore—easier to rely on the vibrations coming through the deck plates into the balls of your feet. The less, the better. Checked the gizmo anyway. On the button. No need for the direction finder: clear weather and we'd have the coastline in sight all the way. I reviewed the acronym in my mind—CREL—Course, RPMs, Engines Synchronized, Levelers Set. All go. I signaled to Carole to take the helm, stood beside her until she nodded she had it, went below and broke out a Coke for me, Tab for the weight-watching crew member.

"Why are we wandering all over the ocean, Cam?"

"You're still working at it too hard, babe. Running a boat is a lot like dancing. There's a rhythm to it. You'll get it—just don't overcorrect every time the boat shifts. Try not reacting at all. You won't hit anything, nobody out here but us and the seagulls."

She found the rhythm quickly, settling into it easily, the small hands far less busy on the spokes of the *Folly*'s destroyer wheel. She grinned at me when she knew she had it, reaching over with a free hand to grab the can of Tab, then back to work, eyes fixed on the horizon, body moving naturally with the *Folly*'s motion. A very determined lady. We plowed on north, in the companionable semi-silence boats produce, alone together on the comfortable island of the *Folly*.

I spotted the landmark Ollie had told me about—a garish pink high-rise condominium, thrusting into the sky like an obscene finger—tapped Carole on the shoulder and slid around her to take the wheel.

Stayed on course until I judged we were dead opposite the condo, then swung northwest toward the reef area, keeping an eye on the flickering face of the fathometer. Nothing at first. Then the water began shoaling—seventy-five feet, sixty, forty-five, thirty. I eased the *Folly* to dead ahead slow, barely making headway, told Carole to take over the helm, dropped the big Danforth anchors fore and aft, with twenty feet of water under us.

"Why *two* anchors?"

"Let me shut down. Okay. Basically to stop us from swinging around during the night when the tide changes. This way I know where the bottom is; otherwise I wouldn't."

"I get it—so we don't bump into coral heads and such. Very clever. Now what, my Captain?"

"First order of the day is a drink. Tall, frosty gin and tonic do you? Or do you want something else?"

"G and T sounds wonderful, but only one, please."

"Think I'm trying to ply you with strong drink, Innocent Maiden?"

"Not hardly. Innocent Maiden is *starving*. I don't know why—I had a monster club sandwich for lunch."

"Sea air. Either that or you're pregnant."

"If I am, we all know who's at the wrong end of the shotgun."

"A chilling thought. Here, stick your finger in it, I forgot to stow a swizzle stick aboard."

"Ummmm, that's nice. You did remember to bring some food, I hope."

"A one-track mind. I'll have you know, Madame, that in

that chest over there is a large pot of Billy's best beef Bourgignon, along with a loaf of French bread and a jug of Inglenook Navalle Zinfandel—their finest hour. Heat up the
Bourgignon and, presto, instant haute cuisine."

"No salad?"

"Tough it out, slim."

Found *I* was hungry, too. Together we gobbled up most
of the chest's contents. Packed everything away and went topside with coffee, sitting in the starboard fighting chair, Carole
nestled comfortably in my lap. A long time of silence, soft,
tangy sea air, slap of the wavelets against the hull, sky strewn
from end to end with a million stars. A dreamer's night. Un-
complicated night, when all the news is good and all the
promises are kept.

"I feel like we're on vacation, Cam."

"Funny thing about the water. You go through the inlet,
feels like you left the rest of world behind."

"A nice world, Cam . . . with you. How about a quick
swim?"

"Not now, sweetheart, time enough for that tomorrow.
We don't know these waters and it's black as the inside of
your hat. Don't need to bang into a barracuda looking for his
supper."

"What have you laid on for entertainment, then—you
should only pardon the expression."

"When I was on that outing with Ollie, I found out if you
go below and stretch out, the motion of the boat rocks you to
sleep in about two minutes. Ollie's theory is that it's a return
to the womb."

So we tried it, discovered that Ollie's theory doesn't always hold. We invented a theory of our own, though, helluva
lot more exciting than Ollie's. Tried it once again to prove it,
fell asleep holding hands.

Ain't science wonderful.

*   *   *

"Cam, Cam. Wake up."

"Whammfff?"

"Wake up, Cam. There's something you *must* see. Upstairs."

"What time is it?"

"Who knows? C'mon, quick. Upstairs . . . before they're gone."

Upstairs? Oh, well, one term at a time. Followed her topside, watching the delicious bottom bobbing under the hem of the short nightshirt. Some things are worth getting up early for.

"Look! Over there. See them? Aren't they marvelous."

Two squadrons of pelicans, grotesque on the ground, incredibly graceful in flight. Soaring along in precise formation at wavetop level, rising and falling with the water's surge, holding their spaces as if programmed.

"Oh, they're coming this way! Look!"

They swept by us, no more than thirty yards away. Close enough to hear the creak-creak-creak of the great wings when they needed to pick up speed. They looked almost prehistoric at their work, continuum of a ritual begun before man could write. A timeless reminder of the natural order of the world.

"They're glorious. What are they doing?"

"Breakfast time, luv. They work the tops of the waves. See a fish and sweep him right up. First pelican to spot a school gets a bonus, the chance to lead the next raid."

"Aw . . . they're going. Goodbye, pelicans, have a great day. Thank you. You're something to see."

"Not the only sight on this bucket either, honey. Love your nightgown. What it lacks in length it makes up for in transparency. Yum."

"You don't have *any* clothes on and . . . Oh, my goodness, best get you *below*."

She'd learned one term. She also demonstrated the new theory works in daytime, too. Very well. May have to market it.

* * *

After breakfast I went forward to the main gear locker, got out the buoy with the red and white flag, tossed it over the rail and went after it, hand over hand down the anchor line to make sure it was secure. Swam back and clambered aboard, only slightly out of breath, watched the flag swinging in the wave motion—a gay spot of color against the pale water.

"What's that, Cam, the red flag with a white diagonal?"

"Diver Down buoy. It warns passing boats to be careful. Doesn't stop the occasional moron but a pretty good insurance policy. Generally used by scuba people but I'm a card-carrying coward—it makes me feel better."

"What shall we do first? Or second, actually."

"Reasonably broad choice. Swim, snorkel, fish—either spear or regular. You pick."

We did everything but spearfish, which was fine with me because blood in the water has a nasty way of attracting the barracuda I'd mentioned the night before. Walk into any bar where the chartermen gather and you'll see why. Missing fingers, ugly puckered scars where the vicious teeth had taken flesh. No thanks.

Took a break for a sandwich lunch, sat in the shade of the wheel house to digest, plunged back in to dive the bottom, watching the streams of brightly colored fish until breath required surfacing.

Somewhere around four, I said we should start getting ready to go home.

"Couldn't we stay another day and go home tomorrow?"

"Only if you've given up eating, luv. We've got two limes and a box of Triscuits left. Not exactly a groaning board."

"I suppose. I hate to leave though—it's so beautiful."

"We'll be back, babe, here and other places. When you get your vacation, maybe we'll go down to the Keys. Looked sensational from the road. Let's go, honey, get home before nightfall."

I retrieved the buoy, turned on the bilge fans, waited five minutes, and fired up the engines. Picked up both anchors, went out to the point I had marked on the chart, and turned south, kicking in the autopilot so we could simply sit and talk.

"What were those things you turned on before you started the engines."

"Bilge fans. Fuel vapor tends to accumulate there. Not so bad with diesels, but in this boat, another chance you don't have to take. You hear the horror stories periodically. Usually a new owner, first timer. Jumps aboard, turns on the engine, spark falls just right and goodbye skipper."

"Ugh."

"What did you like best today? Of *nature*'s wonders, that is."

"The pelicans, hands down. I wish I'd thought to bring the camera. Absolutely spectacular. A memory to last a lifetime. How 'bout you?"

"The look on your face when you landed the dolphin. Hair plastered down, tongue sticking out of the corner of your mouth—you looked about seven years old."

The familiar tower of the Boca Raton Club was sliding by to starboard. Time to get back to work. Took the *Folly* off the autopilot, trimmed the speed back, loafed into the approach to the Hillsboro Inlet. The bridge was up, saving us that chore, and we ran in at the tail end of the traffic.

Swung down past the house, turned her around, and eased back to my dock. Tied up and shut down, sailors home from the sea. End of the mini-vacation. Still, there *was* tomorrow to enjoy before picking up the threads of Horton's death. Time enough.

We finished supper, were sitting on the Lexington with an after-dinner drink, pretending not to notice all the yawning. Carole jumped up and left the room, returning moments later, holding something behind her back.

"I've got a present for you, Cam. A sort of a present anyway. One of the club members works in a thrift shop. She found it."

"Found what? Miss Indirect, you're getting as bad as Dick Ellis."

"This. They came in bubble gum packs, I think."

"I'll be damned. There he is, sports fans, number 88 in

your program, number one in your hearts. Do you believe that crew cut?"

"You look very earnest. And sweet."

"Not so sure the coaches would agree with you . . . Thanks, honey; these cards must be rare as dodos these days."

"Not so fast. I'm getting it framed for you. We'll hang it over your desk there, next to the team picture."

We looked at each other and nodded. Definitely bedtime. I went around the house, locking up, turning out the lights. I was in bed when Carole came into the room. She leaned over, turned off the bedtable lamp, slid in beside me.

"Cam . . . could we make it *just* bed, tonight? I'm so bushed I can barely move. Hold me, though. I want to know you're near me. All the time . . ."

"Good night, Virginal Maiden."

"Good night, Mighty Hunter."

I held her in my arms, heard her breathing gently, felt her drop off.

This is one of the superstars, old friend. Time to do something about it.

Tomorrow.

* * *

". . . then you can go back to sleep until it's ready. Cam, have you heard a word I said?"

In all honesty, I hadn't. Eight-ten of a Sunday morning is not my best time for lucidity. If anything, I had hoped it would be time for drowsy maiden-ravishing, then sleep, then some serious ravishing. Instead I got Susie Homemaker in jeans and checked blouse, questioning me. I certainly hope *this* doesn't get to be a habit.

"Run that by me again, honey?"

"Lazy lout. I *said,* I'm fixing us the all-time Sunday breakfast. Big enough so you won't have to get out of bed all day, Mighty Warrior. But . . . *you* are out of coffee. Can't have breakfast without coffee. Tell me where the car keys are and then you can go back to sleep until it's ready."

"Top of the desk in the front hall. Black leather case. Square-top key."

"That's a good boy. See you in a jiff."

So maiden plundering wasn't out of the question after all. In fact, the maiden seemed bent on doing some plundering of her own. The solid thunk of the front door closing announced she was on her way, probably the Seven-Eleven store—back in twenty minutes at most. I rolled over on my side, forming images of gentle lechery.

The explosion shook the house, a deafening thunderclap of sound accompanying the tremor. I stumbled out to the living room, frozen in shock. The front door had been wrenched off its hinges, all the windows in the front of the house shattered. Flames were beginning to bloom on the curtains. Through the hole where the front door had been, in the driveway, was a twisted mass of burning junk, a hideous pall of thick black smoke. I ran through the living room, oblivious to the glass all over the rug, hurling myself at the car. Just as I got there the world turned shades of orange and red.

*   *   *

"You're nurse . . . where . . . I. . . ?"

"Oh, Mr. MacCardle, it's so good to see you awake. Doctor Duffy said to page him the minute you came to. Be right back."

The all-too-familiar universe of white . . . oxygen tube and drip bottles. The harsh tang of disinfectants. My bandaged hands immobilized in splints, suspended overhead. Body one solid ache, reminiscent of so many Monday mornings in autumns past. But this was far, far different.

Carole. My Carole, gone. Destroyed. Ripped away. Innocent victim of some unknown madman. Irreversible. Irreplaceable. I lay helpless on my back, the big tears flowing down my face. When the indistinct outline of the doctor's face appeared I shook my head. Not now. Dear, sweet Jesus, not now. Later maybe. Just go away. Leave me alone in the sad, still silence, hopefully to pass out and erase the crushing thoughts.

I barely heard them leave.

* * *

I woke next time to brilliant daylight, the sun streaming through the window, casting shadows on the wall. Different nurse, a gray-haired woman, sitting in a chair, watching me anxiously. When she saw I was awake, she rose, motioning me to stay quiet, left the room on soundless feet. Returned minutes later with an improbably young-looking doctor. Red hair and freckles. Tom Sawyer in white. Or was it Huckleberry Finn? Never could keep them straight.

"Afternoon, Mr. MacCardle. I'm Doctor Duffy, Hugh Duffy. Don't talk, save your strength. Let me cover the obvious questions. You're in the Intensive Care Unit at Garber Memorial. It's Tuesday afternoon, Tuesday the twelfth. Three fifteen. As I said, my name's Duffy. This is Miss Shaaps, your nurse. Your night nurse is Mrs. Duncan. Got all that?"

I nodded, somewhat frightened at the two-and-a-half-day gap. That can't be a very good sign.

"The police tell me the car was dynamited. As they reconstruct it, the gas tank blew up when you were trying to open the door. It threw you right through a wooden fence onto a gravel driveway next door. We spent a fair amount of time picking bits of wood and stone out of you.

"The major damage is to your hands. Extensive second-degree burns on your left hand; right's a little less serious. Two nasty lacerations of your left foot. Four cracked ribs—probably thanks to the fence. No concussion but your ears will ring for a couple of days more. Your eyebrows and most of your hair were burned off. They'll grow back, but right now you're no threat to Robert Redford.

"What's all the equipment for? That your question? The hands are immobilized so you wouldn't paw at them while you were unconscious. The drips are saline and intravenous feeding. The oxygen tube can probably come out tomorrow."

"How . . . long . . . Doctor?"

"So far, your vital signs look remarkably sound. You're no longer on the critical list. With any kind of luck, we should have you out of ICU by the weekend—say Sunday—to be safe. Be another week before you can walk on that foot. I'd count on two weeks all in."

"Visit. . . ?"

"No way, not for a while yet. A lot of people want to see you. Stack of messages. Shaaps will read them to you tomorrow. I've told everybody no visitors until you get out of ICU. Enough talk. I'm going to give you something now to make you sleep, hopefully through the night. By then, the worst of the pain should be over."

The needle came with its promise of unconsciousness, of temporary separation from the ache. But no needle, no opiate, could relieve the torment in my heart forever.

*   *   *

They came at halftime of the Dolphins game, Hampton in uniform, Chip in civilian clothes. Looking very grim standing at the foot of the bed. Hampton opened: "Feel well enough to talk, Cam?"

Cam. It took getting blown up to turn him into a human being. Don't think I like the price much.

"Sure, Lieutenant."

"Remember what happened?"

"All too clearly . . . she was going to the store for coffee . . . little after eight o'clock . . . I was in bed when it happened. Great bloody blast, lots of noise. I remember thinking I had to get her out . . . woke up in the hospital. The doctor said dynamite."

"That's the Crime Scene Squad report. Professional job. Somebody wanted you out of the action. Permanently. Unfortunately . . . your . . . friend got in the way. I'm really sorry, Cam . . . I know that doesn't help a whole lot, but . . . for what it's worth."

"Me too, *compadre.* I had our priest say a mass for her

today. Give you the mass cards and the program when you're out of here."

"Thank you. Thank you, both. I . . ."

"Easy, son. You've been through a lot. Don't try to rush the cadence. As of now you're retired, at least from this project. We'll take it from here, that's our job. Just a matter of time."

I knew he meant well, knew they were trying to look out for me. But a week in bed, by myself, had bottled up the words I had to say.

"The hell with that, Hampton. Somebody tried to kill me, which is bad enough. Instead they killed . . . a totally innocent woman—who I planned to marry, incidentally. . . . You want me out? Lock me up. Otherwise, no dice."

"Kinda thought you'd feel that way, boy. Wouldn't think much of you if you didn't. Okay, you can stay in, but on a *very* limited basis."

"As in?"

"As in—when you get out, we stow you in a motel we use as a safe house. Tell us who you want to know you're there—and it better be a short list. No telephone calls in or out. Meals sent in, you can pick the menu. Ordonez will see you every night. He's assigned to this thing only, right up to the finish. Get any great thoughts or urgent messages, give them to either one of the desk clerks. Both guys ours— plainclothes. That's the deal, take it or leave it, son."

"You don't give me a whole helluva lot of choice, Lieutenant."

"Hey, *hombre*, go with the flow. Somebody wants you dead, real badly. You're a wreck. Can't walk, can't use your hands, couldn't defend yourself against a five-year-old. This way you're still a partner. What do you say?"

"I say it stinks . . . but I guess it's better than nothing."

"Good man. Oh, one small thing, Don't worry about your house. Fire department got there right after you went through the fence. Put out the fires, boarded it up. Ellis will tell you more when he sees you tomorrow—they're only letting you have one visit a day until midweek. We pulled rank."

"The house was the last thing on my mind."

"I'm sure, son. One more time . . . I'm mighty sorry this happened to you and yours."

"Thanks, Wade. Appreciate the thought."

* * *

Dick appeared Monday morning as they were taking the saline drip out of my arm. Made him look sicker than I felt.

"I never should have asked you to do this. Here you are, all torn up, almost killed and that lovely girl . . . is *gone*. My responsibility, all mine."

"Quit it, Counselor. You didn't push the button, didn't have any more idea this could happen than I did. So knock it off."

"Very well. But I don't want you to have anything more to do with this investigation. I will not allow you to take further chances. That's it. Period."

"Hampton said the same thing."

"Then *that*'s settled."

"Hardly. I told him to buzz off. We finally made a deal. I don't like it very much, but it's the only wheel in town."

Spent time telling him what the arrangements were, suggested he get all the details from either Hampton or Ordonez. They wanted a short list. They'd get a short list. Ellis and Billy. The Three Musketeers. Huey, Duey, and Basket Case.

"That reminds me—what about the Good Reverend. Where the hell is he?"

"He couldn't make it this morning. Of all godawful coincidences—a funeral. Said he'd be around by three."

"What happened to one a day?"

"Either you're getting better quicker than they thought or else Billy has some clout downstairs. I tend to opt for the latter."

"You're a bundle of cheer."

"Sorry. I hate hospitals—they make me nervous. Now I

know you're all right and properly cared for, I'm going to leave if you don't mind. Be back again tomorrow. One detail before I go. I've hired a contractor and a landscape man for your house, not that you'll be needing it for a while. We'll just go ahead and do it—settle with the insurance company later. If there's any difference I'll pay them. And, Susan said to tell you she's always wanted a crack at your living room. No worry, you know her taste."

"Just tell her no mauve, Counselor. And . . . thanks, I love you both."

"Get well quick. See you tomorrow."

* * *

Billy sat in the chair next to my bed, pretending not to notice my averted head, not to hear the sniffling sounds, waiting patiently for me to get some kind of grip.

"Sorry, I was real *up* this morning. Now this. Teary as a schoolgirl."

"Cam, someone you loved very much has been taken, without any kind of warning. Somebody else tried their level best to kill you. You're in a position where you can't do anything about either. Have to be a robot not to go through moods."

"Maybe. Times when I think I'm losing my marbles, though."

"Some say you didn't have a full sack to begin with, Jarhead."

"Remember what they told us at Parris Island: You didn't have to be crazy to join the Marine Corps, but it was a distinct advantage.'"

"Thatta boy. After this, let's make a pact. Swear off hospitals forever."

"I'll buy that. Were you able to get hold of Carole's dad?"

"Last Tuesday. He'd been off fishing with some friends. Came over Thursday, by bus. He's staying with me. He spent the weekend clearing out Carole's apartment, said it helped to have something to do. He's downstairs, wants to see you. I thought I'd check and make sure you were up to it. He'll understand if you want to put it off."

"Good a time as any. Send him up when you go . . . What is he like?"

"No surprises. Tall, gray haired, kinda weatherbeaten face—looks like everybody's grandfather should. Quiet, soft-spoken man. Incredible mental toughness: he must be devastated, but he doesn't show it. His big concern is for you."

"Me?"

"He knows a good bit about you, obviously from Carole. Said you sound like exactly what she needed. He told me her letters and telephone calls were cheerful for the first time in far too long. You'll like him. A lot."

"Was she . . . buried while I was in Intensive Care?"

"I was afraid you'd ask that. Hang on, Angus, it gets rocky here. There wasn't . . . the explosions and the fire . . . they couldn't find . . ."

"Oh, my God. Not that, too?"

"Afraid so. Her father and I agreed a memorial service would be best. He insisted we wait for you to get out of the hospital. I'll do all the arrangements and invitations if you like."

"Please. I'm sure that's . . . what she would have wanted. Not that anyone gave her a choice."

"Want to skip seeing Jim?"

"Jim?"

"Jim Cummings."

"No, have him come up. And thanks, old friend, sorry to lay all this on you."

"It comes with the collar, Cam."

* * *

Everyone was there. Dick and Susan, Jane, Dana, the people from the tennis club, Max, big George, even Nick the Surly—eventually all the faces became one sympathetic blur. The service was simple but monumentally moving. Billy had written a eulogy, picked out the hymns, had the lovely old church stacked with flowers, knowing how incapable I was of doing any of those things. Jim and I sat together, having recognized a need for mutual support to get through without dissolving.

Only the big gnarled hand on my wrist saved me when Billy's round voice said the ancient words of comfort:

"Jesus said to Martha, the sister of Lazarus, I am the Resurrection and the Life, he that believeth in Me, though he were dead, yet shall he live. And whosoever liveth and believeth in Me shall never die."

I went the rest of the way in a trance. Acknowledged the condolences, said the thanks, waved the goodbyes. Only in my motel room, alone, in bed could I finally give way completely.

The words of the closing hymn had eaten through the pain and numbness, would not leave my head.

> Abide with me, fast falls the eventide,
> The Darkness deepens, Lord with me abide.
> When other helpers fail and comforts flee,
> Help of the helpless, O, abide with me.

Goodbye, Carole. God bless you and keep you safe always. Amen.

15

In my "safe house" confinement, I developed a routine, a schedule with landmarks to make the sections of the days digestible. Up at nine. Breakfast. Merv Griffin, then the game shows. Lunch. Afternoon movies, maybe a sports event on ESPN. Dinner. Ordonez. Back to bed. Repeat the same procedure next day.

The worst part was being alone. Somewhere I had read that the human organism can withstand virtually any deprivation *except* the ability to communicate. True, if I was an example. I found I was holding conversations with myself, talking back to the television set, prolonging my sessions with Chip far beyond any informational worth.

This must be how the felons in solitary feel, I thought, though having to admit it was pretty comfortable confinement. Made the final adjustment one day in yet another mental dialogue. "Why are you here? Because my friends in the police department don't want me shot, stabbed, or permanently damaged. Isn't this a little better choice? Besides, stud, it can't last forever. You win. I agree. Let's see what's on HBO this afternoon." Not brilliant conversation, but what would you expect from someone who saw menu selection as a highlight of the day?

The physical recovery process continued—at an encouraging pace. The stitches had been removed from the big cuts on my foot—I could put all my weight on it without wincing or using the words the drill instructors had taught me. At the end of week two, all the bandages were off the right hand, which was still tender, but at least movable. Then the body wrap went and I could breathe without feeling the Browns linebacking corps using my chest for a hammock. Most of the bruises had disappeared, leaving only the most spectacular as reminders, and even they continued to fade. The eyebrows and hair would take longer, but every day I looked less like something Smokey the Bear had dragged out of the woods.

Ellis sent me an electronic game system—Intellivision— and a stack of game cartidges. Chip wired it to the television set and a whole new dimension was added. Now I could sit for hours, zapping Martians, skiing, playing cards against a villainous looking dealer. My favorite was golf. Nine different hole layouts, variety of clubs, ability to hit short, medium, and long. Slice, hook, straight. Screw up and you push the reset button—start all over with a clean slate. Life should be so forgiving.

Even with the games, the magazines, the books, and the television, I had too much time to fill. At first, all thoughts were about Carole, until I concluded no amount of thinking could ever bring her back, decided to concentrate on what I *could* do to help.

*   *   *

"I had a weird idea today, Chip, let me try it on you. Has to do with the Mayor's Commission on Pornography. We've been guessing all along that maybe it was one of the people being investigated that killed Tom."

"Right. What else is new?"

"What if it was one of the people *doing* the investigating? What if Tom was about to uncover something rotten in John Q. Community Leader's life."

"Starting with the mayor, maybe?"

"Start anywhere you like. You have the list. What do you think?"

"Think you've been cooped up too long, *compadre.*"

"But how do you *know*? They have to be worth at least a look."

"In due time. I'd rather keep pushing against Diaz and friends. Save the civic biggies for in case we come up dry."

"Speaking of dry, how you coming with Goodman?"

"Look, if I want to get abuse, I'll start spending my evenings with Hampton. You're getting worse than him . . . or he is. Whatever."

"Sorry. Just frustrating sitting here playing games while you guys are doing all the work. Let's try again. Has anyone had the opportunity to look into the late Paul Goodman's life?"

"Much better. Answer's yes, results damn inconclusive. His wife divorced him while he was up at Tallahassee, moved the family back to Buffalo. Goodman reported regularly to his parole officer, no history of violations. His last tax return listed him as self-employed, income of thirty-two thousand. Tax-free municipal bonds. Ex-partner said Goodman had at least that much capital before the milking operation, so that seems legit. Neighbors remember him as a quiet man—no girls, no big parties. Spoke civilly when spoken to, otherwise, El Clammo."

"Sounds lousy so far."

"Agreed. Except for one thing. He had the *Miami Herald* delivered everyday by a local carrier, Crane Distributing."

"Didn't know that was illegal."

"Shut *up*. The man from Crane told our Coral Gables man Goodman made a deal with him. Everyday delivery except the middle week of every month—said he went out of town then, didn't want to waste the money."

"Where did he go?"

"We don't know. They tossed his rooms pretty good. No charge slips, no airline coupons, no record, no rental-car receipts. Tried the airlines, no record on a Paul Goodman for any of them."

"So he wasn't in Coral Gables the night Tom was killed. Dammit, Chip, it's the right pattern. Goodman could still be our guy."

"Highly doubtful . . . hate to throw cold water on your theory."

"*How* highly doubtful, Mr. Moto?"

"Dead men don't leave message fish. They also don't dynamite cars."

"Oh. Yeah."

Back to video golf.

* * *

About a week after my Goodman brainstorm self-destructed, Ordonez showed up, this time at noon. "Get your traveling duds on, *hombre,* we're going to spring you for a little while."

"How come? Not that I'm complaining, understand."

"Your boss got a phone call from Mrs. Horton. She thinks she's found something that may be useful. Confusing message, something about a key. We're supposed to meet Ellis at her house around one. Let's *go!*"

"*Con mucho gusto, Senor Ordonez.*"

"Joo're getting better, Jankee."

Feeling better, too. It had been almost a month spent in the motel room; outside would be a more than welcome change. Sunlight, sounds, smells, colors, fresh air. I felt like an astronaut returning from a Skylab stint. Amazing how much the little things mean when you don't have them. I gave Chip the directions to the Horton house, sat back in the right-hand seat, and just sucked it all in. What had Mark called it? A hit. That was it, an outdoors, real-world hit. Sensational.

We got there shortly after one, pulling into the driveway, parking just behind Dick's big gray Lincoln. They met us at the door, Dick reintroducing Ordonez to Linda, shaking my good hand hard enough to hurt, thumping me on the back the while. A most emotional performance for him. Linda's reaction was quite different.

"Cam, I'm right sorry I didn't go to the service for your friend."

"Linda, that's perfec . . ."

"Hush. It isn't all right, it's a mortal weakness. Just felt like I couldn't stand it. First Tom, then them tryin' to do you for helpin' and that poor girl caught in the middle. Can you ever forgive me?"

"Forgiven. And forgotten. I probably would have done the same thing."

"Don't rightly think so. And here you go, takin' even more chances. Dick said he told you to quit and you wouldn't. You worry me sick."

"Relax, Linda. The biggest risk I'm running these days is getting fat. Sergeant Ordonez and his friends are taking all the hard shots. I'm locked up like a prisoner, stowed in some place I didn't even know existed."

"Well, that's some better. Look at us standin' here in the front hall. Forgotten every bit of manners Mama ever taught me. You go on back to the living room now. Got some iced tea and sandwiches for you. Just excuse me and I'll go get it from Tom's den, be right back."

"It" was a small key, no more than an inch and a half long which Linda held out for us to inspect. An old-fashioned key, a straight hollow tube with a pip at the end to turn the lock's tumbler. An ornate head of openwork metal. Brass by the look of it.

"I couldn't find the car keys yesterday, one of the kids probably got 'em somewhere. I'm keeping a box of all Tom's personal stuff—wallet, tie clasp, those kinds of things, that I'm saving for Little Tom. They have the same initials. I took his key case out, put the kids into the car, popped the case open to get the ignition key, and saw this. I got to puzzling on what it fits, wondering if it might be helpful to you. Finally, I figured the easiest thing was to call you—try to work out the answer together."

"Why do you think it might be helpful?" I asked.

"Two reasons. I knew Tom Horton like he was a part of me. Most organized man I ever saw. Used to get on me all the time—'everything to its place and a place for everything.' He wouldn't have a key in that case that he didn't use a lot. The case had car keys, house key, and one I think fits his door down to the office. Plus this.

"Member your askin' me if I'd given you all his diaries, Cam? You seemed to think there was one missin'. So, I thought maybe this fits somethin' where the diary, if there is one, could be. Maybe nothin', but it got on my mind, had to share it with you."

"An obvious question, Mrs. Horton. You're positive there's nothing in this house it could fit? Chest, a desk, box maybe?"

"Sergeant, I about tore this place apart yesterday, believe it. Every closet, every drawer, all the storage places. It's an old timey key, Tom's desk in the den is Danish modern. No fit there. If it goes to somethin' in this house, I'll tell you one thing, I sure can't find it."

"How about his locker at the Club, Linda?"

"No, Dick. We went over there three weeks ago to empty out his locker. It's a combination lock."

"Briefcase, maybe?"

"Two combinations, Sergeant. My birthday and his."

"Well, boys and girls, that would seem to narrow it down to his office at the firm. You and Jane cleaned that out, Linda. Nothing, eh?"

"No. He didn't have all that much down there. Pictures of us, diplomas, some little pottery things Betsy made him in nursery school. Jane said all his work stuff had been parceled out to the others. Files and all, you'd know more about that. What I took is in two boxes in the den. Nothin' even close."

"Hold it. Before we go down to the office. Just thought

of something. How about a safety deposit box, Linda? At your bank. Tom seemed like that sort of guy, super-squared away."

"Wrong kind of key, *hombre*."

"Sorry, Cam. We didn't have one anyway. I kept after him to get one but he never did. He thought it would be a waste of money. My jewelry's all insured, and he kept all the important papers down at the firm."

"We'll be off then, Linda—excuse us if you would, please. Glad you spotted the key, my dear. Tom *was* a creature of habit; whatever that fits was something he used often. We'll simply have to look for it. In any event, I'll phone and let you know the results. I'll call Jane, if I may, let her know we're coming."

On the way downtown, Ordonez asked Dick a series of questions on the firm's storage and security practices, hoping to focus the search effort.

"We have individual offices for the lawyers. The law library and the computer room. Two rooms for small meetings, plus the main conference room. No places for storage other than the individual offices. Anything given to us to hold is placed in the firm's safe. The Senior Partner's secretary has the inventory list of contents. Always up to date, references for additions and withdrawals. I'll check that first thing while you two look over Tom's office."

"It's still empty, then?"

"Afraid so. We've had to go outside to get Tom's replacement, not usual firm policy, but we had no choice this time. We're screening applicants still. Whoever we eventually hire will get Tom's office."

Jane was waiting for us when we arrived.

"Sergeant Ordonez, I have a message for you. Lieutenant Hampton called just after Mr. Ellis. Wanted you to call him as soon as you got here. Shall I put it through?"

"I'll get it, thanks. Dial nine for an outside number?"

"Yes. You can use Ms. Smalley's office. She's at a closing, shouldn't be back until four or so. I'll show you where it is."

So we split up, Dick to review the safe's inventory contents and records, Ordonez to answer his call, I to Horton's office to begin looking. Stripped of the personal touches it looked sterile now, almost forlorn. Bookcases with their rows of reference works, nothing on top of the credenza against the wall, the big desk bare save the student lamp. Not a great deal of options.

"Cam, you look ever so much better. You frightened me at the service. I mean, you really looked awful."

"Careful, lady, you'll turn my head. Actually, I'm about back to normal, except for this hand. Doctor says at least another month—it got singed pretty good. That where you met Ordonez?"

"Yes. Mr. Ellis introduced us. I like him, he seems very dedicated. But several times he called you *El Cojo*. What does that mean?"

"Sort of a joke. It means the man who walks with a limp."

"Not much of a joke, making fun of people."

Chip picked up the last of the conversation as he came in, "I agree with Miss Jane. It isn't much of a joke. And it's getting unfunnier by the minute."

"The phone call?"

"Yeah. We've lost Diaz. I'd like to say he flew the coop, but I'm not in the mood for humor. He slipped the man we had on him yesterday afternoon. None of the snitches know where he is."

"Somehow, I think that wasn't the only message."

"Give the man a cigar. Just before noon, they fished Darvan Williams out of a canal in Coral Springs. Couple of housewives spotted him—shook 'em up some, I'll bet. Hampton said whoever did it wasn't taking any chances. Shot in the heart, hands and feet wired together, tossed in the drink. ME thinks it must have happened sometime late last night."

"Why Williams?"

"Popular theory is the pressure's starting to get to the Sparrow. Williams has a reputation as a hothead—also as a boozer, sometime coke sniffer. Easier to snuff him than worry about what he might say to us or the grand jury."

"Another candidate gone. This is getting more and more depressing."

"More and more dangerous too, *hombre*. Right after we get done this afternoon, back you go to your little home away from home, the city nursery. I may be premature, but I think the balloon's about to go up. Hampton's voice always gets that hard edge to it when things start to pop. Right now, he sounds like George Patton. How you coming here?"

"Just beginning. Might as well tackle that desk first. Seems like the logical place to start."

A big, old Williamsburg pedestal desk. Large file drawer on each side, two smaller drawers above them. Center drawer bridging the kneehole. Huge piece, antique if I was any judge; don't see that kind of detail of handiwork much these days. Completely empty except for a piece of green blotting paper used as a lining for the center drawer. Went over it carefully, looking for secret compartments, like the two fake columns in my Queen Anne drop-front desk at home. Poked and pried, pushed and knocked, even took the handles off. We were taking the drawers out—to look at their undersides and behind them, Chip and I wrestling the cumbersome file drawers, Jane lifting out the middle one. Suddenly she gave a little gasp and dropped the drawer on Chip's foot.

"Ow, damn, that smarts. Miss Jane, we're here to look for things, not break them."

"I'm so sorry, Sergeant. It was heavier than I thought. I just . . . Cam! Look here."

In the fall, the blotting paper liner had come out of the drawer. In the center of the drawer, just past the tray for pencils and whatnot, was a keyhole, brass fitted. Linda's kind of "old timey" keyhole. With the blotting paper gone we could see the outlines of a compartment. A drawer within a drawer. The key fit perfectly, twisted easily, made a nice solid click as the tumbler turned.

Be there, I thought, just be there, you little beauty. And it was—a black and white, spiral-ring notebook, identical to those Linda had given me in the beginning. On the front it said:

Horton Diary
September 9,
to _____

I was waving it over my head like a to-be-spiked football when Dick came in to see what all the noise was about.

* * *

There were entries for each of the days. September 9 and 10, the thirteenth through the fifteenth. The last eerie to read, knowing that the author had been murdered sometime shortly after having written it. The style was all over the lot—from telegraphic to full paragraphs, from factual data to theories and questions. The style wasn't important. The contents were. Key excerpts:

September 9

3 p.m. phone call. A Mr. Dominic Fuselli. Knew I was on Mayor's commission. Wants to talk to me. Alone. Got his number, said I'd call back. 421-9575 D'fld Bch. Ansd 1st ring, prob. legit. Said he worked w/ A. Diaz, knows enuf to put blox to him. Wants immunity in Xchange. I suggested meet— both alone—Mon. nite early, Fuselli said 7, bar at Cross Trees, Fed Hgwy-Sons of Italy bowling jkt.

This could be very promising. My feeling all along is that we must reach the suppliers of the filth. Smash networks and little people will dry up. Think O agrees with me, hasn't said no yet. Wire in the Vice guys? Too early yet. Keep meeting and see what Fuselli has to deal with. Don't forget to tell Linda to hold dinner. Maybe this is break we need.

September 10

All day with Mrs. D. Hand holding time. Not very exciting, but it helps pay the rent. Went alone this time, evidently she doesn't need the banker.

Worried about Mrs. Donaldson. Particularly last 3 mos. Can't predict her moods. Today good example. Snapped at me first thing in the morning, kept right at it. Personal abuse, I wasn't experienced enough, too young why didn't the Firm have a more mature man representing her. Thank God for Smithers. She suggested break after noon meeting.

After lunch Mrs. D. fine, pleasant as could be. Rambling, tho, sometimes I didn't think she knew who I was. Wants to change will. Again. D.E. and S.P. will have a stroke. Her money tho, do what she wants. Wants to change from outright bequests to trust funds for both grandchildren. Bank lady and I to prepare best situation from tax standpoint next month. Everything else same. Foundation, bequests to Mt. Holyoke, Cancer, Heart Fund, Episc. Church. Smithers's gift same. Wonder how long this version will last?

Strange ending to meeting. She just corked off right in the middle of a sentence. Sound asleep. Snoring like that old basset hound Linda had in VA.

Long talk with Smithers after. Told her I was worried about Mrs. D.'s moods. Wondered if it could be health related or some kind of advancing senility. Smithers say Mrs. D. hates doctors. Hasn't seen one since physical last Nov., only agreed to that check-up to please Megan. Passed all tests, healthy as horse, according to doctor's reports, considering arthritis. Still worries me. People her age ought to have twice a year physicals. Look what happened to the Senator. Fine one day, then zingo, gone. Suggested to Smithers we put the old girl on twice a years. Start a day before our next month meeting/recommendation. Smithers said she would try, couldn't make any promises. Mrs. D. still boss. Good woman. Been with Mrs. D. long time, obviously cares a lot about her. Tough old buzzard to handle-this morning prime example.

Better tell D.E. about it. May want to switch me off, don't want to take chances with this client.

"He did come to see me, too. Said he would understand if I thought he could be jeopardizing the relationship. I told him he was doing a fine job—which he was—that we'd sink or swim with him."

"I'm interested in this Fuselli character. Let's move, *hombre,* back to page flipping. You need a speed-reading course?"

"We don't all have advanced degrees, Professor."

September 13

Talked to Linda over the weekend about Mrs. D. Linda agrees on the physicals program. Called Megan and recommended this week. Megan said she almost got her head bitten off last time. She did agree to try though. I feel better already.

Looking forward to Fuselli meeting tonight. Maybe the keystone we need to pull down the arch. Tape it? Bad idea, might scare him off. Time for taping later if he's selling us the straight scoop. Big story in the Sunday paper about a kiddy porn ring bust in NY. Selling 7 & 8 year old—girls and boys—not just their pictures either. Can we be far behind? Recommend to O we beef up Commission's size or establish an add-on ad hoc Task Force. Don't have the luxury of time.

September 14

I think we hit gold—maybe platinum. Fuselli hates Diaz. Will say or do anything we want to eliminate him. Names, dates, places, events. Everything from pimping to loan sharking to drugs to murder. Says pornography is just a sideline with Diaz now. Apparently they headed similar size operations, even cooperated in several ventures. In March, D. gave Fuselli $100,000 told him to disappear, he was out. Say anything, stick around and he was a dead man. Fuselli told me he laughed at Diaz—told him to get stuffed. Stopped laughing when D. produced Fuselli's three Lts. They told F., sorry, but with D. they had a piece of the action, plus territories of their own. That's how it goes, sorry Dom, it all got too big too fast for you. Fuselli took the money and ran. Sent his family back to St. Louis. Doesn't trust D. Thinks Diaz will try to shut him up, family too. Wants immunity from prosecution, new I.D. for him and family, safe house residence—preferably somewhere in Canada. Enuf income to live on, nothing fancy.

In turn, he promises enough to bury Diaz and his 3 ex-Lts. Plus implicate scores of others—retailers, operators, network people and a pipeline to a pharmaceutical house. Deerfield phone number was temporary. Girl friend he trusted. Said he had to keep moving around, didn't want to stay in any one place too long.

I told him I believed him but I needed something tangible to take to the Commission and the police. He asked what. Told him anything of a physical nature. Notes, letters, records, photos, tapes—anything I could show as factual proof. He said it would take some time to get it, it's all stashed in St. Louis. Next steps are to meet this Fri., same time same place-see what he's got.

Then I can talk to Mayor and Vice people.

Looks like time running out for the *bad guys* for a change. Thank God.

September 15

Call from J. Smithers 10:29. Talked Mrs. Donaldson into a physical exam. Oct. 8th. I asked who would do it. Dr. Carman. Robert Carman, Boca Raton. Smithers asked why I needed to know Dr. name. Told her I wanted to talk to him afterwards. Smithers said fine, could she be there too. I agreed. So, that's done.

Lunch meeting with Sgt. Poole, one of the new liaison men Vice assigned to Commission this week. Poole says they're looking into an apparent highschool prostitution ring at Cypress Beach North. Got a 15yr old. For soliciting on Monday. Working with her to try bagging whole thing. Evidently doing it to get money for drugs. Cocaine easy as candy if you have money, Poole says. Little girls. Not all that much older than Betsy. Selling themselves, making scum like Lucchese and Diaz rich. Sickening. Very frightening. Will that be what high school is like when Betsy gets there? Not if I can help it. Friday can't come too soon. If Fuselli really has it, will recommend to O and the Commission we meet his price. *Whatever* it is. Strange note on my desk when I got back after long Follert's Market meeting. Wilma checked with Dr. Carman per my request to try to shift Mrs. D. physical up a day or two, not to conflict with our meeting/recommendation to her on 8th. Carman's nurse says she doesn't have an appointment. Swear that's the date Janice gave me. Somebody's screwed up. Square that away tomorrow, first thing. Why is it little things always cause most the confusion. Easy one to fix. We have bigger and worse problems to solve.

*   *   *

"That's all of it. Next thing he did was walk out of here and get his head blown off," I said. "Who is Wilma, Dick?"

"His former secretary. She's in the steno pool now, waiting for Tom's replacement."

"Hey, Cam, I need to get going. Stuff you back in your motel and get the troops cracking on finding Fuselli. He's the closest thing I've seen to a solve yet."

"What's involved, Chipper?"

"Two-front program. Locals to see if he's still around here, which I doubt. Get on the horn to St. Louis and see if they can run him down. Between us we'll get him, assuming and praying he's still around."

"Think that's why Diaz disappeared? Went after Fuselli?"

"Could be. Anyway, no sense in taking chances with him. Oh, one thing before we go. Call this Smithers dame and find out when the old lady had her exam."

"What for?"

"You know her, for openers. Hampton's a bear on thoroughness. Dot all the 'i's and cross all the 't's'. Better we close that loop than have him chew me out for not."

"Consistency is the hobgoblin of small minds."

"*Vaya, hombre.*"

*   *   *

I called Janice, got Megan instead. "You just missed her. Dinner date with Steve, her boyfriend. Our deal is she gets weeknights off, I get weekends. Can I help?"

"No bother. Ask her to call Sergeant Ordonez in the morning. Number's on that card I gave you last time. Tell her it's about your grandmother's physical—Ordonez has all the details."

"Oh, that. Okay, no problem. Guess what they named the baby."

"Baby?"

"My brother and Ms. Space Shot."

"I give up."

"Iphigenia. Heroine in Greek mythology. Didn't I tell you they were both bonkers? What is that waif going to do with a name like Iphigenia?"

"I'm sure you'll think of something, Aunt Megan."

"I hope. Take care. See you soon, Cam."

*   *   *

Back to the pen. Ordonez couldn't wait to dump me and get back to work. Most excited I'd seen him since we started. Mr. Enthusiasm.

I hoped he was right. I'd almost forgotten how nice the outside world was.

16

I was still in my pajamas when the pounding on my motel door started. So what if it was eleven in the morning? If you're not going anywhere you might as well dress for it. I squinted through the peephole. Ordonez, looking very fierce. Now what? Open the door, boob.

"See that cute little button there. You push it and it makes a nice bing-bong. Don't have to beat on the door."

"Douse the snappy patter, *hombre*. This has been a bad day so far and it doesn't look like it's going to get much better."

"What's with you? Last night you went whistling out of here higher than three kites."

"Yeah? Well, this morning they shot my tail off. Twice. You got any coffee in this pleasure pad? I think I need to get my heart started again."

"Carafe over there on the table. Hope you like it black— otherwise we have to send for."

"Black will do. Where to start? Why didn't I listen to my mother? I could be sitting nice and quiet some place in Virginia, putting pins in the maps to show where the spies were. Not me. Not Cipriano Alfonso Felipe Ordonez Correa. *I* had to be a working cop. With a buzz saw for a lieutenant. My aching back."

"Alfonso Felipe? Sounds like a cigar."

"Careful. My ancestors were royalty in Castile while yours were wandering around worshipping trees."

"We *are* testy this morning."

"With cause. Let's start with shot one. The mayor called Hampton this morning, half terrified and half outraged, according to the boss. Cheery old Oz got a death threat this morning. Man told him if he didn't call off the Commission dogs, he'd be taking swimming lessons from Darvan Williams. Said they'd start with the mayor then go right on through the Commission. Asked Oz to tell the members this morning, else *he* would. The mayor got a little excited, probably only his laundryman knows how excited. Told Hampton he better do something in a pretty big hurry if he didn't want to spend the rest of his tour on a motorcycle.

"I almost forgot the best part. The mayor said the caller had a heavy Latin accent. Just what we needed. It couldn't have taken Hampton three and a half seconds from hangup to landing on my chest. Said if he was going motorcycling I'd be lucky to get a job guarding high school gyms at night. Went on from there."

"So what will you do?"

"What can we do? Maybe the guy is a loco, maybe not. So we put someone on the mayor round the clock. Pull back for now, go underground. Hope the St. Louis guys turn up Citizen Fuselli. Like that."

"Not that I'm totally unsympathetic, but what's all this got to do with me? I'm just a poor man's Prisoner of Zenda."

"Smart mouth. I was just coming to it. Shot number two. Your friend Janice Smithers took off."

"*What?*"

"Vanished. El Foldo. Miss Carter called me shortly after Hampton finished outlining my new career. She got up at the regular time, went down to breakfast—no Smithers. Looked through the house, outside, nothing. Finally went to Smithers's room. Most of her clothes are gone, all her makeup, usually a sure sign somebody's split for good. Miss

Carter thinks she must have left in the middle of the night. She said she waited up last night for Smithers, gave her your message, then went to bed. This morning—poof—gone with the wind."

"Why?"

"That's why I came over here. Let you do some work for a change. Think about it while I get some coffee and try to forget the lumps Hampton put on my skull."

Janice Smithers gone. In the middle of the night. Just like that. No goodbyes, just gone. I had not gotten any sort of feeling that Janice was the kind to do impulsive things. Quite the opposite. Super calm, efficient, everything in order. Megan had mentioned a boyfriend. Elopement, maybe? Nah, she and Megan were too close. She would have said something. What's changed from yesterday, why would Janice Smithers run, what could have happened to make her bail out?

Of course. Had to be.

"Chip! I think I got it. Theory, but one we can check out awful fast. What if Janice lied to Tom Horton about the physical? What if there never was one all along?"

"Why would she do that? She was a *nurse*, that was her job."

"I don't know why, but that's easy enough to check too. Means breaking radio silence though, Captain Kirk; should we risk the *Enterprise?*"

"I'm making a deal with Hampton. After this, no more lousy PI's. Go ahead, comic."

Megan sounded upset when she answered.

"Golly, I'm glad you called, Cam. It's spooky around here."

"Don't worry, probably a simple explanation. Did she leave any kind of note, any feeling for why she left, whether she'd be back?"

"Nothing. I looked everywhere. After I called Sergeant Ordonez, I went back to her room. Her jewelry case is missing. I know because we used to use each other's pins and earrings all the time. It isn't in the usual place. She's gone. Do you think something happened to her? I'm frightened."

"I doubt anyone's out to harm *you,* Megan—stay cool. One quick question. What Ordonez was going to ask Janice. When did your grandmother have her last physical exam?"

"Long time ago. November, as I recall. Last year."

"Horton's notes said Janice had scheduled one for October the eighth—a Doctor Carman."

"News to me, and I would know. Carman's the right man but it never happened. I remember Mr. Horton asking me to try to talk Gramma into it. She wouldn't have any part of it— bit my head off worse than the last time."

"Would you have any objections if I brought Carman over there today and had him take a look at her?"

"Of course not. Why?"

"I don't know, just a hunch. Hold the fort, Megan, we'll be along as soon as we can."

I hung up the phone, turned to Ordonez, "Your ball."

"My ball? I don't know Doctor Carman, don't even have his telephone number."

"The phone book is very helpful that way. If Carman's any kind of good, he'll have a full slate of patients. PI Mac-Cardle won't cut much ice with him . . . Detective Sergeant Ordonez will."

"I think we're really doing this just to get you out of stir for another day, *hombre.*"

"Big part of it."

* * *

An unfamiliar silver Audi 5000 was in the driveway when we arrived. Undoubtedly Carman's, I thought, the MD plates confirming the thought. Megan was waiting for us at the door. I introduced her to Chip, and we trailed behind her into the living room.

"Doctor Carman's upstairs with Gramma, Cam. It's probably coincidence, but I'm glad he's here today. Gramma's been very cranky all morning. She feels dizzy and nauseous. That's why I sent him straight up without waiting for you."

"Good idea, Megan. Anything new on Janice? Telephone call or such?"

"Nothing. I'm afraid she's gone for good. Without so much as a goodbye or even a letter of explanation. That's what's so scary; it's completely unlike her. Do either of you have any feeling for why she left? I'm really worried."

"Closest I've come was elopement, but that doesn't make sense. She would have told you—that's a happy kind of trip."

"Also not very likely. *She* was willing enough but men like Steve Dorn aren't too crazy about the marriage number."

"You said Steve Dorn, Miss Carter?"

"Her boyfriend, Sergeant."

"Tall, slim, salt and pepper hair? Forty or so?"

"That sounds like him. She was forever trying to get him to use that goo you see on TV, takes the gray away. He said he couldn't be bothered. You know him?"

"Unless it's the biggest fluke of the year. He's a cop, works in my section."

"That could be. He said he worked for the city of Cypress Beach. I never asked him what he did there."

"I'll run him down, when I go back tonight—maybe Steve's got an idea of why Miss Smithers would take off."

"Would you call me, Sergeant? Once you know, I mean?"

"Of course."

We were interupted by the appearance of Doctor Carman. A small, stocky man, snow-white hair above a florid complexion. A walking illustration of high blood pressure. He gave us all a disparaging look, one of those "what have you naughty children been doing while the adults were away" glares. Megan began to introduce us. The doctor, making the wave-off signs of someone who wants to get to the point quickly, said, "Miss Carter, may I see you for a moment? Alone."

"Doctor Carman, the only reason you're here is because

of these men. They're friends of ours. What about my grand-mother?"

"Very well. I simply sought to save you some embarass-ment."

"What does *that* mean, Doctor?"

"I have taken the liberty of summoning an ambulance. I have also reserved room for her at St. Aloysius. I chose St. Aloysius because it has the most extensive alcohol and drug detoxification unit in the area."

"I'm afraid I don't understand."

"The arthritis notwithstanding, your grandmother's con-stitution is fundamentally sound. However, I think someone in this household—with or without her consent—has been in-jecting her with some form of narcotic substance. The needle marks are all too plain. I suspect her nausea and dizziness to be a first reaction to withdrawal. I have given her a mild seda-tive, enough to hold her until we can get her to the hospital. The experts there will be able to tell me precisely what sub-stance was used. Of course, Miss Carter, I have no choice other than to report this incident to the police. Even if I wanted to . . . avoid it . . . the recordkeeping process at St. Aloysius is quite strict."

"You just *did* report it to the police, Doctor. I'm Ser-geant Ordonez, Cypress Beach PD. Here's my ID."

"Good, Sergeant, saves that part, then. Perhaps you would be good enough to accompany us to the hospital?"

"Afraid I can't. This man, Mr. MacCardle, is in my pro-tective custody. I can arrange to have someone meet you there. Here's my card. Please let me know when the test re-sults are in. If I'm not there, please ask for Lieutenant Hampton."

"Very well, Sergeant. Meanwhile, I shall stay with Mrs. Donaldson until the ambulance arrives. A most shabby affair, Miss Carter, most shabby indeed."

We sat in the living room, Megan crying softly, as Mrs. Donaldson was loaded into the ambulance. Watched it pull away, followed by the doctor, until the siren faded into silence.

"Miss Carter, I hate to ask you questions right now, but I have my job. I'm going to start by reading you your rights."

"Chip!"

"It's the law, *hombre*. Black and white. Do you understand, Miss Carter? Would you like to call your attorney?"

"No. Go ahead, Sergeant, I'll tell you anything I can."

"Did you have any knowledge that your grandmother might have been taking drugs of any sort?"

"My God, no."

"In your opinion, would your grandmother have taken drugs willingly? Arthritis can be very painful."

"Not Gramma Julie. Never! She was like a Mormon—no stimulants of any kind. Not even Coca-Cola. And she is so strong willed, stubborn. Any pain she would simply fight down . . . disregard. Janice told me she practically had to beg her to take her vitamins."

"Leaves only one answer, Chip. Janice Smithers. But why?"

"I imagine we'll only know that when we talk to *her*. Miss Smithers was entirely responsible for your grandmother's care?"

"Yes, I would take her supper tray up to her on weeknights, make sure she ate. As to anything else, Janice took care of it all. I'd be too terrified to—I'm not trained as a nurse."

"I see. Where did Miss Smithers keep the medical supplies? In your grandmother's room?"

"No, in a specially rigged closet in her own room. She had a big, black satchel, you know, a physician's bag. We joke about it. Doctor Smithers's rounds. What a bizarre thought *that* is."

We went upstairs, into the back of the house, to the suite where Janice had lived. The special closet had a full assortment of first-aid gear, bottles of rubbing alcohol, various body salves, analgesics, multivitamin-complex bottles, laxatives. But no black bag, no hypodermic syringes, no sign of other than over-the-counter drugs. Doctor Smithers had taken the tools of her trade with her, apparently.

Before leaving, Chip asked Megan not to leave the area until Janice Smithers was apprehended and questioned. He was nice enough about it but very official. She could stay home or at a motel, but she must keep him informed as to her whereabouts at all times until all the questions were resolved. A deep, deep look of pain in her dark brown eyes. I tried to soften things a little for her.

"Megan, we know this has been a terrible thing for you. Tough to carry by yourself. Can you get someone to come stay with you? Or maybe, like Chip said, go to a motel. A lot easier that way."

The eyes turned hard as flint. "*Mr.* MacCardle, I'm a Donaldson. We care for our own. I shall stay right here in case my grandmother needs me. Do I make myself perfectly clear, sir?"

Phew!

*   *   *

"You were pretty rough on her back there, Chip. I mean, she's only a kid."

"What did you say that estate was worth? Twenty-five million plus? That's a lot of money to dick around with."

"You don't think she did. . . ?"

"No, I don't think she did it. I'm for Smithers all the way. Megan does seem like a decent, honest person. But until we have Smithers in the bag and talking, I can't afford to overlook any possibility. Stranger things have happened, *hombre,* particularly with all that loot up for grabs."

"But, nevertheless . . ."

"But, nevertheless, your ass, pal. Look, we have a nice easy relationship. Let's keep it that way. However, there are times to be serious. Of all people you should know that—since someone's trying to *kill* you. But I think sticking spikes into little old ladies is pretty grim stuff, too. Anybody who doesn't is playing without a full deck. *Comprende?*"

"You're right. . . . Sorry. Still friends?"

"Goes without saying, *hombre.*"

"What's next?"

"On this deal? Talk to Steve, see if he can be helpful. Wait for the doctor's report. If it goes down the way it looks now, put out an all points on Janice Smithers."

"I can't imagine her being involved in something like this. You don't know her. She is Miss Keep-Your-Cool, get it done properly, English field hockey player. The kind that doesn't get traffic tickets. I don't disagree with you, I think she did it, but I'm damned if I can figure why."

"As I said to Megan Carter, there isn't any use speculating. Just have to hear from the lady herself. Here we are back once again to the Ordonez Hilton. You don't mind my not walking you to the door. Got some work to do. Probably see you around eight, hopefully know a little more by then."

"You were right about one thing."

"What's that?"

"The day didn't get any better."

"Not over yet either, *compadre.*"

*   *   *

Ham steak Polynesian, roasted new potatoes, sliced tomatoes vinaigrette, bottle of Valpolicella for palate lubrication. Not exactly starvation rations. I stacked the leavings back on the tray, carried it outside for disposal. Save the rest of the wine to help me get through the seven o'clock news. Bing-bong. Doorbell. Ordonez.

"Found out how to work it, huh?"

"I'm a quick study."

"How was the rest of the day? Want a glass of this?"

"Shouldn't, but I will. Where do you want to start?"

"Medical report."

"The experts say cocaine. Yeah, I thought people only snort it too. You can do that, or eat it, or inject it, and result's the same. Doctors don't know for sure how long she's been on it. Estimate six to nine months, time to build a tidy dependency."

"How do they get her off?"

"Beats me. I didn't ask that one. Those guys run a crack unit, though. Probably got a detox rehabilitation program for anything, anybody. They seemed pretty confident she'd be fine after a while."

"You tell Megan?"

"She was *there*. In the waiting room. Said she wasn't leaving until she knew. Tough kid, tough in the good sense, that is. This is nice wine, good fruity taste to it."

"What did Steve have to say?"

"Ah . . . interesting coincidence. Officer Dorn called in sick this morning. Asian flu. As common around here as beriberi. I called him at his apartment. Twice. Once from my desk and then from the hospital. No answer."

"So you picked him up."

"For what? Being sick? Malingering? Too soon."

"Too *soon?*"

"Give the guy the benefit of the doubt. Between you and me, civilian, in the gray areas we protect our own. Steve's got sixteen years on the force. He's earned a little leeway,"

"So now what?"

"Depends. He calls in sick tomorrow, I talk to him. Doesn't call in, we go knocking on his door. If he's there, fine; if not, we give the door a little push, maybe it opens up, these things happen. That's how it goes with the terrible locks these days, cheaply made."

"Our Miss Dope Fiend?"

"Once we had the test results, Hampton agreed to an APB. It's been issued by now. I brought Miss Carter in with me to give us Smithers's description. She did that, plus gave me a picture, unexpected bonus. Smithers in a two piece bathing suit. You never told me about that, too bad all we can use is the face. Not that I expect she'll be traipsing around the country in Cole of California."

"Not a bad five hours' work, Sergeant."

"Every once in a while. Finish off the last of that before I go?"

"To be sure, working wino."

* * *

It was a much more somber Ordonez who arrived the following night—tired, with the wounded look of someone deeply disappointed. One glance told me all I needed to know. Definitely not a night for wine and ho-hos.

"I gave him until noon to call in. People oversleep, particularly if they're sick. After that, I couldn't cover for him anymore. Loyalty goes just so far. Took a couple of patrolmen with me and went over to his place."

"Gone?"

"With a capital 'G.' There isn't anything left but furniture and a bunch of old magazines. Must have been planning it for some time. He couldn't clear out like that on a day's notice."

"That's too bad."

"It gets worse. I said he left nothing behind. Not quite true. We found this under a laundry bag in the bedroom closet. Must have missed it when he scooped up the rest."

"What's in the envelope?"

"Cocaine. About a grand of it by the heft. God knows how much more there was."

"Where do you think he got it?"

"Bet your behind it wasn't bought on the street. Not with him supporting every bookie in South Florida. Tomorrow we start looking back through the drug disposal records. Dime to a donut his name will appear on the squad list. They're charged with getting *rid* of it. Burn, dump, flush, whatever— depends on what kind and how much. We get enough of that crap pouring through here every week to make us the biggest source in the country.

"So Mr. Dorn could have plenty to finance their run. Easy to transport, easy to sell, fantastic value per gram of weight carried. Damn it all, Cam, I kept hoping I was wrong."

"A bad cop."

"They say all sectors of society have bad guys. Business, academics, sports, you name it. I even saw the other day they're looking into the Catholic Church in Chicago. Some priest dipping in, evidently. But it hurts when it's one of yours. Sixteen years in uniform. Not a great cop, but a steady one. Now this. A real downer, *hombre*, makes you doubt the whole value system."

"*His* value system. Yours seems to be doing just fine. You put the word out on him?"

"Yeah. Three o'clock. Don't think that's not embarassing, either. Telling the world one of ours went sour and we need *their* help to arrest him. Actually, we issued two, in case they're traveling together. They won't be—doubles the risk. They'll have split up, maybe agreed to meet some place after it's all died down. If we don't nab them, that is, *and* presuming they still have a reason to be together."

"So we sit and wait."

"On this one that's about all we can do. At least for now. I feel like going out and getting stoned, if I thought it would make me feel any better."

"Any news on the Fuselli locating front, or am I depressing you even more?"

"I'd almost forgotten about him. That's the only bright spot today. Reportedly, he was seen yesterday in Clayton, that's just outside St. Louis proper. A definite make, according to SLPD. They think they should have him by the end of the week. At least he's alive. With my luck, I figured he was a gone goose by now—my ticket to life as a gym guard."

"*There's* a hint of the old Ordonez style."

"Shadow of a hint, *companero*. A very bad day. Definitely not one to hold for futures. I'll have to skip tomorrow, Cam. Unless something big comes up. I'm a month behind on the paperwork and we've got the drug disposal project still to review."

"I'll survive, Chip. Make sure *you* do. We're going to see some light at the end of this tunnel. Soon."

"Let's hope it isn't a locomotive."

*   *   *

I settled back into the mindless routine, allowing the days to pass almost without acknowledgement. Watched November die in a flurry of football telecasts and specials about the Pilgrim Fathers.

Blew Thanksgiving, my all-time favorite holiday. A time for reunions, for sharing, for realizing what a fortunate people Americans are, the current economic woes notwithstanding. This was the bleakest Thanksgiving since the one in 'Nam. And at least that had been made bearable by the presence of friends and the special attention the cooks gave to providing a festive meal. Alone in the motel room, I picked at the turkey dinner, finally gave it up as a total loss. Dreary thoughts on death. Carole, Tom Horton, even Goodman. Scant cause for thanks in this year of bloodshed, of violence and death.

News from the outside world was bad and good. The bad news was that Diaz, Smithers, and Dorn were still missing. The good news was they'd found Fuselli, had him sequestered in some "safe house" like this one, were working with him to compile and shape the material for a grand jury. Chip said the inside word was quite encouraging, a lot of trash was about to get swept up. Maybe there was something to be thankful for at that. Meanwhile, it was back to the books, the games, and the wondering. I remembered an old movie, staple fare on all the late, late shows. Starring Sonja Henie and a cast of thousands. A movie called *Holiday on Ice*. It looked as if that was going to be my lot, as well.

*   *   *

December 14 began like all the other days of confinement. Breakfast, television, my sixth attempt to get involved with James Michener's *The Covenant,* finding it still very tough to slog through, putting it away for assault later on. ESPN was televising the World Series of College Rodeo. A little much, even for an avowed sports fanatic. Maybe a round of golf on the Intellivision. Watch the fourth hole, it's the one that always louses up the score.

Thump, thump, thump on the door, someone kicking at it. Five o'clock. Far too early for dinner. To the peephole, men, prepare to repel boarders. Ordonez! Features twisted into the first grin I'd seen in over a month.

"Pepperoni pizza? Half a case of Amstel? You get promoted, Chip?"

"Much, much better news, *compadre,* though I truly do deserve a promotion."

"Come in, sit down. Quickly—what we don't need is cold pizza and warm beer. What we do need is the cause for all this revelry."

"Call from the San Antonio PD. This afternoon. They nailed Janice Smithers at the Trailways station. Holding her now while we execute the extradition papers. We should have her in two days."

"Aww . . . right! Dorn with her?"

"No. Didn't think they'd travel together. But we got one of them anyways. Truly a cause for celebration, *hombre.*"

"*Verdad,* as we used to say in the San Juan office."

"*Salud.* To Janice Smithers and the SAPD."

"I'll drink to that."

17

I stalked around the room all day Thursday, counting down the hours until Ordonez's arrival. Tried to do a thousand things and put them all aside, unable to concentrate. Smithers's statement could be critical or only marginally helpful. What were they asking? What was she saying? Why wasn't I there? Nothing to do but pace and fret and stew, all tasks at which I had become highly skilled, willing away the interminable hours of the day. Six o'clock, then seven and eight—where was he? Nine, nine thirty, ten—surely there's a limit to the nerves' endurance.

When the doorbell rang, I didn't even bother with the peephole routine, just popped the door open and dragged Ordonez inside. He looked bone weary but very, very pleased.

"Where in hell have you been, it's after ten, for Godsakes."

"Long day, *hombre*. She had a lot to say. You'll see. We got it all down, played the tape for the Assistant DA, then transcribed it. *That's* what took the big chunk of time. Fumble-fingered typists. Wish we could go back to females again—Women's Lib has not been a total blessing for us."

"Will you stop blathering? What did she say?"

"It's all here in the transcript. She also threw in some freebies. Thank God for true love."

"What does that mean?"

"You'll see. You read and I'll help myself to one of the leftover Amstels. Skip the first two pages—it's just background junk to establish her identity, all stuff you already know. Start at the top of page three and happy reading, *compadre*."

A standard Cypress Beach Police Department format, legal-sized transcript, bound with a blue cover. As instructed, I flipped to page 3, settled back to read.

Page 3 (of 13)

Q. That completes the personal identification portion, Miss Smithers. We will now turn to specific questions.

A. I should like to make a personal statement first, if I may.

Q. Certainly, providing it is relevant.

A. I must let you be the judge of that. I am prepared to offer certain information on a matter related to the reason for my detention. In return, I request leniency in my judgment. What I believe the American television police programs call "copping a plea."

Q. In that you are familiar with that term, Miss Smithers, you also know we cannot promise anything. However, I can assure you that a cooperative attitude on your part will be recognized. Is that understood?

A. Very well. Where shall I begin?

Q. You left your place of employment with no notice. Strange behavior for a trained nurse, charged with the physical well-being of your employer. Why?

A. A message that a policeman was inquiring about Mrs. Donaldson's medical history. That meant to me the nightmare was about to occur again.

Q. Nightmare?

A. Any reputable physician examining Mrs. Donaldson could not fail to notice it. It simply cannot withstand scrutiny.

Q. What can't withstand scrutiny, Miss Smithers?
A. The physical and chemical evidence. The presence of
    narcotics in her system. Such discovery would mean the
    end of my career and my incarceration, Mr. Dorn was
    quite specific on that account.

                                        Page 4 (of 13)

Q. Mr. Dorn?
A. Officer Steven Dorn of your Cypress Beach Police De-
    partment.
Q. Please describe your relationship with Officer Dorn, Miss
    Smithers.
A. We are . . . were . . . lovers.
Q. You may be aware that Mr. Dorn is currently a fugitive
    from justice. Have you any knowledge of his where-
    abouts, Miss Smithers?
A. No. In hell, I hope. This dreadful affair is entirely his
    doing. I curse the day I met him.
Q. Miss Smithers, this is becoming confusing. What does
    your relationship, or former relationship, with Officer
    Dorn have to do with your flight the evening of Novem-
    ber 23?
A. It has everything to do with it. The forfeit of an honor-
    able position, penury and prison—none would have oc-
    curred were it not for Mr. Dorn.
Q. Miss Smithers, please try to be more specific.
A. Perhaps if I might be allowed to describe what occurred
    from the beginning . . .
Q. Certainly. Whatever you think will help us. Please do try
    to stick to the major points, however. We will raise ques-
    tions if pertinent details seem missing.

A. Quite. As you know, I have been in Mrs. Donaldson's employ for over ten years. It has not always been the easiest of relationships. Over time, it has become workable and, I dare say, could have been described as mutually satisfactory. On the eve of my fifth anniversary of employment, Mrs. Donaldson informed me at supper that I was to be a beneficiary in her will. Specifically, I was promised a bequest of two hundred fifty thousand dollars, a promise later confirmed when a new will was drawn. The amount was increased to four hundred thousand in the following years, again as a mark of faithful service. This bequest is contained in her will extant. Thus my welfare and future security were provided for amply. Good salary, comfortable residence, lodging and meals included. A most comfortable estate, with financial independence assured.

Q. Officer Dorn, Miss Smithers?

A. Just so. I thought you would find the background appropriate to what I shall be relating. Shall I proceed?

Q. Please. Again, with a caution as to relevancy.

A. I met Mr. Dorn in May of last year, at a small pub friends of mine own in Delray Beach. I found him quite likeable, then. Quiet, polite, most pleasant. When he asked me to dinner, I was pleased to accept. We continued to keep company, sporadically at first, eventually

often and exclusively. We became lovers—the first such relationship for me since breaking my engagement eleven years ago. I even entertained thoughts of marriage and ultimately a shared retirement in our own home. Spinster lady's fantasy, as subsequent events bear out. If only I could have known, all would be quite different.

Q. Miss Smithers.

A. Do try to be patient. I discovered Mr. Dorn to be an inveterate gambler, hopeless really, like an alcoholic. Apparently he wasn't very good at it, often complaining of his poor luck and receipt of incorrect advice. All of his salary went into betting on horses. My money furnished us the few dinners and entertainment we could afford. A year ago, October, he came to me and begged my help. He told me he owed $25,000 to a bookmaker who threatened his life if the debt were not repaid. He swore to me he would stop gambling if I would clear his debt. It took almost all my savings, but I did it. Sounds foolish, of course, but I loved him. People in love do foolish things. In January of this year, he came to me again. This time the amount was smaller, nine thousand dollars, but one impossible for me to cover. Mr. Dorn suggested we sell some of Mrs. Donaldson's jewelry to discharge the obligation. He argued she must have chests full—quite true—and wouldn't miss it. I was to give him the

Page 7 (of 13)

jewelry, and he in turn would sell it confidentially. Once more only—after that he would be quits with gambling. I wanted so badly to believe him. I did it. And so the nightmare began.

Q. Miss Smithers, for the record, you stole the jewelry and Officer Dorn effected its resale? Can you describe the article or articles in question?

A. The first occasion?

Q. There were others?

A. I'm afraid so. It was the one in early March which precipitated the real trouble.

Q. Perhaps you could describe that for us, then?
A. Entirely too well. It was a diamond ring with two emerald baguettes flanking. When I described it, Mr. Dorn assured me it would be ample to account for his current debt. A tragic choice, as it happened. Unknown to me, it was the first major piece of jewelry Mr. Donaldson gave his wife—enormous sentimental value. I had never seen her so much as look at it before, but one afternoon shortly after we sold the ring, she asked for it. A dream about her late husband had triggered the wish to hold something dear. I brought her the appropriate chest, feigned shock and dismay at the ring's disappearance. Fortunately, Mrs. Donaldson is a frightful bigot. Her feeling was that Obeliah, our maid, was responsible for the theft. "Darkies have been stealing from me for years" were her actual words. Rather than go to the police straight off, she planned to confront Obeliah the following day when she came to work, *then* turn her over to

Page 8 (of 13)

the police. That night I told Mr. Dorn what had happened. He felt we could allow neither the confrontation nor any subsequent investigation. Tracing the missing jewelry would eventually implicate him and lead to me as the accomplice. Result in dismissal and criminal charges for both of us. I had no notion what to do, I was terribly afraid. I wanted to make a clean breast of it to Mrs. Donaldson and hope for her mercy. Mr. Dorn wouldn't hear of it. He said wealthy people had no concern for servants, that Mrs. Donaldson would surely ruin us both. Then he told me he could secure a supply of cocaine, sufficient to see us through a month, from a street contact of his. Interim, he could get himself assigned to one of the disposal units for drugs at the Police

Department. He said he could only utilize that source once, but that it should be enough to last the duration.

Q. Again, for the record, Miss Smithers, Officer Dorn intended to divert quantities of cocaine from their mandated disposal?

A. Intended and did so. When we fled, he estimated the remaining stock in excess of three hundred thousand dollars worth. "At street" as he called it. It was to be our escape fund, if it ever became necessary.

Q: We're getting ahead of sequence. What was the use Mr. Dorn proposed to make of the initial cocaine?

A. An appallingly simple plan. Controlled injections twice a day, under the guise of vitamin B–12 injections her doctor had recommended in November. The only medical treatment she would permit me. May God help me, I acceded to the plan. The thought of the loss of my in-

Page 9 (of 13)

tended husband, occupation, my future, and a jail sentence was too dire an alternative to consider.

Q. Weren't you concerned about being discovered, Miss Smithers?

A. No. Perhaps I should have been. I knew that Mrs. Donaldson hated doctors, refused to have anything to do with them. She was well along in years, though healthy, save the arthritis. But she was beginning to lose the will to live, husband and most friends departed, cooped up in bed, capable of doing little unaided. So the plan was to keep her under control until she died a natural death. At her age—it seemed not too long a wait. At which point, I would inherit my bequest and all would have reached a natural conclusion. I even rationalized that the cocaine would help her through the arthritic pains. That, indeed, I was doing her a service.

Q. Weren't you concerned that when she did die, examination for cause of death might have revealed the presence of cocaine? How could you explain that?

A. Straightforwardly. My patient was an elderly, wealthy woman, in constant pain. She asked me to purchase drugs for her and I did. I would admit to injecting it, at her request, saying I acted under the orders of my employer who was a consenting adult. What was I to do? Either comply or be sacked, including the probable forfeiture of a sizable bequest. Under those circumstances, I can't believe a single juror would vote for punishment.

Q. Then you received the message to call Sergeant Ordonez?

Page 10 (of 13)

A. Yes, and realized we had no choice but to abandon the plan and flee. It had happened once before; I shall cover that subsequently.

Q. Where did you plan to go, Miss Smithers?

A. Mexico, then on into South America. We traveled separately, planned a final meeting in San Antonio. Mr. Dorn was to sell the balance of the cocaine, purchase false identification papers for us; we would then live on the rest of the proceeds. Mr. Dorn said one can live quite handsomely in several South American countries on comparatively little.

Q. What went wrong?

A. I arrived per schedule at the agreed upon motel in San Antonio. Once I had stayed a week beyond the assigned date, I knew one of two terrible things had happened. Either he had been apprehended, or I had been duped, abandoned. I made a long distance telephone call to the Cypress Beach Police Department. I told them I might have information as to the whereabouts of a fugitive named Steven Dorn, but did not choose to get involved if he had already been apprehended. They assured me he had not been. I made up a vague story placing him in Atlanta somewhere and hung up. At that point, I knew I had been betrayed, that I could count on nothing further from Mr. Dorn. My one thought was to exit the country, decide where to go once I got out. I was apprehended one hour before departure of a three day charter, a round trip I had no intention of completing.

Page 11 (of 13)

Q: All quite clear so far, Miss Smithers. Frightening as well. Previously, you said "It happened once before." Specifically, what had happened?

A: That is the additional related information I mentioned. I hope you will bear it and my previous responses firmly in mind. That I am volunteering this information. A young barrister, attorney, you would say, was assigned to handle Mrs. Donaldson's legal affairs. Horton was his name, Thomas Horton. He began pressing me about her physical condition, urging me to arrange to have her examined. In my capacity, I could scarcely refuse, although I had no intention of doing anything of the sort. He kept after me and Miss Megan until I had to do something or look terribly suspicious. I gave him a ficticious date on which Mrs. Donaldson was to be examined, hoping it would give us time to think. Mr. Dorn's immediate choice was to kill him, in such a manner as to be untraceable. He told me he had been an expert marksman in the service and that he had the appropriate weapon to execute the mission without detection. I wanted nothing to do with murder and I said so. Anything but that. I urged Mr. Dorn to devise a better solution. I reminded him we were running out of time. Later, I received a telephone call from him saying the matter had been taken care of. The following morning's paper told the story. When I reproached him, he said it had been the only way all along, that I was foolish to have pretended otherwise. I asked him what had become of the weapon. He said he'd given it for safekeeping to a former army friend in Cypress Beach. Curious last name, Hogg. His first name is Albert, as I recall. I imagine you can locate him easily enough.

Page 12 (of 13)

Q. Why murder, Miss Smithers? Why not simply take off, as you did this time?

A. We had to react so quickly. We hadn't been prepared. We had no contingency plan because we never thought there was the slightest chance of being discovered. Had we, I should never have agreed to any part of it from the first.

Q: Once more, Miss Smithers, are you saying that Officer Dorn did, in fact, murder Thomas Horton.

A. I am.

Q. One last topic, please. You are aware that a Mr. A. C. MacCardle was hired to investigate Mr. Horton's murder?

A. Yes. I have spoken with him on more than one occasion.

Q. Are you aware that an attempt was made on Mr. Mac-Cardle's life, notably the implantation of an explosive device in his automobile. And that a woman was killed as a result?

A. Yes, I read of it in the newspaper. Despicable affair.

Q. Miss Smithers, were you involved in any way with that attempt on Mr. MacCardle's life?

A. I was not.

Q. To your knowledge, was Officer Dorn involved in the attempt?

A. He was not. If he had been, I would be delighted to tes-tify against him. Please be assured of that. I did ask him after I read about it if he was in any way involved. He swore not. It would also seem far more likely, had he tried, that he would have attempted to dispose of Mr. MacCardle in the same manner as that of Mr. Horton. In any event, I cannot, in honesty state that Mr. Dorn was responsible.

Page 13 (of 13)

Q. That about finishes our first session, Miss Smithers. Would you care to add anything before we wrap this up?
A. Only that I hope you agree I have done my utmost to be cooperative. I wish you good luck and Godspeed in the apprehension of Steven Dorn.

END INTERROGATION SESSION I

I'd gotten so fascinated with her story, I read it straight through. Now I laid it aside, uncapped the last Amstel bottle, and walked around the room, thinking.

A dismal reason for Tom Horton to die. Killed because of his concern for an elderly client's health. Killed because of a spinster's dependence on an unsuccessful horse player. An ironic, dingy way to die. The poor, well-meaning bastard.

And what a lousy trade Janice Smithers had made—a lifetime of dignity and security for disgrace and a stay in the jug. She had said something about love making people do foolish things.

Love that English understatement.

* * *

"What do you think, Cam?"

"Helluva story, Chipper, a helluva story. Funny thing is, I feel sorry for her. She was no child. Guy comes along that makes her feel like a woman again, somebody she could maybe share the rest of her life with. . . . Doesn't excuse what she did, but easy to see how she got there. Agree?"

"You forgot one thing. This was only the first session and all we got was her side of it. She could be lying through her teeth."

"Hello, Mr. Cynicism. You got to admit she sure *sounas* plausible."

"That she does. But I'll feel better when we have Steve Dorn's version to compare it with."

"You said, 'freebie' information. What did you mean?"

"She didn't have to mention Tom Horton's murder or tie it to Steve. She could have admitted to the thefts and the drug ministrations—which are de facto anyway—let it go at that."

"You're right. Wonder why she did it?"

"Put yourself in her place, *hombre*, assuming what she said is true. She risks everything because of Dorn. Even when they split, the intent is to get together. So he sends her to a phony meeting place and takes off. She sits in a motel room, scared to death, waiting for him to show and make it all right again. If he misses by a day or so, that's understandable, no sense taking high risks to meet a tentative timetable. As the days wear on she gets the sinking feeling she's been dumped, that she gambled it all and lost. One desperate hope, perhaps 'my darling' has been captured. Doesn't make her situation any easier, but at least she feels better mentally. Slam *that* door. Right now she'd hang the Brinks Robbery on him if she thought it would stick."

"What will happen to her?"

"For now, nothing. Bind her over, no bail, hold her until we get Dorn. If that takes forever, they can always try her for the thefts and the drugging of Mrs. Donaldson. That's enough to put her away for fair."

"Where does that leave us?"

"On the bright side, Old Lady Donaldson's safe. We get this Hogg character to verify Smithers's story about Steve's weapon, find out what it was. Tie that in with his drug theft and fencing activity. Not ironclad, but a pretty good case."

"What's the dark side?"

"If what she said hangs together, we've got Horton's murderer. So your job's over.

"But *our* job's far from over. We still don't know who's trying to kill *you.*"

I could hear the words of my great aunt Fiona, not one of the world's all time optimists, quoting Robert Burns:

> Now a' is done that men can do,
> And a' is done in vain.

I sure as hell hope not, Aunt Fee.

18

I'd been right about the year end. Holiday on ice. Estranged from the real world, observing it only through Chip's nightly visits, the newspapers, and television. They weren't doing a very good job of managing the world without me. Interest rates and unemployment up, productivity and the GNP down. Layoffs, cutbacks, strikes. A jumbo jet crash in Spain, riots in Nicaragua, escalation to near-war levels of the crisis in the Middle East—again. All things considered, I might be better off staying in my room permanently. It worked for Howard Hughes, didn't it?

"Tonight on 'Sixty Minutes,' we'll be talking to Mr. A. C. MacCardle of Lighthouse Point, Florida. Mr. MacCardle has been in protective custody for the last fifty-seven years. Tonight we'll get his views on the new morality, President Julie Eisenhower's foreign policy, and the savage war raging in Antarctica."

Lunacy, sheer lunacy. Legacy to a shut-in.

Christmas cards reached in to touch my world. A photographic one from my brother in Chicago—clearly Tess was about to make me an uncle for the fourth time. Cards from former teammates, retired and scattered across the country. Hammering Henry teaching sociology, curious for a defensive back who majored in maiming at Grambling. Big Bob Bucciarelli, a corrections officer at Attica, uniformed to the end. The Main Man, now a State Farm Insurance agent in Dallas, good hands indeed.

Even got one from the Pearl, the Sacre Coeur Cathedral print of Yuletide past, a reflection of her fine eighteenth-century mind. At least she didn't complain about the late alimony payments.

The best wasn't a card at all. It was a semi-grimy piece of ruled paper apparently torn from a pocket notebook.

Dear Cam,
　　It's late at night here at the fish camp and I'm more than a little drunk, so please excuse the stationery. It's been a tough two months since Carole died. Probably just as tough for you. Tonight my partner, Henry Pappas, gave me a piece of Greek philosophy I want to share with you. The way he said it—half full of ouzo—goes something like this. God grant me the · strength to accept what I cannot change and the courage to live the balance of my days in dignity. God bless you, son.

Jim Cummings

Maybe the best Christmas present I ever got.

The pipers piped, the choirs sang, the revelers wassailed. Office parties, Christmas trees, expressions of good cheer. They let me out for Christmas dinner with the family Ellis, enjoyable except for the presence of the black and white parked in front of their house.

I watched the Giants win their semifinal Conference Play-off game, their best showing since the middle sixties. Just two more to go, boys. Gettem, Big Blue.

The ball of light came down the pole as the Times Square crowd welcomed in the New Year. Screams of joy, party hats, noisemakers, and champagne. The announcer's breath frosty in the night air as he described the passage. Then inside for scenes of celebration and earnest clergymen calling for peace and good will. I knew what was coming but it got me anyway. "Auld Lang Syne" always does—even in a good year.

An orgy of football games on New Year's Day. Halfway through the Orange Bowl, I realized I'd lost track of who was playing. Let's see, Nebraska are the red and white suits but . . . sensory overload.

One more attempt at the Michener book. Page 500 and we'd gotten all the way to 1821. I hoped he got paid by the word, decided the Boers could do without me for a while.

Back to television, where I saw more of Merv Griffin than the legendary Miss Miller. One program was about mysticism and the occult, two favorite topics of mine. I also believe in UFOs, in life somewhere other than on Planet Earth. Monumental conceit for man to believe that His handiwork could be confined to an insignificant segment of an immeasurable cosmos. The highlight of the program for me was a Polaroid picture of a vacationing family, Mama, Daddy, and little girl. The problem was, there hadn't been any little girl when the picture was taken. No real girl, that is. Tim Tourist had asked a stranger to take a shot of him and Martha—show the folks back home they'd really been to Yosemite. When the picture was developed, seconds later, there she was. Who? You figure it out. Meanwhile, I'll just sit here with my goose pimples.

Doctor Duffy came by to remove the last of the bandages from my hand. The new flesh was pink and supersensitive, but he assured me it would toughen quickly. Besides, old man, you're not doing manual labor these days. I think that was what finally pushed me over the edge. Unfortunately, I took it out on Ordonez.

"Goddammit, Chip, I've been here for three months. How long are you people gonna keep me here? I'm going bananas in this crummy room. How about I go home while you guys are wrapping up all your little details? Save the good taxpayers some money, free up your watchdogs to do some honest work for a change. What do you say, warden?"

"I'd say you have a good case of cabin fever, *hombre*. It's really two and a half months, but who's counting?"

"*I* am. Every lousy day seems like a year. You're supposed to be my partner. Put the screws to Hampton and get me out of here while I'm still reasonably sane."

"Tough order. We still have a lot of those 'little details,' as you call them, that bother me. The Fuselli packages are almost ready, but the key word is *almost*. Meanwhile Diaz and friends are still very much at large. As is Steve Dorn."

"Steve Dorn? He could be in Tierra del Fuego by now for all you guys know. He's been gone for two months, APB and all. You out to break the Patty Hearst record for nonapprehension?"

"I'll talk to the man . . . do the best I can. But don't get your hopes up."

"I'm starting to *like* the *Simmy the Clown Show*. Think Hampton would mind if I sent away for my SimmBeany? It's got a bell and everything!"

"I'll *talk* to him, *chico!*"

*   *   *

Home. Home sweet—at long last—home. Be it *ever* so humble. I took a shower in *my* bathroom. Went out to *my* kitchen and made coffee. Sat on *my* couch drinking it, looking out the window at *my* canal.

I wasn't totally free. Hampton had been adamant on a number of restrictions. No phone, no visitors, no car, mail still being diverted. The world was to think I was still in close custody. Nightly visits from Chip, now toting in groceries and whatever household products needs I mentioned. Curtains drawn at night, no outdoor cooking. Garbage disposal à la Ordonez, which didn't thrill him. Stay inside, pray they don't have binoculars trained on you. Otherwise, do what you like. Last of the great American humorists.

The Lighthouse Point police couldn't give me constant coverage, but they promised Hampton a car would swing by every hour. I had told him both my immediate neighbors were home most of the day, could be called on to help if something came loose. On one side, a fifty-year-old ex-Eastern Airlines captain, forced to retire after twenty-plus years because his eyes weren't up to FAA par. On the other, an enormous hulk named Kribbens, contractor who hit it big building shopping malls and retired. Complained bitterly about my pool parties when they got too raucous, but probably could be counted on if I needed him. I'd never hear the last of it, though.

Susan Ellis had done a splendid job of reconstructing my living room. An off-white wall-to-wall carpet in place of the original brown that I'd always thought too dark. Tan grass-cloth wallpaper, drapes in a light sand color that pulled it all together. Now it fit with the open tone of the rest of the house, as if planned all along. A new desk in the front hall, exact copy of the original. A magnificent ship print hanging over the desk, I leaned in to read the calligraphy. "The First Journey of HMS *Victory,* 1778." Rendered by Dunthorne and Sons. Silvered wood frame, matted in black with a gold interior border. Gorgeous.

The print reminded me of my own small navy, moored at my dock. Two to one, Billy forgot to run the engines every week. Batteries will be finished, bilge pumps won't work, the *Folly* will sink like a stone the first good rain. I looked out the windows, saw nothing very sinister, decided I could violate one of Hampton's commandments just once. I expected the click-click sound only sick batteries make but the engines both started on the first try, burbling along happily in neutral at low revolutions. Both bilges dry as a Baptist wedding reception. He *had* remembered. One less chore to worry about. I shut them down, went back inside, and locked the door again. It may be prison, but at least it's *my* prison.

* * *

The routine was still the same, only somehow not so crushing in familiar surroundings. *Too* familiar once. Susan had cleaned out all of Carole's clothes from the guest bedroom, a thoughtful gesture which, in retrospect, I appreciated. But on the night table was the dog-eared bubble-bum card she'd planned to frame. I sat with it cradled in my hands the rest of that afternoon, the half-forgotten knives of pain returning with a vengeance.

*   *   *

"Well, my friend, the trap is about to be sprung. The assistant DA has all the Fuselli testimony now, working on his presentation to the grand jury."

"Can't come too soon, Chip."

"Don't get antsy. Today's the 28th, and he's shooting for a February 15th date. So we're talking two weeks."

"I still can't believe Diaz could have been that stupid."

"He didn't know the St. Louis PD had the house in Clayton staked out. So, he hires two locals to torch it, never figured they'd get nailed. His mistake was not leaving the hotel, wanted to make sure the job got done, I guess."

"Half payment now and half later? He might as well have put up a neon sign."

"The Sparrow is frightened. He has every right to be. Fuselli came through, according to Hampton. Enough to finish Lucchese, the Sparrow, and a whole lot more. Put one huge dent in Action Junction. So be patient. A matter of days now, *hombre*."

"Still no word on Dorn?"

"None. Maybe you're right. Maybe he is in Tierra del Fuego. Hope he brought his woolies. So . . . what do you want me to bring you tomorrow?"

"Got the list in the kitchen. You anxious to go home? Thought we might have one more game of cribbage. For the championship of Lighthouse Point."

"Not tonight, *compadre*. I'm whipped. Home to the sack and sleep till noon. I'll get your list on my way to pick up the garbage. Sleep tight, don't let the bedbugs bite."

"Bedbugs? In this little number out of *House and Garden*? You impugn my househusbanding ability, sir."

"We all got our shortcomings."

*   *   *

The searchlight caught me full in the face, stayed on me no matter how I twisted and dodged, the brilliance of its beam making my eyes tear. Lousy dream. I came awake but the light didn't go away. Someone was in my bedroom—someone shining a strong flashlight in my eyes.

"No queek moves, *por favor, senor.* Thees gon hass a hair treeger and I om in a horry."

Now I was wide awake, the fear pushing adrenaline through my body, heart racing. Queek moves? I'd play statues if that's what it took to get rid of him.

"Wha . . . what do you want? Money? Liquor? Whatever it is, you got it, just don't get nervous."

"Money I got. Liquor I don't use. What I want is *you,* MacCardle. You and your boat. Now turn on that table lamp and we'll talk."

Steve Dorn.

I did as I was told, sitting up in bed, looking at Dorn standing near the door, training a very ugly pistol at me. A changed Steve Dorn, one with collar-length blond hair.

"That's better. We're going on a fishing trip, MacCardle. To Nassau. Only neither one of us is coming back."

"Nassau?"

"First step in the chain. I hear the authorities there aren't nearly as vigilant as us cops. Nassau, then Jamaica, then Trinidad. From Trinidad it's a quick trip to Venezuela. From there, *quien sabe?* By that time, I'm Esteban Dario from Barcelona. Independent oil producer. Got all the papers to prove it. I speak fluent Spanish, thanks to the neighborhood where I grew up. Terrific passport, ·picture and everything. Too bad you won't see it—you're getting off—halfway to Nassau."

"Why not just take the boat and go? You've got a fifteen hour head start until someone comes here. Tie me up and split. By the time I could say anything you'd be long gone."

"Nice try. You screwed up my life, MacCardle. Hadn't been for you, I just cruise along, wait for the old lady to die, marry Janice, and that's the ball game. Not any more. The cops have her and I'm running. Live the rest of my life scared. Because of you. Tried to warn you off, but you were too dumb to take the hint."

"The fish?"

"That and the car, except I got a little careless there. Ordonez told me what you were working on. Figured I'd make it look like mob-style moves, get you guys going the wrong way. I even called the mayor. Talk about terrorized. He thought I was Latino, like you did when I came in tonight."

"An innocent woman got blown up in that car, Dorn."

"Yeah, I know. Told you I got a little careless. One stick probably would have done the scare job. I used six. Aimed it at you, got her instead. How was I supposed to know you were shacked up?"

"Dorn, if you didn't have that gun . . ."

"Right, cowboy. Just hold steady where you are. It's got a silencer on it. One jump and you're cold meat. Let's be getting dressed, MacCardle. Slow and steady. Jolly fisherman gear, please."

Jolly Fisherman got out of bed, started pulling on clothes, wondering if I could throw a shirt or a shoe at Dorn, decided not to. He was out of range, fully on guard. I had no doubt he'd use the gun.

"You look real nice. Very convincing. Sporty, even."

"Dorn . . ."

"Talking bother you? Better take advantage, it's the last conversation you're ever going to have."

"Okay, tell me something. How did you know I'd be away when you planted the fish and dynamited my lady."

"Still playing detective, huh? Not a real good one, either. You forgot who ran your car home when you went to Charlotte? Besides, you told the Carter girl you'd be out of town. The car return was a bonus for me—that's when I saw your boat. Never figured I'd have to use it, though."

"The dynamite job?"

"Your big mouth again. You turned down Miss Carter's invitation to a party. Said you were taking a friend snorkeling. Galleon Reef, I believe. Pretty place."

"How the hell do you know all that?"

"Janice was there both times. Whatever you said I heard an hour later. Made everything a lot easier. My turn. What tipped you we were doping the old lady? I thought we had that sealed off for good when we hit that lawyer."

"We?"

"Janice and me. Might not believe it, but she can be pretty bloodthirsty. She stalled him as long as she could. Then she said we had to kill him, he wasn't going to give up. She knew about my sniper rifle, saw me cleaning it one time when she showed up to go to the track with me. She convinced me if we did it right, no one could trace us. Nobody can either."

"Wrong. I saw her statement. You made a big mistake dumping her. She told the police all about it."

"Bullshit. Even if she did, which I doubt, it's her word against mine. Anyway, the rifle's in a safe place."

"With Hogg? Guess again."

"I'll be damned. Maybe she did talk—good thing I got rid of her after all. Doesn't make any difference now. C'mon, MacCardle, next step's the kitchen."

"The what?"

"Kitchen. Jolly Fishermen always take coffee and sandwiches with them. Part of the cover, just in case we get stopped. Besides, that's a long run to Nassau, liable to get hungry on the way. You can tell me how you found out about the old lady while you're at it."

And maybe find a way to chuck a knife or some boiling coffee at you, I thought; give me half a chance.

He gave me no chance. No chance at all. Took up station at the back of the kitchen where he could see everything I was doing, the gun constantly at the ready. An eerie scene. Making a meal I'd never eat, telling a man who was going to kill me about how a lawyer kept diaries.

"Well, who would have thought it. A diary. Be damned.

And you had to get lucky and find it. 'Fraid you used up all your luck. Leave that stuff on the counter—I'll pack it into that chest there in a little bit. We gotta get ready to go boating, coming up on four thirty. Ignition keys?"

"In the desk in the front hall."

"Let's get them. Very cautious now—gun's got a one-pound trigger pull. Put 'em on the desktop where I can see them. Switches marked on the dashboard?"

"Uh huh. Just put the keys in and twist."

"And up we go in a nice fat boom. Where are the blower switches, smartass?"

It had been a desperate move, the thought being that if I had to die at least I could take him with me, get even for Horton and Carole. I had hoped he hadn't grown up around boats. Strike three. Maybe five. And it suddenly got worse, if such was possible.

He had me stand, legs spread apart, eighteen inches from the wall. Told me to put my hands in back of me, hold them out as far as I could, then lean until my face and upper body pressed against the wall. Try it, or believe me. An absolutely helpless position. I felt the cold metal of the handcuffs, winced as they bit into the still tender flesh of my left wrist.

"You can straighten up now. Here's how this thing is going down. Take you out to the boat, give you a little tap with the butt of this thing. Stuff a gag in your mouth, wire you to one of the fighting chairs, pull that big hat down over your eyes, come back, get the keys and the food, lock up the joint. Anybody sees us, it's two old buddies going fishing. One at the wheel, the other taking a little snooze before the action. Couple hours out, you get the deep six and I'm on my way to Venezuela. Let's go boating, MacCardle, it's almost dawn."

So this is how it ends. Last act in a grim melodrama. With a nasty plot twist, the villain wins. Chip wouldn't come by until at least six tonight. A twelve-hour-plus chunk of time for the future Esteban Dario of Barcelona to get to Nassau and start his trip to anonymity. Chip would find me missing and the boat gone. Even if he put it all together, it's a mighty big ocean and lots of ports to alert. And he wouldn't know to tell them to look for a blond man with a Spanish passport. A nice tight plan, with no loopholes.

I'm sorry, Carole, I did the best I could. Just wasn't good enough. Please try to understand and forgive me. The man who killed you is about to kill me. I couldn't do anything to stop him then and nothing now. A lousy ending to the play, darling. Would that I could change it for you.

Dorn opened the back door, signaled me to proceed him through it. We were on our way to the end.

19

A soft, tranquil Florida night. Crickets chirping, dock lights glowing all along the canal. Last of the stars twinkling out, false dawn promising a clear, sunny day. A lovely day to die.

"Lead the way, MacCardle. Don't even think about getting cute. One twitch I don't like and you've had the course. Move out, now."

I started down the concrete walkway leading to the head of the dock, the familiar shape of the *Folly* becoming clearer as we approached. The last, the saddest voyage, I thought.

And remembered a very happy voyage, a dazzling Sunday in September, a stunning girl rocking back and forth in agony, nursing an injured ankle . . .

Where was it? She'd jumped down from the foredeck, facing aft. Should be about five feet ahead of us. Gently now, no room for error. The next plank. Bet all the marbles. I stepped over it, went three steps beyond, heard a muted crack as the rotted board gave way under Dorn's weight, a gasp of surprise and pain as he went through. Prettiest sounds I'd ever heard.

The gun went skittering past my foot, stopped just short of the big white wooden dock box. No time for heroics, laddie, keep it simple. I spun around looking for Dorn. He'd caught the weakened board with his left foot, the fall slewing him sideways, head facing away from the *Folly*. I aimed carefully, took a three step approach and did my best to punt his head into the Intracoastal.

A great roaring wave of pain surged through me, knocking me off my feet. The Knee. Gone, again. If God didn't design the knee to play football, He certainly didn't have head-kicking in mind either. Get up, Angus, dammit, gotta finish strong. I scrabbled myself over to look at Dorn, realized I could have taken my time about it.

He lay unconscious on his back, jaw twisted grotesquely, obviously broken. What to do now? The gun, dumbo, the gun. But first, the handcuff problem. I lay down on my side, pulled my hands as far apart as the handcuff links would allow, worked my hands past my butt, started on the legs. Drew them up tightly against my chest, strained to somehow make the arms longer, felt them touch my heels, the limit of their extension. I thought. A grunting sound from Dorn put it over the top. I gave one convulsive jerk and the cuffed hands cleared my feet, back in front where they could be at least semi-useful again. I hopped over to the dock box, found the gun, and picked it up. Hopped over for another look at Dorn. Still unconscious, the grunt must have been some involuntary action of his nervous system.

I needed help. I knew I'd never make it up to the house. Besides, the telephone wasn't working. Thanks, Hampton. Thanks a heap. You can always *shoot* Dorn if it comes to that, you know.

But I doubted I could, no matter what he'd done. Shooting at people who are shooting at you was one thing. I'd seen enough of that in 'Nam. Shooting at an unarmed man, even one as dangerous as Dorn, was quite another matter. The thin veneer of civilization. Slim margin separating man from the brainless, amoral predator.

A puff of wind pushed the *Folly*'s bow against a piling, with a soft thud. Of course. The Coast Guard requires that all owners operating boats longer than sixteen feet carry emergency signaling equipment. Mine was in a big Olin canister clipped to the bulkhead opposite the wheel station.

I stuffed the gun into my waistband, levered myself aboard the *Folly*, retrieved the canister. Clambered back onto the dock and hopped over to sit on the dock box. Unscrewed the canister top, fished out the Very pistol and the clips of flares.

Simple process now. Fire and reload. Fire again, the flares arcing in graceful parabolas overhead, bursting and floating gently down, lighting up the area like an out of season July 4.

The shout meant I finally hit the jackpot.

"Goddammit, MacCardle, this time you've gone too far! It's five thirty in the morning, you stupid clown! This time I'm calling the cops on you! Right now!"

"Kribbens, my man, that's exactly what I had in mind."

20

Back to the all too familiar world of white.

Meals at ungodly hours, people waking me up to give me sleeping pills, the tang of Lysol a sharp reminder of where I was. I loved it.

Tuesday Snoopy came by to give me the results of the arthroscopic tests on my knee. His real name is Doctor Herbert Sterne, one of the best orthopedic guys in the country. The players call him Snoopy because of his permanently lugubrious expression, the sober brown eyes and big jowls contributing to the portrait of a man who's seen it all, found none of it very heartening.

Snoopy rebuilt my knee after the linebackers put me out for good. I'd called, told him I was afraid I'd just undone all his good work, and he'd flown down from New York to have a look. That kind of doctor.

". . . not so bad after all, Cam. Severe ligament strain, to be expected granted what you subjected it to. But no tears, nothing time and resting it won't take care of. Not like the last time at all."

"That's great, Doctor Sterne. How long?"

"Until you can leave? End of the week. Saturday, say. I'm having them put a walking cast on, just to play it safe. A cane, of course. Might make you look almost respectable."

"Just the medical news, please."

"Month or so, it'll be good as new or as good as that knee can ever hope to be. Check in with Shroyer weekly, here at the hospital. Should be routine. Any complications, let him know right away. Maybe I'll write this up for the *Medical Journal*. MacCardle's Syndrome. What happens to knees that kick someone in the head."

"A one-time, nonrecurring experience, I hope, Doctor. Nothing of real interest to the medical community."

"Yes. Well, my boy, if you'll excuse me, I have a plane to catch. Back to trench warfare, not to mention my private practice."

"You were great to come down. Say hello to the troops and wish them luck for me. Awful close this year. Maybe the Super Bowl next time out."

"'Bye, Cam, take care."

"So long, Snoopy, thanks a million."

A steady stream of visitors, all seeking to brighten my day, all of them successful.

"You look officially wounded, *hombre*. Want me to write something funny on your cast?"

"That went out with crew cuts and penny loafers. I'll settle for a bulletin on Dorn's status."

"Singing like a bird, in a manner of speaking. 'Course he can't really talk, jaw's all wired together where you belted him. But boy, can he write. I've been busy as a one-legged man in a butt kicking contest. Telling Dorn what Smithers said, showing her what he wrote. Right now, it's an implication contest."

"Who's winning?"

"We are. The only question left is whether both of them get maxxed or just Dorn. We have the weapon, his and her testimony, and your story to cap it off. There won't be a defense attorney in the country wanting to take on either one of them unless he needs the money real bad."

"You know, I would have bet all my pennies on Diaz or one of his people."

"Dorn made a good job of it. The fish, the bomb—never knew he had that much imagination. Won't do him much good where *he's* going, though. What's the scoop on your knee?"

"Going to be fine, just a bad strain. Check out Saturday. Gotta use a cane for a month, give or take."

"So you really will be El Cojo, eh?"

"Looks that way. Chip, I want you to know how much I appreciate all the help you gave me. No way we ever would have solved this thing without you."

"You too, *hombre*. Hampton said you were the luckiest man he ever met. Hadn't been for that board you'd be some fish's dinner by now."

"The Lord watches over procrastinators. I don't even like to think about what could have happened. More than delighted to settle for what did."

"Me too, we're getting used to your ugly face downtown. Got to be going, *compadre,* catch up on the latest episode of 'Sniper Faces Life,' with an all-star cast of two. Be well, come and see me."

"How about lunch when you have all the final pre-trial details?"

"Only if you buy, *hombre*. I'm just a poor cop, trying to scratch out a living. Fighting the forces of crime in the big city."

"Bah."

                    *   *   *

Billy and Dick Ellis dropped in, Dick bringing along a rule-breaking six-pack of Amstel that Sheila, the day nurse, managed to ignore when she came to take my temperature. A true angel of mercy.

"We had a pact, Cam. No more hospitals. Before I can blink an eye, you go breaking it. Whatever happened to trust?"

"Talk to Dorn, Padre. Sure as shootin' it wasn't my idea. Does seem like old times, though, doesn't it?"

"Too much. You're getting out Saturday? I'll come fetch you. I need an audience for a new recipe. Veal Marsala à la Mrs. Gianfriddo. She swears it's sensational."

"Listen, after the chow here, I'm ready to eat an old rug. With no sauce. You're on. Doctor says anytime after ten."

Dick and I had talked the day before. A long talk, serious on his part, full of words like gratitude, sacrifice, staggering losses—that kind of talk. Today was social, or at least it began that way.

"Now that this dreadful affair has been concluded, Cam, what are your plans? After your knee recovers, of course."

"That and I promised Jim Cummings I'd go fishing with him. He says the tarpon are running wild over there, needs my help to bash 'em back in line. Never went after tarpon before, I'm looking forward to it. Be nice to see Jim again, too."

"Yes, an admirable man. On all counts. Well, that seems like a pleasant pastime. Restful, even."

"Counselor, I don't like the sound of that. Is there something you want me to do? Like a job maybe?

"As a matter of fact, there is. A lady, named Marilyn Hoak, close friend of Susan's. Seems Porter, her husband, has been a bit lax in the child-support payments. Nineteen months lax, to be somewhat more precise."

"And?"

"And she's suing him. We're representing her. I need someone to serve papers on Mr. Hoak personally. I could use a local, but I'd rather have somebody I know and trust to do the job. Be more reassuring to Marilyn."

"You said something about 'local.' Mr. Hoak is not living around here?"

"Moved after the divorce was final. New location's in the town of Waipahu, in. . . ."

"Yeah, I know, South Dakota. Waipahu. Even *sounds* Indian. Just what I need. Gimping around in snow up to my armpits."

"Actually, Waipahu is on an island. Called Oahu. Part of the Hawaiian Islands, it appears. Think you're up to it?"

He thought he was crafty enough to hide it, but I caught his wink at Billy, saw the answering grin. Reassuring to Marilyn, my foot. She probably wouldn't care if the Avon Lady delivered the papers. A little bonus from the boss. Grab it and run like an Arab, sport. Michelle's at the Colony Surf, the Kahala Hilton, the waves at Makaha—first-cabin rest and recreation. Mr. Hoak, stand by for a visitor.

"Right after the fishing trip, Dick. Say around the fifteenth?"

"Sounds fine. Jane will make all the arrangements. Free for a drink Sunday afternoon? Ricky's itching to talk to you about the Pro Bowl. Pick you up four, four thirty?"

"You got a deal, boss."

*   *   *

She came shortly before the end of the afternoon visiting hours Friday, standing in profile against the window with the pale winter sun setting behind her. Told me she was going back to Virginia, bring the kids up on the farm outside Charlottesville. Open up the big house again, not being used by the tenant farmer she'd hired to work the place. Too many memories, good and bad, better to build a new life for them on old familiar ground. She came over to the bed, took both my hands in hers, the gray eyes gone soft with tears. "God bless you, Cam MacCardle. You came into our lives a stranger, but you're family to us now. We're beholden to you. Ever have troubles, or need anythin', there's three Hortons ready to bust their backs for you. You gave us back a purpose, a cause for livin'. And what a terrible price you paid . . . have to leave before I break up completely . . . but, thank you, Cam, from the very bottom of our hearts. God keep you today, tomorrow, and all the tomorrows.

"One last thing, then goodbye. Please tell Mr. Cummins Toby's fine. It was thoughtful of y'all to give him to Betsy. Don't reckon I know who owns who, but he's a joy to us."

"I bet he turns out to be a great mouser on the farm. Linda, I *will* tell Jim when I see him. Somehow, I think Carole already knows."

*   *   *

I lay awake the last night, trying to sleep, unable to shut out all the events of the last six months. Triumph and tragedy. Laughter and tears. Friends and enemies. Luck and disaster. Misguided woman and a cop gone sour. A promising attorney and a lovely lady dead.

Remembered a fragment of a poem from a college English course, centuries ago. The words seemed to sum things up, for me, anyway. A poem called "Paresis," written by a minor American poet, Eugene Fitch Ware:

> The highest of renown
> Are the surest stricken down,
> But the stupid and the clown
> They remain.

I finally fell asleep, dreaming about a sunlit field in Virginia and a little girl laughing at her cat chasing a gaily colored butterfly.